Lilith Angel

KRISTEN HOUGHTON

Skylight-NYC Publishers, LLC

LILITH ANGEL

Skylight-NYC Publishers, LLC

Copyright © 2019 by Kristen Houghton

Library of Congress Cataloguing-in-Publication Data Houghton, Kristen, LILITH ANGEL, fantasy mystery novel/ Kristen Houghton-1st. ed.

1.ilith Angel (Fictitious character)-Fiction 2. Hunter Hollis Hopper (Fictitious character)-Fiction 3. crime solver part-witch 4. female with magical powers 5. Vampire parents and werewolf boyfriend supernatural cozy mystery 6. YA fantasy mystery 7. California

First edition

ISBN: 978-1-7324166-4-2

Cover art by 2Hopper Production & Design Studio
Typesetting by KH Koehler Design

Contents

Books by Kristen Houghton

CRIME & MYSTERY

CATE HARLOW PRIVATE INVESTIGATION SERIES
Sins of the Fathers: For I Have Sinner
Grave Misgivings
Unrepentant: Pray for Us Sinners
Do Unto Others
Murder in Hawai'i (July, 2019)

FANTASY

THE TEDDY JAMESON CHRONICLES
Welcome to Hell, Teddy Jameson
Leaving Hell with the Angel of Redemption (coming in 2020)

SHORT STORIES ANTHOLOGY

Stolen Property

HISTORICAL ROMANCE

The Anchoress: A Romantic Tale of Terror

ANTHOLOGY

And Then I'll Be Happy! Stop Sabotaging Your Happiness and Put Your Own Life First
No Woman Diets Alone-There's Always a Man Behind Her Eating a Doughnut

YOUNG ADULT NOVELLA

Remember, Hetty? A Ghost Story

Dedication

Dedicated to all the magical and other worldly creatures in our lives—Believe.

"Magic is believing in *yourself*—if you can do that, you can make *anything* happen.

—Johan Wolfgang von Goethe

ONE

I remember so much more than what I was told. I was found on the steps of an abandoned church in a very bad part of the city of San Francisco. My wrist was tied to the rusty railing that trailed upward from street level to the broken church doors. Pinned to my dress was a piece of paper with writing on it that I knew was my name. I remember that I was scared and was very uncomfortable. I had to pee and at almost three years old I already knew that only babies wet themselves. I was a big girl, that's what I had been told. Big girls don't wet themselves. Mommy would be so mad at me. She would make me go to bed without supper again. But I had to go so badly! Where was mommy? Where did she go?

When the male and female came walking up to me I became more afraid. They stopped in front of me and bent down to sniff my clothes. "I want mommy!" I screamed loudly. "Where's mommy?"

The male smiled softly, "Why, what do we have here? A little angel come from heaven? Tied to a church railing!" I screamed again, a long piercing howl that had the male put his fingers in his ears in mock surprise.

The female bent down and looked into my eyes. Her own eyes were glittery-bright green. "Don't be afraid, little one. We won't harm you. Who has tied you to this railing?" She worked quickly, and easily untied the dirty rope around my wrist. "There, now, see? No one will hurt you."

She looked so kind and smiled so gently at me, but I was still afraid and my bladder let loose a torrent of urine that splashed onto the steps and the female's shoes. I thought she would be angry and slap my face like mommy would, but she just moved closer to me and whispered, "Poor baby!"

The male laughed lightly; he had a pleasant laugh. He was standing, leaning casually against the railing. The female caressed my hair as she removed the pin and read the paper. "Her name is Lilith." She straightened up and handed the paper to the male. "That's all it says."

"Lilith, hmmmm, interesting name." He looked at the church and laughed again. "Lilith of the Angels!"

He sniffed the paper then handed it back to the female who did the same. She whispered something to the male who looked at me and shook his head. "Later. This person will be easy to track."

"Well, we can't leave her here," whispered the female gently stroking my hair.

"No, indeed. She is special." He looked at me intently as if he saw something distinctly unique about me. "Very special it seems. We'll take her with us and then decide what has to be done."

The female bent down and gently touched my face. "We're going to take care of you, my darling little girl. Don't be afraid. Come with us."

The male took one of my hands and the female took the other. Slowly we began to walk away from the church but, halfway down the block, I began stumbling with exhaustion. I was so tired. I sank down onto the broken sidewalk and began to cry the way only an overtired, frightened child can cry. The male bent down and gently scooped me into his arms.

"Lilith of the Angels," he said smiling at me, "why walk when we can fly? Would you like to fly?"

Deep in my tired mind came the thought that only birds could fly. People couldn't fly—we had no wings! I think I may have said that about people not having wings because I remember he laughed and said, "But Lilith of the Angels, *we* don't need wings!"

And with me in his arms, the three of us flew straight up into the night sky. For some reason, I wasn't afraid. Maybe because he said that I was from the angels. I thought perhaps that we were going to Heaven and I closed my eyes feeling the gentle night wind on my face.

I didn't know it at the time but being rescued from the church steps by these two powerful creatures was the luckiest thing that could have happened to me and that magical happenings were to become a big and amazing part of my new life.

Later that night, I was sleepily aware that I had been fed, bathed, dressed in a soft garment, and gently placed in a warm, very large bed. I felt safe and quickly fell into an exhausted sleep that lasted until something strange happened. Sometime in the early morning hours, I came fully awake to find my face touching the ceiling. Terrified, I screamed loud and long as I fell downward into the comforting arms of the female.

TWO

I've done it again. I'm kissing the ceiling. In the middle of a sweet dream where my lips are about to touch the soft, greedy lips of my boyfriend Hunter, I find myself smack up against the ceiling, kissing cold plaster. Hell's Bells!

Concentrating hard, with my eyes squeezed tightly closed, I will myself to drift lightly back to my bed. It almost works this time except, instead of landing on the soft pile of pillows and blankets on the bed, I somehow miscalculate and land with a loud thump on the floor. I glance at the softly-lit numbers of the digi-clock on my nightstand. 2:05 in the AM.

The house is quiet. There's no sound from the master suite at the rear of the house. No one is home except me. Not surprising—it's nowhere near sunrise yet.

My spirit cat Lively lazily lifts his head and peeks over the side of the bed to gaze at me lying on the hardwood floor. He's changed his look again. This morning he's a ginger-colored cat. I wonder if I'll ever get used to the fact that he's never the same cat more than two weeks in a row. Sometimes he changes his look in a matter of a few days. It all depends on who needs to see him.

As a spirit cat, Lively represents all of the myriad types of cats, one by one. He's been many different cats throughout the years—a Persian, a Tuxedo, a Siamese, and any type of mixed breed ones. You name them, he's been them. It has something to do with animal spirits which live on and on. He visits his former owners in dreams and sometimes in person, appearing to them exactly as he was when he lived with them. They miss him and grieved when he died. By visiting them, he's letting them know that the cat they loved and lost still lives on and on. His visits bring them comfort.

I sigh. My power is erratic. Power. Huh. I've been rising and falling since I was a child. It's gotten worse as I've gotten older, happening much too frequently. At seventeen, all I want is to be a normal person and not have this so-called power. It's an annoyance and something I try very hard to hide.

I get up from the floor, flop back into bed, miscalculate again, and smack my head on the headboard. My day hasn't even begun and already it seems as if I'd better be extra careful in what I do.

"Amsterdam, Rotterdam, damn, damn, damn!"

"Lilith, hey Lilith! Are you up yet? C'mon, we're going to be late!"

The sound of Hunter's voice shouts outside my bedroom window followed by a rain of pebbles hitting the glass. I open one eye and look at the digi-clock. Hell's Bells! I've got Advanced Calculus in forty-five minutes and I haven't even showered yet.

Bounding out of bed, I rush to the window and open it just as a handful of pebbles is thrown again. "Hunter! Be quiet! You're going to wake the dead!"

"Your parents? The shades in their room are up. They're not home yet."

Not home yet? The sun's already up and I can feel the heat. This is a little weird. They're always home before sunrise. I shake my head. I guess I shouldn't worry. They are adults and over twenty-one, after all. I mean, *really* over twenty-one.

"I'll be ready in fifteen minutes," I call down. "Wait on the front steps."

I run to the bathroom, shower, brush teeth, and go back to my room to dress. No time for anything fancy. Jeans, a cute yellow tee that says 'Smile', and orange-colored sneakers. A quick dab of lip gloss and mascara, and putting my red hair into a high ponytail is all I have time to do, and I'm ready to go.

Lively follows me as I run down the stairs into the kitchen. I've had him for five years. He appeared in the garden one rainy night when I was twelve years-old. He was just a kitten, a tiny ball of fur who immediately cuddled in my arms letting me know we were destined to have a special bond and we do. Our spirits are attached.

Opening the 'fridge to grab a water and an orange, I move glass bottles containing a dark red liquid aside, and note that we're running low on the stuff. I'll have to remind Mom and Dad to pick up some more.

Before I get ready to leave, I fill one cat bowl with Kitty Crunchies and another one with water for Lively. I snuggle my spirit cat for a brief few seconds before stuffing the orange, water, and an energy bar into my backpack. Then I grab my iPad and run out the door smack into the waiting arms of Hunter Hollis Hopper.

"Wow, babe! You are a speed *demon*! Less than 15 minutes!"

"Who's a demon? Me?" I tease as I kiss him full on those greedy, soft

12

lips I dreamed about. "Let's go."

As we zoom off on Hunter's motorbike, a beautiful Vespa, I look back at my house. The sun is high and already hot. I think about my parents being out and about in the sunshine and hope they remembered to put on sunblock. *Lots* of sunblock.

THREE

"**A**ngel, Lilith Angel," drones the voice of Mr. Mendelsohn, my Advanced Calculus teacher. He's focused on the roster on his laptop.

"Here."

He looks down his glasses at me, then hits a key and checks off my name. The man is so brilliant that even the Honor's List, brainier-than-thou, highly mathematically-inclined kids in the class are totally intimidated by him. You can imagine how I, math-phobic Lilith, feel when I sit in my assigned seat and look at today's calculus problem prominently displayed on the smart-board.

· *Let A and B be two compact subsets of Rn. Define the distance between A and B by*

(A,B) = inf\'7b|x−y| : x ∈A,y ∈ B\'7.. Show that if A∩B = Ø then · (A,B) > 0.

2. Show that $f(x) = 2\sqrt{x} - 3cosx + ln(x2 + 1)$ is uniformly continuous on $(1,\infty)$.

Seriously? Hell's Bells! My palms begin to sweat and a wave of dizziness comes over me. My mind goes blank and I begin to panic. Suddenly I feel the desk wobble as my body tries to levitate out of the chair. This can't happen! As far as I know, Hunter and I are the only 'different' students in the school. We keep that a secret. The girl next to me sees the desk shaking and mouths, "You okay?" "Leg cramp," I mouth back, hooking my legs firmly around the metal base of the heavy desk chair in an effort to stay grounded. Emotions, good, like kissing Hunter, or bad, like a stressful situation, make me rise upward.

I take slow even breaths to calm myself. Finally, the desk stops wobbling and I'm able to avoid flying upward. Thank goodness! But, just in case there's a chance of unexpected levitation, I still keep my legs hooked tightly around the chair. Just in case. Lilith Angel needs to stay grounded for now. Relax, Lilith Angel.

About my name—I was registered in school as Lilith Angel purely by accident. The secretary at Montfaire Elementary School was an elderly woman named Mrs. Ellsworth who was well-loved by the staff and the myriad of students. She was a lovely, efficient woman who only had two problems. One was her hearing. She wore a hearing aid but, since she frequently forgot to change the batteries, it sometimes went in and out causing her to make mistakes. Mistakes like names. Her other problem was that she loved to gossip.

The day the male and female registered me for kindergarten, Mrs. Ellsworth was there to welcome us. After gossiping about various people in the school, including faculty and parents, she began the process of registration.

"And the name of your sweet little girl?"

She tapped her hearing aid and smiled over to where I was sitting on a child's bounce-y chair, sucking hard on a lollipop she had given me. The chair had been Mrs. Ellsworth gift to the school. She felt a comfy, fun, child's chair was something every principal's office should have.

"Lilith," said the female smiling behind her dark glasses. "Her name is Lilith."

"Can you repeat that, please?" she asked politely, tapping on her hearing aid.

"Yes, of course, her name is *Lil-ith*," the female said enunciating my name carefully.

"Lilith. Pretty name for a pretty girl. A darling daughter you have there," said Mrs. Ellsworth.

"Yes," said the male flashing a charming grin, "she's our Lilith Angel."

"Let me just finish typing this up, Mr. Angel, and Lilith will be officially registered for next Fall. Now how do you spell Angel? Just one l, correct? A-n-g-e-l?"

"Angel? Yes, but—" began the male.

"Just one second," she admonished gently, staring intently at the computer screen. "You can ask any questions you may have after I'm done."

I watched in awe as her fingers flew over the keyboard. Then she got up and went to the small copier. "Now, let me make a copy for you. Make sure you put it in a safe place at home, Mrs. Angel. I know you will. Mommies always keep all the important family documents!"

As she turned away to retrieve the paper from the copier, the male and female looked at each other and then at me. I giggled and they laughed quietly.

"Ah, here you go," said Mrs. Ellsworth. She smiled and handed the copy to the female. "Now then. Any questions, Mr. Angel? Mrs. Angel? No? Oh! All right then."

Mrs. Ellsworth tapped her hearing aid again, then shook hands with all of us. "It's been lovely meeting you both, Mr. and Mrs. Angel. And you too, Lilith. Please don't hesitate to call if you *do* have questions."

Truthfully, at that time, I didn't know my parents' real last name or even if they had one. Angel suits us just fine and Angel we became. Victoria and Christopher Angel and their daughter, Lilith.

Hunter is nowhere in sight when I exit my class. He's usually waiting outside the door so we can walk to Criminal Justice, the one class we have together. I'm kind of exhilarated because I was actually able to solve one of the problems on the board and I'm dying to tell him. I scan the crowded hallway. Nope, he's not here.

Hunter and I have been dating for almost a year now. It began at the spring sports rally picnic, the end of our junior year. I was standing in line behind him over at the food tent.

"I'm a vegetarian," said Hunter declining a hotdog being offered by the girl behind the food table. He reached instead for a wrapped sandwich.

"Oh, sorry," said the girl. "That's egg salad. Let me get you a veggie-burger. My sister's a vegan and I know that vegans don't want any type of animal products."

"That's okay. I'm a lacto-ovo vegetarian—I eat eggs, cheese, and stuff. I'm not a vegan. There's a difference."

He grinned nicely at the confused senior and went on to tell her about vegetarianism vs vegan-ism. I liked him immediately. That only increased when I found out that he was 'different' too. Hunter's your average all-American teenage boy with one small exception. He's a hyper-sentient humanoid with the essence of a wolf's spirit in his body, who has the ability to shapeshift into a wolf when the gravitational forces of the moon are at a certain point. Whew! Full-moon running Hunter calls it. Actually, Lycans, more commonly known as werewolves, are one of the most common otherworldly creatures around. As for how he feels about my ability to levitate, he actually thinks it's pretty great. And when he found out about my parents, he was happy and excited to meet them. How's that for a special type of boyfriend?

"Lilith, hey. Sorry I'm late. Had to get something out of my locker."

"I solved the problem in Calc."

"You did?" Faked shock. "Wow!"

A bit of sarcasm, but that's okay. Hunter is a numbers guy while I'm more a word person. He needs more of my help with his English essays than I need his help with math.

"It is a wow, wise-ass," I say, nudging him forcefully with my hip. "*I'm* definitely wowed by it. Now if I can pass that final, four months from now, I can concentrate on graduation."

The class that takes up the last two periods of my afternoon is my Criminal Justice class. Both Hunter and I love this class and have seriously talked about becoming criminologists. It's a fascinating profession, including the part about forensics, and not at all boring.

I used to think that a crime, and the justice that followed it, was a cut and dry operation but that's not the way it works at all. A person who commits a crime is not always caught or, if he or she *is* caught, the justice they receive doesn't always fit the crime. Sometimes, an innocent person is imprisoned simply on mediocre evidence or mistaken identity. Other times, a guilty person gets off with no jail time at all. I find all the angles, mistakes, and problems encountered by law enforcement and the legal system to be fascinating puzzles that I want to solve. Unlike the complexities of calculus with its numbers and symbols, these puzzles contain words and that's always been a cinch for me to work through and solve.

Hunter says that I could solve calculus problems as easily as I solve word problems and that they're basically the same. But they're really not. Plus, I have a little secret that no one knows. It has to do with me, words, and languages. Even my parents didn't know about it until I was six years-old.

I can read and understand any language. No matter what the language is, I *know* what the words mean. I just *know*. I have no idea how. When I was a child, I thought everyone could read and understand any and all written words. I didn't know I was different. For me it was normal.

The male and female found out about this part of me one day when we were in the book shop they own. While they were poring over an ancient scroll, they gave me a child's book about a bunny that had simple sentences and mostly pictures to look at and to keep me occupied.

I grew bored with reading the same sentences over and over again and wandered over to where they were sitting to see what was so interesting to them. My dad absent-mindedly patted me on the head and my mom gave me a quick hug. They were so engrossed in looking at that scroll that they didn't mind when I scooted between them to take a closer look.

It was very pretty with its fancy words and delicate drawings. I liked it. No wonder they kept looking at it. I leaned closer to the scroll.

"Who's Astarte?"

They both looked up, surprised. "Who, darling?" asked my mother.

"As-tar-te." Pointing to the words on the scroll, I slowly read, "'*This temple and statue have been dedicated to Astarte.*' Who is Astarte, mommy?"

The male and female stared at me astonished as well they should be. The words on the scroll were written in the ancient language of Etruscan and I knew exactly what the words meant.

As I said, calculus is hard, but words are easy.

FOUR

Midnight Ink is the book shop owned by my parents. It's where I go after school. It's a perfect place to study. I love the smell of old paper and book bindings—it is a familiar, safe smell from childhood. It's also a great place to daydream, something I seem to do a lot of lately. So I sit in the window seat and do just that.

Hunter usually hangs out with me and helps with the occasional customer. It's only a little after three and we're usually here until closing time which can be anytime between 6:00 and 8:00 at night.

The first floor of the book shop is divided into two rooms, the large front one where most of the books and all the magazines are kept. There's an area in a far corner of the room where we have an electric teapot, a small refrigerator, and a shelf that holds a few boxes of cookies and things needed for tea.

In the back of the shop is a smaller room, the rare book room, which houses special editions, ancient books, and ornate manuscripts. A special glass case containing fragile scrolls which are magicis scripturam or magical writing, are kept in a locked cabinet there. In fact, that's what we call the room in the back, the Magicis Scripturam That room has a mystical aura about it that I like. I feel very comfortable in there. Only certain customers enter that room. Most people coming into the shop assume it's an office.

There's a circular staircase in the rare book room that leads to a round turret-like room enclosed by floor-to-ceiling windows. Inside is a desk, a small sofa, a bookcase, and two chairs, but nothing else. That room was supposed to be the office but it's never been used. It looks as if it truly does belong to a magic castle and in my mind I call it the castle turret. As a child it was my favorite place to be.

After having watched Disney's movie *Sleeping Beauty* a million times over, I used to go up there in my princess costume, lie on the sofa, and pretend to be the sleeping princess. It was fun being a princess but, I pretty quickly grew annoyed with just lying around and waiting for an imaginary prince to show up. When my mom asked me how I liked pretending to be Sleeping Beauty, I told her how boring it was to wait to be saved.

"It's no fun, Mommy. All I do is wait and I don't think any prince is coming to save me."

She laughingly told me that a princess didn't *need* a prince to save her. "A princess has the power to save herself, my darling Lilith. Always remember that."

The chimes over the door make a charming sound as a man and a woman enter the shop.

"Hey, Mr. and Mrs. Angel. You're early today."

"Hello Hunter." The voices are soft and mesmerizing. I glance up from the book I'm reading.

"Mom! Dad!"

They are incredibly gorgeous creatures, the male and female whom I call mom and dad. Stunning. And very young looking.

"Hello, darling," says my mom, taking off an enormous pair of designer sunglasses and coming over to give me a kiss. Her eyes are that incredible piercing green I remember from the first time I saw her, the color of grass brightened by a fierce sun after a drenching rain. She leans over and ruffles Hunter's hair. He adores my mom. I remember him telling me that his own mother died when he was barely two years-old. I didn't ask him any more about it because I saw how sad he looked when he told me. His dad, he says, is a little overprotective but he adds that he understands the reason. "After my mom died, I'm all he's got."

"Sweetheart." My dad gives me a hug and removes his own pair of sunglasses, revealing startling crystal clear blue eyes.

"The sun's still out," I say. "You're up early."

"We had a few things to take care of. Some special things that needed our attention. No sleeping in for us today, darling."

"You came home late, too" I continue.

"Yes, Lilith of the Angels. As your mother said, there were some things that needed our attention. Last night as well as today."

My mom gathers her beautiful full silky blonde hair into a ponytail and walks past me to open the box of books that arrived a short while ago. Those books are special and they are kept behind the closed door in the back of the shop. I study her as she passes me. She looks as lovely as ever.

"But you were careful? I mean lots of sunblock, right?"

"Lots and lots of it, our beautiful Lilith Angel."

Sunblock was the best thing ever invented for those like my parents. Truthfully, they sure do love the heat. My dad smiles at me, his perfect white teeth dazzling. Well, almost perfect.

"Dad? You have a spot on your tooth." I point to the dark stain on his left canine tooth.

He moistens his finger and rubs the tooth. "Better?"

"Yup. All gone."

"I'm going to go help your mom with the new arrivals. Can you and Hunter handle any customers who come in?"

"Sure thing, Mr. Angel," says Hunter. "We've got this."

The soft melodious voices of my mom and dad drift back to me as I watch them walk toward the rear of the shop. They are beautiful creatures, my mom and dad. Beautiful creatures who cast no reflection as they pass the mirror on the back wall. No surprise there.

My parents *are* vampires.

I grew up with the male and female who rescued me one scary night when they found me all alone, frightened, and tied to a church railing. They brought me to their home and took care of me as if I were their own little girl which is who I became. They nurtured me and protected me, making my childhood as normal as possible. I like normal. I consider them my real parents and the fact that they just *happen* to be vampires has never once bothered me. The fact that some otherworldly creatures are frequent customers at our book shop is also part of my life. No one coming into the shop can even tell they're any different from anyone else.

As a little girl, I thought that all children had parents who slept most of the day, could fly up into the night sky, race faster than the wind, and who had lived a really, really long time. My parents explained their *life* style to me when I was about nine years-old and, as only a child can, I was fine with that. I still am. They really are perfect parents.

About age, let's face it—most kids think their parents are old anyway. Kids think thirty is old. Add a zero to the number thirty and you have an approximation of how old my mom and dad really are. Trust me they are nowhere near the human thirty.

I don't know too much about the woman who tied me to the church railing with only a note that read, 'Her name is Lilith.' Either my parents couldn't find her, which I find kind of odd since they have excellent tracking and hunting senses, or they chose not to do so. Maybe they saw her and decided that any woman who would tie her child to a railing and abandon her, wasn't fit to be a mother. Who really knows? They've always said that they decided the second they took me to their home that I would be their child.

"You're our Lilith of the Angels, our very own precious child," the male, my dad would say to me. "We love you. You have nothing to fear, we will always take care of you."

And I never feared anything or anyone because I believed him. I feel completely safe being their child.

As I grew older and levitation became a more frequent annoying occurrence, the female, my mom, told me that she believes that someone in my ancestry had some sort of powers that were passed on to me.

"You inherited the gift of levitation from someone, darling. Ancient wisdom says that witches have the gift to levitate. I believe that you are part witch, Lilith my darling, and that you have more magical powers lying dormant within you. Good powers, good gifts. They usually become stronger right before the possessor of those gifts turns eighteen. You are indeed a special person, Lilith."

Part witch? Magical powers? Oh no! "I don't want to be special in that way."

My mom came over to me and kissed my head. "But you are, Lilith, you are."

I sighed. I don't want to be special. I just want to be a normal person, no otherworldly talents, no gifts other than what other kids have. Music, art, sports, you know, normal gifts.

The sun is just beginning its glorious descent when the chimes above the door ring gently. I see Old Mr. Paget pause in the doorway and sniff the air. Even though it's a pleasant 82 degrees, he's wearing a long wool coat, scarf, gloves, and hat. With his long sparse whiskers, he resembles a large beaver dressed up as a human. But he's a gentle old soul and kind. He's an otherworldly healer. His passions are ancient books and feeding all the vast variety of birds who visit his garden. Mr. Paget communicates with them the same way I do with Lively.

He shuffles forward, his nose inhaling deeply. Then he sees us. "Ah, Lilith and young Hunter." His nose quivers ever so slightly toward Hunter who raises a hand in greeting. Inhaling deeply again, he looks anxiously at me. "Are they here? Has it arrived?"

I know he is asking if my parents are here and if some obscure book he had ordered a week ago has been delivered to Midnight Ink. I get up from the window seat where I'm daydreaming and go over to him.

"Yes, Mr. Paget, my parents are here but I don't know if the book you ordered has come in yet. Let's go see."

I take his arm and escort him to the back room, walking slowly to accommodate his shuffle. He really *is* an old soul.

As soon as he's in the open doorway of the rare book room, he calls out, "Is it here? Has it arrived?"

My parents welcome Mr. Paget into the back room and after he is seated, my dad winks at me before he closes the door. I hear the rustle of paper and then a gasp. My mom's soft voice gently asks, "Is this what you wanted, Mr. Paget? Exactly what you requested?"

"Oh yes, oh yes, my dear. Exactly!" I hear him cough gently. "I must tell you that this book is so rare, so very rare that I am overwhelmed that you were able to procure it for me. How can I ever thank you? The price of the book is hardly enough payment for what you must have done to get this for me."

I hear my mother murmur that it was "our pleasure", no need for any payment other than the cost of the book. My parents make their real living, so to speak, on being able to find old and rare books, scrolls, and manuscripts. Their customers for those items are interesting creatures.

I glance at the front of the store and see Hunter staring intently out the window at the beginning sunset. There's a full moon tonight and I know he wants to get home. He's an interesting creature too.

For someone whose parents are vampires and whose boyfriend is a werewolf, I lead a relatively ordinary life and I want to keep it that way. I'm cautious and careful; a kind of normal girl with normal fears, especially about anyone finding out that I can levitate. I have a few school friends but no one too close. I'm a little bit of a loner and that's fine for me.

As I walk back to the window seat I am struck once again by the solid fact that I live in two worlds—the ordinary every day one, and the one that's filled with magic, myths, and mysterious creatures.

And both worlds have their advantages—and dangers.

FIVE

Kissing Hunter is sweet, so sweet. We're snuggled together on the window seat, holding onto each other and looking at the last rays of the sun disappear over the housetops. It's so comfortable being anchored in his arms—it keeps me from levitating. He's a good person. I lay my head on his shoulder and feel the muscles move in his arms and on his chest. The moon will be rising soon. He has to get home.

"Hunter?" I raise my head and look up at him.

"Yeah?"

"Be careful tonight, okay?"

"I was born careful," he says laughing and kissing me again.

"No seriously, be careful. Last time you almost got caught. What were you thinking anyway?"

He looks out the window at the faint pink remnants of the sunset.

"Don't worry. I just got a little reckless. It was stupid of me. Won't happen again."

"Okay."

We get up from the window seat and both of us stretch. Hunter takes my face in his hands and smiles into my eyes.

"Be on time tomorrow. No oversleeping. I'll be at your house at 7:00 sharp. Remember that we're going on that class trip to a real crime lab. That's going to be great."

I love our Criminal Justice class. Our teacher has arranged a trip to the Hall of Criminal Justice for a lecture and workshop. Both Hunter and I have been eagerly waiting for this trip for weeks. I promise him that I'll be up and ready to go and he gives me a quick kiss before leaving. I hear his totally cool Vespa motorbike start up and I watch through the window as he speeds off toward his home. My feet are barely touching the floor as I hold on to the window frame to keep from floating up to the ceiling.

I'm still staring out the window when I hear the sound of voices coming in my direction. I come down to the floor with a soft thud and turn toward the sound. My parents and Mr. Paget have just emerged from the back of the shop. In his arms is a large wrapped package which must be the book he had ordered. He sniffs the air, making his nose quiver rapidly like a tiny mouse, and looks around.

"Well, Lilith, I see young Hunter has already left here. Full moon rising. A wise decision on his part." Mr. Paget inhales and exhales deeply, his sparse whiskers vibrating with each breath. "Yes, yes, good decision by young Hunter. Good decision. He must be careful though, must be very careful. Well, have to be going now, have to leave. Good-bye to all of you." Turning to my parents he says, "Thank you, thank you for finding this. It is so, so precious to me. Thank you."

"No thanks necessary," says the melodic voice of my mother. "We're happy to have been able to have it returned to its rightful owner."

Waving a hand in good-bye, Mr. Paget shuffles slowly to the door. The chimes ring softly as he exits Midnight Ink and I am alone with my parents. My mom turns to me.

"What would you like for dinner, darling? It's getting late and you must be starving. Let's order something from Cho's, all right?"

"Sure, okay. I *am* hungry. Want your usual?" I look at the beautiful creatures in front of me, the male and female I call mom and dad.

"Yes, sweetheart," says the male handing me money. "You know what to get."

"Got it. Back in a few."

Outside Midnight Ink, a soft breeze brings the tangy scent of salt from the ocean. It's so warm. What a beautiful night, I think as I jog across to Cho's. I look at the rising full moon and make a wish. *Keep Hunter safe.* The moon winks back at me as a cloud passes in front of it. Wish granted.

At Cho's I order two cheeseburgers well-done and a side of curly fries for me. Then I order my parents' usual. "Two thick double burgers, *very* rare, and two orders of steak tartare."

"Just take a few minutes to prepare, Lilith. Your parents' food, quick, yours takes longer, you know. No problem. Wait at your table over there. Ming will be over shortly."

Mr. Cho is a nice guy and he always has me wait at a special table by the window, where his wife will bring over a hot platter of French fries and an ice tea, free of charge.

I'm in the middle of the absolutely delicious plate of hot cheesy fries when Cho calls out, "Lilith, order ready."

Ming hurries over with a waxed bag and puts the remaining fries on my plate inside it while I go to pay for the food and grab the take-out order.

"Here you go." Ming is standing next to me holding the tightly sealed bag with my leftover fries and shaking it lightly. "Still hot."

"Thanks Ming, Cho. Maybe I'll see you tomorrow."

Outside the moon has almost risen to her highest point. It is a beautiful sight. I stop and sigh. Beauty has its price though. Some creatures are moonstruck when the moon is full. Animals act differently, turtles lay their eggs, dolphins swim closer to shore—the gravitational pull of a full moon has awesome powers on all creatures.

The warm breeze picks up and I walk quickly across the street. Lively has appeared in the window of Midnight Ink. I love how he can transport himself from one place to another. He knows Cho put some shredded chicken in a carton just for him. He'll eat with us at the small table in the shop.

From somewhere on the outskirts of town, I hear dogs barking. A cacophony of woofs and ruffs intensifies as I reach the door of the shop. Suddenly, there's a different sound, a piercing sound that makes me catch my breath in excitement. Out of the night comes a strong and fierce howl.

Hunter.

My parents are good 'appear-eaters'. That's vamp-talk. The point is that to the human eye they 'appear' to be eating. They suck the blood from the burgers and steak tartare delicately and discreetly, gently crumbling the meat and bun with their fingers. Anyone dining with them would simply see two people who eat what they want and, when they're full, leave the rest of the food on their plates. They're good at pretend-drinking too although I do know that vampires can, and will, drink water. It's another vamp myth of things they can't do, but that I know they can. There's a whole list of myths detailing what the average person truly believes vampires are and what they can and can't do. Here're are just five myths I can debunk.

Myth number one: They're the evil undead and creatures of Hell.

So not true. Vampires are alive and they aren't creatures of Hell. Being a vamp is a biological thing. As for being evil, my mom told me that once you're bitten you have to make a choice about how you're going to live. "Simply put, Lilith, if you were a good human, you'll be a good vampire."

Myth number two: Their bodies are ice-cold.

Only sometimes. They can, and will, warm themselves up more easily than a human body can, when needed. In fact, they *enjoy* the heat. Maybe that's why we live in Summer Valley, California.

Myth number three: They have to drink human blood.

Well, okay, partly true. They *o* drink human blood, but they don't kill any creature when they do 'take a small sip'. It doesn't hurt anyone—their victims simply go to sleep for a few hours. Sometimes, they need more than just a little blood to sustain them. I liken it to a craving, the same kind of craving I get for a hot chocolate rum raisin sundae. I don't eat it every day but when I get the craving, I have to have it. When the craving for a larger quantity of liquid nourishment comes upon them, Rudy down at the blood bank, our friendly and discreet neighborhood supplier of blood, will give them what they need.

Myth number four: They can't cross water.

Can and do. No problem. I mean, they even swim!

Myth number five: Sleeping in a coffin is a must.

Maybe for some vamps but my parents prefer a comfortable king-sized bed in a room with black-out curtains. They do like black sheets, though.

But there are three myths that *are* absolutely true. One of those is an unbreakable vampire rule. Vamps *cannot* enter any building unless they are specifically invited inside. The invitation doesn't have to be formal and it doesn't even have to be uttered by a human. A good example of this is the sign over the local library, "Enter in all who seek knowledge." That's a good enough invitation.

I've gotten used to being the 'invitor' for my parents—stores, school and office buildings. I'm the one who goes in first and then extends the invitation to my parents. The good thing is that the invitation to enter any specific building only has to be extended once. Then vamps can enter the same place any time they want. Neither my parents nor I know why invitations are necessary but that's one vamp-myth that is absolutely true.

Cast no reflection is true—most of the time. They cast no reflection in mirrors but, if a picture is taken of them, their reflection can be seen. A bit fuzzy, sometimes out-of-focus looking, but there. It has to do with their ability to project heat toward the camera so that they can be photographed.

The last myth, the 'forever young one, *is* true. Victoria and Christopher will never, ever age. They will always look as young as they were when they first became vampires. That can present a problem. Usually my parents use a simple vampire trick—they can make people believe an image they project from their minds, making the observer see them as older. It's a type of vamp hypnosis. But occasionally they can be caught off-guard. This happened one night, last month when my mom and I were out shopping at a mall a few towns away.

"Mrs. Angel? And little Lilith! Well, not so little anymore! Hello! Hello, how have you been? It's been quite some time since I've seen you, my dears!"

It was old Mrs. Ellsworth, the sweet secretary from my elementary school, the woman who inadvertently gave us the last name of Angel. We stopped and smiled at her.

"Lilith, you've grown into quite a young lady, haven't you? So nice to see former students from Montfaire School all grown up. I don't get to see many of the children any more now that I've retired. How are you, dear

Lilith?" She peered closely at me and smiled.

"I'm fine Mrs. Ellsworth. How are you?"

"Oh, well, old but still spry. Can't help getting older!"

She turned to my mom and looked startled.

"Oh my, Mrs. Angel," said Mrs. Ellsworth, staring hard at my mother in wonder. "*You* haven't aged a day! You look as young as the day I met you when you registered Lilith for kindergarten! My goodness, that was, what? Almost thirteen years ago! You still look so *young*! How do you do it? So young!"

My mom gets close to Mrs. Ellworth and whispers, "Facelift."

"What was that dear?" She taps her hearing aid. "I didn't quite catch that."

"Facelift," says my mom louder. "Shhh, don't tell anybody, Mrs. Ellsworth!"

"My goodness, you look wonderful. No, of course I won't tell. But let me say that your cosmetic surgeon is a genius to be able to keep you so young-looking."

"And terribly expensive," smoothly lies my mother.

"Well, he's definitely worth every penny, I'm sure."

"Oh yes, I think so." My mom checks her watch. "I'm so terribly sorry, but we have to run. So nice to see you, Mrs. Ellsworth."

"You too!" She leans toward my mom to take another scrutinizing look and says, "Don't worry, your secret's safe with me."

"I trust you." We both know that Mrs. Ellsworth will tell everybody she knows. "Good-bye, Mrs. Ellsworth."

"Bye now!"

"Facelift? Seriously, Mom?"

"All I could think to say, darling. Besides," she raised an eyebrow, "we know my secret is safe with her."

We both laughed all the way to the car.

We're lazily finishing dinner when a long, delicious howl is heard through the open windows of Midnight Ink, rattling the glass panes.

"Hunter," says my mom smiling with her mouth closed so as not to show teeth that are bloody from the almost raw burger.

"Can't mistake that howl," agrees my dad.

Just be safe, Hunter, I think, be careful. The night is beautiful— but dangerous for a werewolf.

SIX

Lively wakes me up by sitting on my chest. When this spirit cat materializes, he takes on the weight of a normal well-fed house kitty. I open one eye and look at him. He's still a ginger-colored cat today but that will change in another week.

"Are you awake?" His mind communicates this to me as he gently paws my face. Most of the time I can understand him. It's like the transfer of thoughts from one mind to another. My mom calls it mind-talk.

"Yes. I am definitely awake."

"You had a very restless night." Lively begins to delicately bathe his face with a paw.

Restless, huh. He's right. I didn't sleep well because I was listening for Hunter's distinctive howl all night long and taking stock of my life. Stress makes me levitate. I am so happy to see that I'm still lying in my nice, soft bed and not on the floor. I don't remember levitating but if I did, at least this time I landed well.

The last time I heard Hunter's howl was probably around Midnight. I knew that last howl was him saying good-night to me. I sigh, wishing that we just used a cell phone or text message to say good-night to each other like every other couple I know. But then, every other couple I know isn't like us—me, Lilith Angel who levitates and whose parents are vampires, and Hunter who is a werewolf. We're definitely a distinct pair.

"What time is it, Lively? Let me see," I say reaching for my cell phone. Good, plenty of time. It's only 5:30 but already the sky is lightening up with the sunrise. I'm up earlier than usual. I wonder if my parents are home yet.

I look at my phone again, this time checking the local news feed. Weather, traffic, news. No mention of strange wolves or large dogs running wild. No breaking news of a large wolf having been captured—or worse. Hunter is okay.

Lifting my arms over my head, I stretch every muscle in my body, hoping to get out all the tight kinks associated with a restless night. A nice hot shower, a good breakfast and I'll be ready to face the day.

"C'mon Lively. It's going to be a helluva full day for me."

Lively jumps off the bed and I throw the rumpled sheets aside and head for the shower.

I'm outside at a quarter to seven, sitting on the front steps and waiting for Hunter. The sun is up and the day is crystal clear with sunshine. Not one cloud in the brilliant sky. A beautiful late spring day in California.

The male and female, my parents, aren't home yet—another night/day where they're out late. What's going on with them? It has to be important. What did my mom say yesterday when they came to the book store? Oh, right, "We had a few things to take care of. Some special things that needed our attention."

Now that's intriguing right there. What kind of special things cause them to stay out after sunrise? Books? Finding manuscripts that are so old, the writing is indecipherable? Returning old books to the rightful owner as they did for gentle Mr. Paget? What? It has to be something really important.

The soft purring sound of Hunter's Vespa motorbike comes around the corner of our street. He stops the bike on the curb and quickly gets off. Hunter looks happy and exhilarated. His run last night has been good for him.

"Hey there, Lilith. What a great day, huh? Blue skies, all-day class trip—I'm psyched! You?"

I sling my backpack onto my shoulders and stand up to kiss Hunter. He smells different, the way he always does after a night run. It's a good smell. Grass, moist earth, and all the subtle smells associated with the night. I grab his hand and check his nails. Clean, no mud. He must've really scrubbed them this morning.

"Good run?"

"The best! I feel incredible." Hunter gives me a serious look. "You know, Lilith, I just wish you could run with me. It's one of the best feelings in the world. You'd love it."

"I guess I would but—I don't know Hunter, sometimes I just want to be normal like everyone else."

"Normal? That's boring! Don't ever be normal, Lilith!"

I heave a deep sigh. Hunter's having adventures that I can only imagine. And me? All I can do is try to control the annoying power of levitation. Totally unfair. Hunter senses how I feel and brings me into a warm hug. Then we climb onto the bike and head for the school.

And, even though I don't know it yet, today is going to signal a major change in my life. A change that will begin to turn my annoying power into something unbelievable, something that will change my entire world and everything in it. Something incredible that will truly start me on my journey to becoming the real Lilith of the Angels.

SEVEN

"**Y**ou have an hour for lunch and I expect all of you to be back at the Hall of Criminal Justice entrance on time. We have a specific time slot reserved for this last lecture so, absolutely no latecomers will be admitted to the hall once the lecture starts. Now go!" Our Criminal Justice teacher checks her watch and then waves all of us toward the exit.

Hunter and I break away from the crowd of students and chaperones and rush out the door. We're both starving. Hunter says that, on the bus ride in, he saw a food truck that is selling Philly Cheesesteak a block away from the building. I love Philly Cheesesteaks.

Luckily the line is short. Ordering one cheesesteak, three large pitas stuffed with zucchini and cheese, two large orders of cheese fries, and two ice teas, we make our way to a small park nearby and find an empty table.

The three pitas and both orders of fries are for Hunter who literally, no joke intended here, begins to wolf them down. He always has a huge appetite after a full-moon night run.

"Lilith? You're kinda quiet today. Everything okay?"

I play with the inside of my Philly cheesesteak, pulling out the beef and melted cheese with a plastic fork and eating it before I answer.

"I'm okay. Just tired. I didn't sleep all that great last night."

"My fault. That Midnight howl? I just wanted you to know that I was okay. Sorry if I woke you up."

"You didn't wake me, Hunter. I'm not really sleeping well. I've got a lot on my mind. And yes, I do worry about you but that's not all. It's the uncontrolled levitation, my parents not coming home before dawn—what's with *that* anyway? And, passing Advanced Calculus, college next year. My mind is a whirling mess of my entire existence right now."

Hunter stops eating for a second and regards me seriously. "Wow, Lilith, I had no idea. But listen," he reaches across the table and his fingers touch my face, "don't worry about me, okay? I know what I'm doing and, after what happened last month, I'm more careful. I seriously didn't know that guy had set a trap."

He's talking about a man who had actually *seen* him running. Even though his father, Gideon, had always strictly forbidden him to go anywhere near the area, Hunter had traveled farther than usual on last month's run and ended up racing through the woods near a place called Ringwood Hills Club, an upscale riding academy owned by C. Thomas Ringwood.

The owner of the estate is always called C. Thomas; the name *Mr.* Ringwood is reserved for his father, even though that man has been dead for the last fifteen years. Sixty years old and, from the gossip I've heard, extremely superstitious, C. Thomas is a man who lives large, loves gambling, and has to have absolute control over everything in his life. To do that he is willing to do anything. There are wild stories of him having traveled to New Orleans and Jamaica to have his Tarot cards read by high-profile Voodoo queens to foresee any dangers that might occur in the future. He leaves nothing to chance and has a lot of fears, one of which is wolves. The eyes of wolves, he has been warned by one voodoo queen, can see into your very soul. Only by being in control is he able to allay his fears.

At the last full moon, Hunter had gotten a little too close to the stables and spooked the beautiful, high-spirited horses boarded there. C. Thomas came out to see what all the fuss was about just in time to see Hunter run past. He sent out an alarm to the stable hands, shouting, *"That wolf! It's come back to get me! But—it can't be, it's not possible! I thought it— last time I saw that wolf—no, no. Catch the ᵊamn thing. Now!"* The hands immediately set out wolf traps.

"He was so weird, Lilith. He kept saying that *it* had come back to get him. As if he thought I was some wolf he'd seen years ago or something."

Hunter raced to the shelter of the thick band of forest trees and waited there, watching the hands put out traps, carefully noting where each one was set. C. Thomas stood inside his house at the large picture window armed with a set of night-vision binoculars and all was quiet.

Hunter waited until the hands went back to their rooms. He should have just left and continued his run away from the riding academy grounds but the moon can sometimes make a young werewolf reckless. They don't think about the consequences of an action the way an older, more mature werewolf does. Hunter was definitely reckless that night, filled with the strong effect of the moon's power. He'd heard about how superstitious C. Thomas Ringwood was and couldn't resist the opportunity to make one more run past him, meaning just to scare him a little. The man was standing at the glass door to his house, loudly cursing all wolves. Just a quick scare, Hunter reasoned, and then he'd be gone.

But Hunter underestimated Ol' C. Thomas and it nearly cost him his freedom. While his attention was focused solely on the men setting the traps, he failed to notice that C. Thomas Ringwood himself had set a trap a short distance from the steps to his house.

Hunter raced toward the steps of the veranda, easily avoiding where the other set traps had been placed. He intended to run up onto the veranda, stop, let out a long, scary howl, and then take off. As he got closer to the house, a glint of metal caught his eye and, too late, he tried to make a turn to avoid it. But he was running too fast to make a complete turn and he brushed against the side of the trap. The metal teeth of the trap immediately snapped shut, pulling a large clump of long fur from Hunter's leg. Hunter was able to get away before anyone came to investigate the sound of the trap snapping, but C. Thomas Ringwood saw him and immediately came outside to inspect the trap and the long strands of fur caught in it.

He laughed like a crazy man. *"A wolf your size isn't easy to miss. I'll get you. I swear I'll get you this time."*

"This time?" I ask surprised.

"That's what he said."

It scares me to think what would have happened had Hunter been caught. He says that from now on, he will stay away from the Ringwood estate and I have to believe him. I have no choice.

"Hey, Lilith? I'm serious. I can promise you that I learned from that foolish mistake." He reaches across again and grabs my hand.

"Seriously? You know there's a Blue Moon coming the end of this month."

The Blue Moon, so-called because it is the second full moon in a 30-day time span—one at the beginning of the month and one at the very end, but still in the same calendar month. It's considered lucky but, the power of the Blue Moon can have some very strange effects on werewolves, more so than just a regular full moon. I worry about Hunter.

"I love the exhilaration the Blue Moon brings me! The thrill of power I feel speeding through the—." He stops when he sees the worried look I must have on my face.

"Umm, sorry, forget what I just said. Seriously, Lilith, don't worry about me or the effects of the Blue Moon. That mark on my leg will always remind me to steer clear of people when I'm out on a run. I promise and a promise means a lot to me."

I nod at him. The raised reddish mark on his calf where the fur was pulled out. That's a reminder all right.

"Okay." I glance at my phone. "We'd better get back, Hunter. That criminologist who's a specialist on poison is going to speak next. Let's go."

We hurry back toward the building with a quick stop at the food truck so Hunter can get two chocolate bars and a hot pretzel. His appetite is scary the day after a full moon run.

"Poison can come in many forms," says the criminologist, a man who gives a direct, unflinching look to the group of high school seniors seated in front of a large screen. "It's not always a product you buy in a hardware store. The most innocent looking things in nature can be used as a poison if a criminal knows how to extract a lethal quantity. This morning you learned about the poisonous flowers Larkspur, Foxglove, and the sweet-smelling Oleander which is particularly deadly and native to California. You also learned about deadly mushrooms, such as the Death Cap and the Destroying Angel." Someone yells out to Hunter that he better be careful around me and there's a bit of good-natured laughter as my classmates glance in my direction. I laugh too.

"We're also familiar with Belladonna, a Eurasian perennial with reddish, bell-shaped flowers that bear glossy-coated, black berries. Crushed into food or drink, it is highly lethal. In fact, the use of Belladonna to secretly poison someone has been a favorite of assassins throughout the centuries. The Borgias were famous for their use of Belladonna. A small dose of the crushed berries in a cup of wine served to their enemies, or to anyone they felt was a threat to their ambitions, was all that was needed. Potent stuff that Belladonna.

"But as I said, there is poison in the most innocent products of nature. Poison is a naturally occurring composite of some fruits and vegetables which we consider harmless. For instance, did you know that the simple apple contains poison?" There's stirring of interest in the assembled group. An apple? Poisonous?

"How is that possible?" asks a girl who has a skeptical look on her face. "A lot of people eat apples and they don't die."

"Yes, but it's not the fruit, the apple itself, that is poisonous. It's the seeds. Apple seeds contain a substance that can convert into poisonous hydrogen cyanide in the intestine and it isn't only apples that can be poisonous. Cherries, apricots, peaches, and plums—all contain cyanogenic glycosides that create cyanide in the pits." He stops and lets us ponder this for a moment before he continues. Poisonous fruit. Who knew?

"Raw lima beans are another product of nature that can be used as a poison. They contain a product called limarin. Just a handful of raw lima beans can make someone violently ill, more can induce death. However, when the lima beans are well-cooked, they're harmless. Just don't drink the liquid in which they were boiled, which contains the liquefied poison, and you'll be okay."

I hear a boy mutter, "Here's my excuse to never eat lima beans again. They're disgusting anyway."

I raise my hand.

"Yes? You have a question for me?" The criminologist asks.

"I do. Can you get sick if you eat the seeds in just one apple?"

"Not really. Most bodies can handle that small amount without any harm. Others may experience a slight gaseous stomach upset."

"So then, how many apple seeds are we talking about that would create enough poison to kill a person?"

The criminologist looks hard at me, then smiles. "Are you planning to poison someone, young lady?"

"No, sir, not at all. I like the science of criminology, how it works to solve crimes—and I'm fascinated by it all. I want to be a criminologist."

He shakes his head and smiles again. "Right. Well, then, I'd say for an average size adult the fatal dose of hydrogen cyanide from apples seeds would be about 50 milligrams or less than a teaspoon. Of course the seeds would have to be *pulverize* first to ensure the cyanide was absorbed by the body."

There's a question and answer segment with the criminologist that goes on for another hour and then it's back to the bus. It's going for 4:00. Time to head to Midnight Ink.

EIGHT

Lively is in the big, bay window of Midnight Ink catching late afternoon sun rays when Hunter and I arrive. He rises and stretches, then bats a paw at the glass in greeting. The beautiful creatures I call mom and dad are somewhere in the back of the book shop and, from the sound of voices carrying to me, it seems that they have a customer with them.

"Hey, it's just us," I shout out in case the tinkling of the chimes makes them think that another customer has come in. "We're going to do some inventory before Hunter has to leave."

I know Hunter can't wait until the moon rises. It's day two of the full moon. He's anxious to run again tonight.

"All right, darling," calls my mom, her voice sounding as lilting as the chimes above the door. "Hello Hunter. All good?"

"It's all good, Mrs. Angel. You and Mr. Angel?"

"Fine, we're fine, Hunter, just—well, busy at the moment."

Hunter grabs a stylus and the iPad we use for inventory and follows me as I go up and down the shop, checking off current titles or writing in the names of new ones that have yet to be catalogued. It's nice to work with Hunter and I envision a day when we might open our own agency that deals with criminology. The two of us helping to solve crimes.

We'd certainly have an advantage over other criminologists, especially when I learn to control my power of levitation and Hunter gets a little older. My dad told me that older werewolves can control their transformations better. Hunter's father never does a full moon run any more. He still experiences the pull of the full moon but it's more in terms of stronger mental powers, a heightened sense of smell, and physical strength.

There are so many books to inventory and we keep at it as late afternoon turns into early evening. I see Hunter start to twitch just a little, quick sudden ripples in his muscles that let me know the change will be coming over him in a couple of hours. I haven't seen him make the change, not yet. Changing from human to wolf, that's a big deal in a relationship. But, I am determined to do so this summer.

Looking at Hunter makes me know that he needs something to eat before he heads out for the moon run. The energy he expends on these days is phenomenal. I touch his face gently.

"Hunter? Let's go grab something to eat. You have some time before the moon begins to rise."

He puts down the iPad and stretches. "Yeah, good idea. I need some fuel for later. My dad's on a business trip and he did cook a lot of food before he left, but I really want some Italian cheesecake right now. I am *starving*."

I let my parents know we're going out to get something to eat. Hunter reaches for my hand and we leave Midnight Ink for the pastry shop two blocks away. The sun is getting low toward the horizon and I can feel the magic of the moon who will soon begin her steady ascent to take her place as the dominant celestial body in the night sky. Hunter's hand trembles slightly as we run across the street.

Back inside Midnight Ink, I place cut up pieces of roast beef in Lively's bowl and get him fresh water. After promising me once again that he'll be careful, Hunter has gone home to get ready for the last moon run of the month. I sit down in the window seat and look out at the street. It's quiet tonight. I know Hunter won't go by the Ringwood Riding Academy again. My sincere hope is that C. Thomas has forgotten about seeing a wolf or at the very least, has put the incident in the recesses of his mind and is not actively seeking Hunter with a group of armed goons leading the way. Hunting is against the law in Summer Valley but you never know. From what I've heard about him, C. Thomas is just crazy enough to break that law.

There's a soft, warm breeze blowing through the open side windows of our book shop. I close my eyes. It's so peaceful that, for a moment I forget about dangers and dangerous people like Mr. C. Thomas Ringwood, and doze off.

"Lilith." The soft voice of my mom wakes me. She kisses my cheek. "Did you and Hunter have dinner?"

I rub my eyes and sit up. "Yes, we went to the pastry shop." I look at her. Her beauty is diaphanous and gossamer-thin tonight. She must be really hungry. Why hasn't she fed yet? Quickly I ask, "Can I go get you and Dad anything?"

"Thank you, darling, but no. We're all right for now."

My mom stands looking at me with the same gentle kindness she has shown me since the night she found me and brought me home. I have no idea what made the male and female love a disheveled, dirty little girl tied to a church railing so much that they decided to raise me as their own. All I know is that they are my true parents, people who have always made sure I was protected and cherished. That love and kindness dispels another vamp myth—the one that says vampires are cold, cruel, emotionless creatures. Not true at all.

"Is your customer still here? I didn't hear the chimes."

"She's more than a customer, Lilith. She's someone special and we'd like you to meet her. It's time. We searched the world for her. Come in the back with me and I'll introduce you."

"Sure, okay."

It's time? Time for what?

Time for me to find out something I guess.

"Levitation can be a defense mechanism, Lilith," says Professor A. J. Reed. "Your mind is controlling it. Like most normal people who are in a tense situation, it's a fight or flight action. In your case, it's a *real* flight!"

A.J. Reed is a tiny, elf-like woman with a mass of dark curls that she keeps brushing back from her face. Dressed all in a pastel lilac, she looks as if she stepped right out of a Victorian era children's book. As delicate as she looks, I sense a strength and determined will in her. There's something about her that makes me feel at ease and I like her immediately.

"But I also levitate when I'm happy or—," I hesitate, slightly embarrassed.

"Aroused?" She smiles at me.

Aroused?! Wow! I wouldn't have put it so bluntly, but yup, aroused is the word for it. When Hunter kisses me, I start to levitate. I nod yes, grateful that my parents have left. After making small talk with us and making sure that I was comfortable with the professor, they have gone out to feed.

"Well, yes, that will happen too. Hormones, you know. All it means is that your emotions are overloading, *pleasantly* overloading when aroused, but still causing you to take flight. A flight of joy as it were." She nods knowingly at me.

Oh boy!

"Did you know that levitation is only the beginning part of your gift? You have the actual gift of flight. Compare this gift to a baby's progress. The baby crawls before learning to walk. So, in essence this levitation is your crawling stage. Flight, actual flying-through-the-air flight, is the next part."

"But if I can't control my levitation, how can I control this gift of—of flight?"

"Ah, Lilith, there *is* a way to control this power of yours. It is a remarkable power, you can be sure, but it shouldn't control *you*. You're the boss of *it*." She pauses and looks steadily at me for a few minutes. "Are you aware, has anyone told you that you can will your own feathery wings to appear for flying? Once you learn to use them, they can certainly aid you in any flight."

"Wings? Like—*real* wings?" Hell's Bells!

"Yes, real, solid, absolutely perfect wings. As real as you are right now, standing in front of me. All you have to do is visualize them just once, see them in your mind's eye, and then concentrate on the image. They'll appear and become a part of you. When you don't need them, they disappear. The wonderful thing about that is that you only have to imagine them once and anytime you need them, they'll simply reappear!"

I must have looked extremely skeptical because the prof hurried to continue. "Lilith, you have been *blessed* with the gift of flight. Up to now you've seen it as a bother, an annoyance that was hard to control. But you must believe me when I tell you that this is a wonderful gift you have."

"My parents can fly and they don't have wings," I say completely unconvinced that I can just imagine a pair of feathery appendages and they'll magically appear. I remembered the night I was found and how I told the male that only birds have wings. He had replied, *"But, Lilith of the Angels, we ￼on't nee￼ wings!"*

"Your parents are different. Their power isn't really about flight. It's more a matter of willing themselves to zoom into the air and rush away at great speeds or to simply to float on the air currents. Theirs is more a mind over matter vamp power. Your speed, however, is limited and, will always be limited, even with wings. You'll never be as fast as your parents are." She pauses. "But your wings might even give you a greater advantage in soaring the skies than they possess. You have other powers as well as levitation and flight, your red hair and green eyes attest to the magical possibilities in you. Your mother believes that you are part witch, and I believe she's right." She looks at me with a knowing smile. "Once you take the time to learn about, and use, your powers, you will be amazed at what you can do. You'll find that you have superior fighting skills, strong powers of observation, a powerful sixth sense, eyes like a hawk, and an uncanny instinct concerning people and all creatures."

"What about math?"

"Math?"

"Calculus to be exact. I have a hard time passing calculus. It drives me crazy."

"Well, your mind *will* be sharper and you'll be able to learn faster, so that should help you pass calculus. The gift you possess for knowing words in any language will increase as well. That gift seems to be one that you aren't afraid to use, am I correct?"

"Words are safe," I say rather defensively.

"Yes, but they're also powerful. And, here's a fun fact— your mind-talk with your cat, Lively will become stronger."

"I can understand most of what he says now."

"Yes, I know but, with your increased powers, you will be able to communicate much more easily and you'll understand *everything* he tells you. That's a great asset. I know because I have two cats. Their advice is very practical, you know."

Professor A. J. Reed smiles at me when she says that, then she turns serious. "One more ability, and this is crucial, you have the power to sense the supernatural world and all its otherworldly creatures and inhabitants. You'll begin with all the many of them who live around here."

I look at her in complete surprise.

"*What* other inhabitants? You mean like Hunter, Mr. Paget, you, and my parents? Like," I hesitate, "like—me? How many others are there?! I have met *some* otherworldly inhabitants, customers, here in Midnight Ink but, are you saying that there are a lot of others I don't know about?"

"Oh, Lilith, many, many others. Haven't you sensed us? Sensed that there was a world other than the physical one we see here? Haven't you sensed that there were others who were—for want of a better word— different?"

I think about the people I know, teachers, classmates, the small circle of those I see almost every day. Except for my parents' customers, I've never sensed that anyone else was an otherworldly inhabitant. I shake my head. "No, sorry."

Professor A. J. Reed smiles at me. "That's all right, Lilith. We creatures do tend to blend in wherever we live. And, as for you not sensing us, well, you're probably blocking that knowledge. But now, you're almost at the age when your powers will begin to manifest more strongly. Eighteen is usually the key age. With my, and your parents' help, your senses will begin to expand day by day. You will be able to train your mind and your will to allow them to enter your life. I think perhaps that you were unconsciously blocking your powers because you were afraid of them."

"You're saying that I didn't realize that I had any powers because I was afraid of them, that I blocked them. Wouldn't the powers just, I don't know, manifest themselves anyway, whether I wanted them or not?"

"Well, no. Look at the way you seem to want to block your power of levitation. You're afraid of it, of what it can do. Any power that you fear, your subconscious will try to block."

"I almost rose to the ceiling in Advanced Calculus yesterday. I don't want anyone seeing me do that!"

"No, and you're quite right about that. Unless your classmates and teacher have certain supernatural powers themselves, then of course you wouldn't want them to see you levitate." She takes my hand and says, "Lilith, your parents have asked me to help you learn about your powers and how best to use them. I can also teach you how to center yourself with calmness in order to better access your powers."

"But—" I paused thinking about all she was saying to me. Thinking about what she called my gifts. It was overwhelming and mind-boggling trying to understand all that these gifts would mean to me and how they would change my life.

"Yes?" Professor A. J. Reed looks at me, nodding encouragingly.

"What if I don't want to use these powers? Can I refuse these—gifts—if I don't really want them?"

"You can, of course, refuse these powers, dear Lilith. You have that right."

"No disrespect, Professor Reed, but I just want to be normal."

"But you *are* normal, Lilith. Having these powers *is* normal for *you*. I know you don't believe it but you're perfect just as you are. Normal is subjective to every species. Take cats and dogs as a simple example. They're very similar in a lot of ways and they co-exist well. But make no mistake, they each have certain gifts, certain powers that are different from each other. Their special abilities, if you prefer that word over powers, are normal for them."

I shake my head. "Maybe you're right but, actually using these powers, I don't know about that. I'm not brave enough to use them, really Professor Reed, I'm not at all brave. My big ambition is to someday open an office with my boyfriend Hunter and work as a criminologist. Hunter could gather information, you know, do all the legwork, and I'd sit at a desk sifting through clues, maybe do some lab work, and solve crimes. That's all I really want."

Professor Reed looks at me steadily, almost as if she's seeing into my very core, seeing what I am really am, seeing into my future. She seems to go into a mystical trance and when she speaks again, her voice is strong with conviction.

"You're braver than you think you are, Lilith, much, much braver." Her eyes glaze over slightly and she seems to be looking into some future time. She shakes her head and continues. "You have a bravery that will protect and help our kind and humans as well. I see that in you. You will use your powers well. Let me tell you that you will make an excellent criminologist and you won't just be sitting at a desk. You'll be out there with Hunter because you will love the action, what you call the legwork. I see this for you."

I want to ask her to tell me what else she sees in the future when I strongly sense something behind me. The sixth sense Professor Reed just told me about? I turn to see my mom and dad standing in the doorway of the rare book room. Their vamp stealth allows them to enter without being heard. The pallor that had plagued them earlier tonight is gone. They must have fed well. They come over to me.

"Your powers are a rare gift. Very few are blessed with these gifts. I think it would be such a terrible disregard of their beauty and strength to just ignore the fact that you possess them."

My dad lifts my chin gently. "You yourself are a rare gift to us, my Lilith of the Angels. Remember that I called you that the night we found you? Lilith of the Angels. I think you owe it to yourself to learn about your powers first and then make a decision about using them or not."

"Yes, Lilith. It will always be *your* choice." My mom's crystal-clear green eyes look deeply into my own. "We can advise you but you are the only one who can choose what to do."

"Give me a little time."

"Of course, my darling."

I walk out the door of the rare book room, through the main area of Midnight Ink until I stand in front of the shop's door. Opening it, I breathe in the night air, the smell of new jasmine and lilac tickling my senses. I hate making decisions. Amsterdam, Rotterdam, damn, damn, damn!

Lively jumps down from the window seat and circles my legs, purring softly. I get the feeling that he's encouraging me to learn how to use my powers. I think about all that the powers would open up to me. How the world would change for me and how, maybe my powers would turn out to be something wonderful. Maybe.

Suddenly a long howl fills the night followed by another and then another. Hunter. How appropriate. Talk about otherworldly creatures! A heavy sigh of longing that seems to come from the very pit of my core escapes through my mouth and, with it, a deep calm seems to descend on me. I close the door and walk back to where my mom and dad are patiently waiting.

"Okay. Maybe it is time I learned about whatever powers I have." I turn to my mom and dad. "I'm ready."

NINE

"**R**eady or not, here I come!"

I fly up, up, up. The earth below me looks so far away and the night sky so vast that, for one awful moment, I feel a thrill of fear. Then the moment passes and I fly and circle up and down, feeling the wind against me, feeling the awesome strength of my wings. My incredible, beautiful black wings. Below me, Hunter lets out a howl of pure joy as he runs in ecstatic circles beneath me on the earth below.

For the first time since I learned how to harness and control my powers I feel as if I am truly worthy of the name, Lilith of the Angels.

The Blue Moon is here, a time of magic. Tonight is its last night. It's been three weeks since my last daily lesson with Professor A.J. Reed. She gave me the knowledge and taught me all I needed to know. Now it's up to me.

"All you have to do, Lilith, is visualize, concentrate, and work at controlling your powers every single day."

Everything about learning how to release and control my powers was intense. That, coupled with my school work took all of my time. I missed Midnight Ink, but every day after school, Hunter dropped me off at home where I did my homework—calculus was still not clicking for me, last test I got a 76—then worked on my powers with A. J. Reed.

The first power I had to learn to control was levitation, I needed to stop fearing it and make it work for me.

"Think of your powers as electricity, something you can simply switch on and off. You're in control of turning a light on when you need it, and off when you don't. It should be the same with your powers. Your concentration is the switch to use with your powers. On. Off."

So, I concentrated and concentrated and concentrated. I learned that if I found myself up against the ceiling in the middle of the night, I could concentrate my way down slowly to my bed and not land haphazardly on the floor. By concentrating on grounding myself, I could keep the levitation under control at school and everywhere else I went. I still levitate when Hunter kisses me and we snuggle together in each other's arms—that's the hardest to control—but I'm working on it.

The part about having a sharper mind is true except, as I said, for Advanced Calculus. As far as the other powers, physical strength, observation, and instinct, they're slowly coming out. I can just barely sense the supernatural world but that's getting stronger. It's a little strange to realize that there are so many others, otherworldly beings like me, in the world.

The best thing of all, the power that I really doubted would be mine, were my wings. Eyes closed, I sat on the floor of my darkened bedroom and visualized them in my mind. The first two times, nothing happened. No feathery wings appeared and attached themselves to me. I was disappointed.

"You fear this power. Your fear is blocking it," said my mom very late one night after I had failed yet again to create wings. They had just returned from feeding and their strength was a great source of comfort to me. My dad sat on my bed and Lively jumped into his lap. He's a Tuxedo cat now, black and white, and mind-talk with him is one of the best gifts from my powers. His green eyes regard me with interest and in my mind, I hear him say, "Concentrate. It will come."

"Try it again, darling. Clear your mind of all negative thoughts, and visualize the most powerful, beautiful wings you can imagine."

"We'll stay with you," said my dad. "There's nothing to fear. Just keep your eyes closed and don't open them until you can clearly see your wings in your mind's eye."

They sat on the floor across from me and each took hold of one of my hands.

I closed my eyes and felt a warm calmness I knew was being radiated through the hands of my vamp parents. I began to breathe slowly and methodically, visualizing a fantastic pair of wings, feathery soft but powerfully strong. I saw them in my mind's eye, just a glimmering at first and then the image began to slowly grow more vivid until I felt a tingling sensation in my shoulder blades and I saw, actually saw, the wings. Strong, black wings of an indescribable beauty.

I heard my mom inhale a quick breath and my dad murmur, "Incredible."

"I see them in my mind! Can I please open my eyes now?"

"Wait, Lilith. Let us help you stand up before you open your eyes," said my dad quickly. "You need to see yourself in the mirror." I felt them pull me to my feet.

"Now, darling, now you can open your eyes," said my mom. I did as she requested and stared.

I was standing in front of the long pier glass mirror I had gotten as a present for my fourteenth birthday. How many times had I stood there looking at my reflection while I tried on clothes or did my hair a different way! How many times had I practiced my English Lit. presentations over and over again, looking at my expressions in the mirror! I knew exactly what I looked like. Now I looked a bit nervously to see a 'new' me.

The reflection in the mirror was still me, me in a pair of soft jeans and a tee-shirt, but with a significant difference. On either side of my body rose a jet black wing in graceful arcs of incomparable beauty. I moved a little, shifting my body from front to side. The feathers shimmered in the bright moonlight which shone through my window. The wings seemed to be attached to my shoulder blades.

My mom picked up a hand-mirror lying on my dresser and held it so that I could see a back view of myself. I was stunned. I had wings, wings! Like a bird, I was a winged creature. I was thrilled and I felt—powerful!

A howl splits the quiet of the night. The Blue Moon. Lots of power and strong vibes.

"I want to go outside. I have to feel them in the night air. I want Hunter to see me."

My parents lead the way but stop outside my room when they see me hesitate at the doorway. What if the wings are too big to pass through? They are certainly higher than the door frame—they almost touch the ceiling! Would they break if I try to push through? They didn't feel stiff, they felt remarkably supple. But—oh, Hell's Bells! What should I do?

"Mom? Dad? I don't know if they'll fit through the door!"

"Darling." The soft, gentle sound of my mom's voice calms me. "Remember what Professor Reed said? *You* are in control of your powers. Imagine passing through the doorway with your wings."

"Yes, Lilith of the Angels, concentrate on passing through," says my dad. "Just visualize it."

I close my eyes and try to envision myself walking through the door with my wings. I even imagine them brushing ever-so-lightly against the door frame. Okay, I have to try. I open my eyes, stepping forward and placing one foot over the threshold. My wings gently drop to my side as I go through the doorway. Encouraged, I run outside to try them out.

"Remember Lilith, flying with wings is the same as getting a license to drive a car. It's a privilege that comes with responsibility."

"Okay, Dad. I know!" He's told me this several times already. After careful consideration and a long talk, it was decided by the male and female that I should fly only after 11:00 at night. The houses in our neighborhood aren't close together and our backyard is basically hidden by foliage and high trees so the chance of anyone seeing me fly at that time is minimal.

The male and the female are excellent navigators. They flew, or, as Professor Reed explained, leaped up into the air before me. They wait, their vamp power allowing them to hover motionless in the air.

"Responsibility and precautions. You need to know the risks and the rewards of winged flight."

"Got it, Mom."

Once I'm out of the house my wings rise once again to their magnificent beauty then spread out in a breath-taking display. They are awesome. I move them up and down just to get a feel of how they will work for me.

I sense a presence near me, that powerful sixth sense Professor Reed mentioned. I turn and there's Hunter in his wolf form, over by the rose bushes, standing completely still and calmly watching me with his wolf's eyes. I wave and then point to my wings.

"Watch me, Hunter. I'm going to fly!"

I concentrate, eyes closed, and cautiously flutter my wings up and down. Slowly I feel my body rise into the air. Opening my eyes, I find I am level with my mom and dad. Hell's Bells!

Levitating is one thing and I'm happy to see that I can control it. Now I just need to actually fly. Can I control that too? I picture myself swooping slowly around our backyard and to my surprise, I begin to do just that! Fly until, my shock at what I'm actually doing hits me full force and I lose control, smacking hard into the upper branches of the oak tree and falling to the ground.

"Owww! Hell's Bells!"

"Lilith?" The soft voice of my mom floats down to me.

"I'm okay. Seriously, I'll be fine."

I lay there for a few seconds, breathing hard and being scared. Hell's Bells! Amsterdam, Rotterdam, damn, damn, damn!

I am furious with myself. I have to conquer my stupid fears and do it now. I get to my knees and then to my feet, shaking my wings. A few feathers fall off but otherwise they're fine. I glance at the back door where Lively is perched on a chair looking at me. Over by the roses, Hunter stands still as a large statue and waits.

That's it! Fears be damned, I am determined to master flight. Walking to the middle of the yard, I spread my wings and hear them rustle the air around me. It's almost as if they're waiting for me to give them the command to fly. I concentrate.

I feel my body rise vertically through the night air. I flutter my wings toward the left and, like a turn of the steering wheel of a car, I fly left out over the yard and then flutter them to make a right turn. I do this over and over again, making wobbly circles. Gaining confidence, I fly higher and faster, suddenly realizing how Hunter feels when he does a Blue Moon run.

Exhilarated!

My parents separate quickly, avoiding a head-on collision with me, as I fly straight toward them. I swing to my left.

"How beautiful, darling! You're really flying!" says my mom proudly.

"Lilith of the Angels," laughs my dad in absolute joy. "We named you well!"

I rise and swoop a bit erratically, trying hard to be confident in the power of my incredible wings.

Hunter throws back his head and howls with joy before copying my flight circles with perfect precision on the ground below me.

Soaring hesitantly above the ground, with the night breeze against my face, I feel free and brave. The stars brilliantly twinkle down at me and the full moon glows with a beauty that is luminescent. Heady with the power of flight and an unbridled joy, I wonder why I was so afraid of releasing my powers. How ridiculous to be afraid of possessing these special gifts!

What is there to fear anyway?

TEN

I flew until early morning. Amazingly, after I landed in the backyard my wings magically disappeared. Just a brief thought in my mind that I didn't need them and they were gone. I didn't even have to concentrate! Is controlling powers really this easy?

Surprisingly I wasn't at all tired. Again I thought of Hunter and how, after nights of a full- moon run, he's energized and ready to go once the morning comes and he changes back to his human form. I feel as if I could run a marathon!

My parents watched me on my solo backyard flight to make sure all went well, then left just before sunrise. I don't know where they went. Their mysterious journeys are a little unsettling. I had thought that, in the past few months, they came home past sunrise because they were searching for Professor Reed so she could teach me about my power. They *ha* said they searched the world over just to find her. What could they be searching for now?

Hunter left soon after I landed in the backyard. I heard his distinctive howl about an hour ago, letting me know that he was running toward home. There's just me and Lively here now and that's okay. I need to shower and change. Classes begin in two hours. But first, I have to eat—I'm starving.

From the refrigerator, I grab a bagel my dad bought for me yesterday. It's stuffed with Swiss cheese and smoked salmon. I had intended to eat it after school but then got distracted with concentrating on making my wings appear. Lively's dish is full. My mom must have filled it, and his water dish too, before they left. I sit with Lively and we eat in contentment and peaceful quiet. I go over my calculus homework from last night—it's getting a bit better. Maybe the sharper mind gift is really starting to work on my understanding of calculus.

Later, I take a shower and shampoo my hair. I decide that I'm just going to towel dry it, brush it smooth, and let it simply fall. I have no time to be fancy today. I just want to get through the day so I can fly again tonight. I'm so psyched!

The front doorbell rings just as I'm getting out of the shower. Who's ringing the bell at this hour? It can't be Hunter. Glancing at the clock in the hall, I see that I have almost an hour before he shows up. Plus, he never, ever rings the bell. He either throws pebbles at my window or does a rapid staccato knock on the door.

Wrapping a towel around me I cautiously peer through the upstairs hall window which is directly above the front door. There's no one there. I open the window and lean my head out, looking up and down the street. I don't see anyone.

But as I turn away from the window, I feel the hair on the back of my neck rise and a brief chill goes through my body. I smell a certain barely remembered scent, something flowery but distinctly unpleasant. A fluttering memory tries hard to surface and then fades away just as quickly as the chill. Is that sixth sense alerting me to something otherworldly? Is it warning me of impending disaster?

"Relax Lilith, everything is all right."

It's Lively, purring and rubbing himself against my legs.

I bend and pick him up, burying my face in his soft fur. A calmness surrounds me and my mind goes blank. I shake my head. What just happened? What was I doing? Oh, yes, okay. I have to get ready for school. I walk slowly to my bedroom, totally forgetting the fear I felt. The only thing that remains in my mind is that faint decaying flowery smell that seemed to waft upwards and through the open window.

"Calculus is the study of how things change. For instance, when we deal with an object moving along a path, its position varies with time. It's calculated. The following are three examples."

I diligently copy down the statements projected on the white board at the front of the room listening to the droning voice of the narrator explaining what they mean. I once read that you'll remember information if you actually take the time to write it down. Something to do with hand, eye, brain coordination or something. These will be on the final exam and I am determined to pass this with at least a B-.

While I write, I keep my legs hooked around the chair base just in case I unconsciously start a rise to the ceiling. I pretty well have this power under control—most of the time anyway. I read over what I have written, *the study of how things change.* I smile thinking about my first winged-flight. I was an object moving in circles, my position varying with time. I trace small circles on my notepad, then draw larger ones.

65

"Very good, Lilith. You're demonstrating a calculus proof for the area of a circle. There's an equation for that, you know."

Mr. Mendelssohn is standing behind my desk and, involuntarily, I feel myself rise upward just a little. I hug the chair tighter with my legs.

"Um, yes, it was in the last chapter, right?"

"Yes, it was. I'm glad to see you are finally catching on to the immense joy of learning advanced calculus. It is a powerful gift."

"Uh-huh, yes, I know."

He walks away and I take a deep breath, letting it out slowly. Powerful. Mr. Mendelssohn if you only *knew* what a real powerful gift is like! I daydream about the wonder of being able to fly.

"Lilith?"

A boy next to me, who has been looking at his phone for the last half hour, asks to see my notes. I hand them over and he takes pictures of what I have written. Lazy!

"Thanks." He puts my notebook on my desk and goes back to checking his phone.

"What's so interesting on your phone that you can't take your own notes?" I ask grabbing the notebook. He puts his hand up in a 'wait-a-second' gesture and keeps reading. Then he turns to me, all excited.

"Lots of shit going down. You haven't heard? My friend works at a riding academy on the weekends—it's way out of town. He just texted me. That filthy rich guy, C. Thomas Ringwood, is offering a reward to anyone who captures or kills a huge grey wolf who attacked him and his horses. Ten thousand dollars! Happened a couple of weeks ago. He's been putting out traps for the wolf himself but hasn't had any luck. Now he's offering this big reward. He put up signs and everything. Even put it on social media. He says the wolf barely escaped from a trap he set. 'This damned wolf won't get away from me again,' is what he told my friend. Man, would I like to get that money!" He laughs.

Hunter.

"My friend says that C. Thomas said his father was killed by the same big grey wolf years ago and he's hated them ever since. Says that he got a tuft of fur from this wolf and it matches the one he's kept, the one from the wolf who killed his father. People are setting baited traps all over the area. They're—hey!"

I stand up and, over his protests, I grab the boy's phone to look at the text he received. Hell's Bells! C. Thomas Ringwood hasn't forgotten about Hunter's visit. I think about last night's second full moon of the month, the powerful Blue Moon and take a deep breath. Hunter was with me all night and only did his Blue Moon run going back to his house. No chance Ringwood saw him last night. So, he hasn't seen Hunter since the time my werewolf boyfriend almost got caught in a trap. But—according to the text message—he's been searching for Hunter in his wolf form ever since. And C. Thomas lied! Hunter never attacked him or his horses!

Oh Hunter! My heart pounds hard with fear for him and anger at C. Thomas Ringwood. Before I can control it, the strong emotions I feel make me rise a foot in the air. The boy whose phone I have looks at me in utter shock.

"Lilith? *Lil?* Did you, uh, did you just like, *float* up?! I mean, did your feet leave the *floor?!*"

I take a deep breath, grab onto the desk, and as Professor Reed has taught me, I concentrate on switching that power off. Turning to my classmate, I feign disbelief.

"What?! That's ridiculous! What are you *thinking?* Nobody floats!"

"Yeah, but I just saw *you*—"

"You saw *me* stretching and balancing on my toes, silly. My back aches from sitting too long." I deliberately stretch upwards as high as I can. "My muscles are so tight!"

He looks at me quizzically then lets out a sigh of relief. It's easier for the practical part of the human mind to believe a lie than to question the truth of what the eyes really see. No one wants to believe anything that can't be explained rationally. It's too scary and unnerving.

The dismissal bell rings and I reluctantly hand back the phone. Gathering my stuff, I leave class. Outside the classroom door Hunter is waiting for me.

"How's the queen of the nighttime sky?" he whispers happily, putting his arm around me. "You were fantastic! What do you have to say about last night's flight?"

I look him in the eye and answer, "Amsterdam, Rotterdam, damn, damn, damn!"

Then I pull him into an empty custodian's closet and tell him about what Ringwood is doing.

ELEVEN

"**B**ut it's been almost eight weeks since I was there. I was nowhere near the Ringwood stables last night. I did my run from your house to mine. C. Thomas Ringwood is *still* looking for me? Why?"

"Because you got away, you escaped the trap he had set! Because a wolf killed his father. Why in the world did you ever run up and scare him anyway?"

"What are you talking about? His father was killed? I don't understand what you mean about a wolf killing his father. When?"

"It didn't happen now. The text said it happened some years ago. I don't know all the details but it said that he saw a big grey wolf kill his father. You're the only big grey wolf I know. Plus, he says he has an old tuft of fur from that wolf that matches the one caught in the trap from you.

Were there others like you? I mean—have you ever seen any other Lycans around here?"

"I don't run with a pack—there are no other werewolves around here anymore. The packs, for whatever reason, seem to have gone to other areas. No Lycans and definitely no Canis Lupus, the regular wolves, that I've seen a few times. Believe me, I'd sense it if either kind was in the area."

"Maybe your father might know about other Lycans that may have been here or near here."

Hunter muses, tapping his fingers against one of his books, trying to take in everything that I'm saying. "Maybe, but he's never mentioned anything about others like us in this area." He pauses. "You're saying it was a grey wolf like me?"

"Yes! A big grey wolf like you!"

"And his father was *killel* by this big grey wolf?"

"Yes!" I say in a loud whisper. "That's why he hates wolves and why he put up a reward for your capture or—Hell's Bells! He wants you dead or alive!"

"But, how can he think that wolf is me? You said his father was killed years ago." Then Hunter is silent for what seems to be an eternity. My heart is pounding like crazy while I wait for him to say something. But when he finally speaks, his voice is low and very strange.

"This big wolf, the one who looks like me, it was never—caught?"

"I guess not. That's not the point, Hunter. The point is this C. Thomas Ringwood is looking for *you.* Hunter! Did you hear what I just said?"

But Hunter seems to be miles away in thought. He's standing there shaking his head and whispering softly to himself, "Memories, grey werewolf running, running. Freedom. Fear."

I tug his arm to get his attention. "What are you saying, what are you thinking about? Hunter, talk to me."

He takes my books and his and puts them on a utility shelf. Then he gathers me in his arms. "Do you mind if I don't go to Midnight Ink with you? I'm curious about something and I want to find out if—never mind, I'll see you later. You have to practice flying and I love seeing that." He smiles gently into my eyes.

"Fly? How can I fly tonight when I'm worried about you?"

"Everything will be okay, I promise. There's just something that I want to check out. But I don't want you to worry about anything, okay? "

"What's wrong? You're not going to see C. Thomas Ringwood, are you, and try to find out what he's doing?"

"That might not be a bad idea, but no, I'm not going anywhere near him in any form, human or wolf. I'll come by later tonight and explain everything. I wonder why my dad never told me about a wolf attack around here. I'm just curious to—." He doesn't finish the sentence, just kind of stares off into space as if he's trying to remember something important. He kisses me, picks up his books, and leaves without any further explanation.

I walk into the hallway with a feeling of dread deep in the pit of my gut. My increased senses intensify the feeling one-hundred fold. Two girls walk past me, chatting and laughing, on their way out the door. They smile and wave to me and I give them a half-wave back. Damn! I wish I was normal like them, just normal! A normal life with simple everyday activities is really what I want. Why do *I* have to have powers? Professor Reed said that the powers I possess are perfectly normal for me, but that's not the normal I want right now because, truth be told, I'm scared! Plain, old simple, boring normal seems really good to me right now.

Even though my parents are vampires, for the most part they have always acted like an average mom and dad. And Hunter, my werewolf boyfriend. Except for his full moon runs, he's pretty normal too. *I'm* the one who's weird with this mostly, unwanted power.

Walking out the double doors of the school, I step right into a warm wind that makes the leaves on the trees sway and make me stop suddenly on the stairs. There's a fleeting feeling that someone otherworldly is nearby. Otherworldly, supernatural. Great, I think. Now I have to deal with that feeling as well! Hell's Bells!

"That killing was over fifteen years ago, darling, two years before we came to this town with you and before we bought the house and Midnight Ink. I do remember hearing something about it from customers coming to this book shop. People do talk, and that killing was something that had never happened before in this area. Yes, there were wolves here, both kinds, but there's never been a wolf attack that I know of because both kinds of wolves tend to stay away from civilization."

The female cups her chin in one hand and looks at me, her green eyes mesmerizing. We're sitting in the Magicis Scripturam where I've just told them about C. Thomas Ringwood and the wolf who killed his father. Vamps are wonderful at keeping secrets. If you have a secret you don't want anyone to know, tell a vamp.

"Do you," I swallow hard, "do you think Hunter's *father* is the wolf who did the killing?"

The male shakes his head no, emphatically. "Gideon is what legends call a Ghost Wolf—his pelt is pure white, so white it glows. He's a type of werewolf that is very, very rare. I've never seen it, but I have heard another vampire say that when a Ghost Wolf is angry, his fur will glow blindingly white. Over the centuries there have been many legends about the Ghost Wolf. Some humans even believe that a Ghost Wolf comes to exact vengeance, to punish a grievous wrong. It's said that he will drop whoever committed an evil deed into the pit of Hell. Funny how legends can be believed." I shake my head in wonder at what my dad is telling me. A Ghost Wolf.

"So, Lilith, no one could mistake Gideon for a *grey* wolf. Some type of wolf may have killed that man, but it wasn't Hunter's father."

"You remember hearing the story?" says my mom directing her clear crystal gaze on my dad.

"Parts of it, yes. But the otherworldly beings I know never said that the kill was made by a *werewolf*. It could have been a regular wolf, possibly infected by rabies, poor creature."

"Some Canis Lupus *are* as big as a werewolf," muses my mom. "Genetic changes over time, and better food sources for hunting, have helped. I remember seeing them years ago in the forests in Europe and in the northwest areas here in the United States. The thing is though, that most wolves never attack humans unless, as your father said, they're rabid."

"Or unless they're provoked in some way, Victoria. Baited traps, hunting parties. Any wolf worth their pride will fight back if they feel they or their children are threatened or in real danger."

"That goes for werewolves as well, Christopher. You know the saying. *'To try to trap a werewolf is to try an· trap a raging torna·o. Devastation will prevail.'*"

"Unless they have a silver bullet," I whisper. "Then it's all over."

"That's a myth," says the female gently. "Legend had it that silver was pure and the werewolf was evil so silver cured the supposed curse."

"Or killed the werewolf!"

"No, darling!" She takes my hand. "That's just Hollywood movie fiction. Silver only immobilizes, like an anesthesia. It won't cause—real harm." She means death.

My dad looks at me with concern. "Lilith, honey, Hunter's a smart boy, he won't do anything foolish. Your mom and I will pay a visit to Gideon and the three of us will talk to Hunter, give him some advice. Certainly Gideon is old enough to know lots of survival tricks."

"Perhaps we should go see Gideon and Hunter now," says my mom. Turning to me, she asks, "Darling, will you be all right alone here? I don't want to close the book shop. Mr. Paget is coming by to pick up another package and it is really important to him."

"Sure, I'm okay. I'll wait for Mr. Paget."

"Thank you, darling. The book is over on that table waiting to be wrapped. We won't be long."

After my parents leave I spend some time looking through the book Mr. Paget ordered. It's called *The Sworn Book of Honorius*, a grimoire which is basically a textbook of magic. The illustrations are beautiful as are the handwritten spells. I can see that the book has been used, the pages bear the mark of fingerprints, but the condition of it is surprisingly good. Someone cherished it and kept it safe. I wrap it carefully in soft linen and then heavy brown paper.

The chimes above the door make that magical sound signaling the entrance of a customer and I get up.

"I'm in the back, Mr. Paget," I call out.

There's no answer.

I poke my head out the door and call his name again. Still no answer. Walking into the main room of the book shop, I don't see anyone. Perhaps Mr. Paget decided to browse the book shelves? I wander around to the side, Lively right next to me.

"Mr. Paget? Are you trying to find a book or something? I can help you."

No one answers. Mr. Paget or whoever came into Midnight Ink has to still be here. There was no sound of chimes indicating that someone opened the door and left. That's odd.

"Is someone here?" I search the entire shop but find no one. I stop and lean against a bookcase. Who opened the door?

Suddenly, even though there's no physical evidence of anyone besides me in the room, I have a sense that I'm not alone. A feeling of uneasiness grips me as I smell it. That same rotting roses, unpleasant scent I smelled this morning! It seems to float in the air around me. I love the smell of flowers but this scent is different—it's floral all right but it's mixed with an odor of decay. I know this scent. I know it! But try as I might, I cannot remember from where.

I rush to the door and throw it open, looking up and down the street. All I see are kids skate-boarding and some people running errands on their way home from the scattered offices on the street. The scent surrounds me once more. It slowly fades but as it does, an irrational fear comes over me.

Gripping the door handle to keep my panicked body from floating upward, I yell loudly, "Mom! Dad!"

TWELVE

The male and female are by my side in a heartbeat, their vampire speed making them appear in the book shop as if by magic. My mom closes the door and my dad takes my hand leading me to a chair. I see both of them sniff the air and then exchange an unreadable look. What are their senses telling them that my own aren't?

I put my hands over my face and take a few deep breaths. The presence of my vamp parents is reassuring and I feel the warm safety they've always provided wash over me. What indeed did happen?

"Lilith? Are you all right?"

"I guess so. I heard the chimes and I thought Mr. Paget came. But he wasn't here, nobody was here but me. This is weird, just weird." I look at the male and female. "Were you at Hunter's house?"

"We were almost there when we heard you call us. It's all right Lilith."

"We'll talk to Gideon later. We just wanted make sure that you're all right."

"But, Dad, someone opened the door. I heard the chimes!"

The female looks at the door and rattles its ornate handle. As she does so the chimes sound softly. "Perhaps it was the wind, darling. Look!" She shakes the handle again making the chimes ring.

"But it wasn't only the chimes, Mom. There was a—smell. An odor like flowers but not like flowers. It smelled like something gone bad."

They look at me but don't say anything. I'm not making myself clear and I wrack my brain trying to think of an example of that smell.

"A smell like, like, those roses!"

"Roses?"

"Yes. Remember that vacant lot we used as a short cut to get to the lake when I was a little girl? Remember the roses?"

"I know that lot, "she says cautiously, "but I don't understand what you mean. You love the scent of roses."

"I do, I do, but those roses were sitting in a glass jar and they must've been there for a long time because they were drooping and they smelled funny. I didn't like it at all. When I asked you why they smelled so badly, you said it was because they'd been left to wither in the sun. You said they had rotted. Remember? I got scared and you took me home."

The female looks at me, an unwilling recognition in her eyes. "Yes, Lilith, I remember."

"That smell was here! In Midnight Ink! I smelled it."

A look passes between the male and female, a look that is filled with a secret knowledge of something I don't understand. They both nod as if they have come to some type of agreement.

The female toys with a slim bracelet on her wrist. "Perhaps the smell is coming from someone's compost heap. It has been very warm and, you know, that odor can travel."

"That's it. Those compost heaps can emit a powerful odor." The male smiles at me, revealing his bright-white vamp teeth.

"I guess," I say doubtfully knowing they're trying to soothe my concerns. Why, I don't know. "But, Mom, Dad, who came in here when you were gone?"

"Oh, darling, I told you. It was more than likely the wind."

I'm unconvinced but I answer, "Maybe. It could've been that, I guess."

The chimes over the door ring out and all three of us turn at the sound. A figure walks toward us. "Ah, so glad you're here." The figure comes closer and I see that it's Mr. Paget, smiling at us and asking in an excited voice, "Has my package come in yet?"

"Mr. Paget? Did you come in here earlier? About fifteen minutes ago?"

"Earlier? Earlier?" He wrinkles his tiny nose, confused. "No, no, I just arrived. Is everything all right?" He inhales deeply and frowns.

"Yes, Mr. Paget," smiles the female. "Everything's fine. Your package is in the Magicis Scripturam."

I stand up. "I'll get it. Come with me, Mr. Paget."

"Thank you, thank you Lilith." He sniffs the air again. "Where's young Hunter this afternoon?"

"Oh," I say trying to be casual, "he had to do something at his home."

"Ah, yes, industrious young lad. Very reliable, very reliable indeed."

"Come on in the back, Mr. Paget. I've wrapped it up for you."

My parents gather the mail that's on the table and tell us they'll be with us in a few minutes.

"By the way, my dear Lilith. I am so happy for you, dear girl. I heard that you've begun flying!"

"How did you know?" I ask curiously.

"Oh, ah," he chuckles a little, "a little bird told me. He winks at me. "The night is alive with those like us."

The male and female stand a distance away from the Magicis Scripturam and speak in hushed tones.

"I sensed it," says the female. "This can be a problem for which Lilith is unprepared. Should we—?"

"We'll just keep watch and protect her, Victoria."

"We should have done something about it a long time ago, when we first found her."

"Yes."

"She is *our* child."

"And we must protect her always in all ways."

"And we will."

"We knew this day might come, Victoria. Her biological mother knows what Lilith is and what her powers are. She also knows that her eighteenth birthday is when Lilith will have full possession of those powers. Her birthday is this summer. That woman wants to use Lilith's powers for evil purposes. She mustn't get to our child. Lilith has already smelled the rotting roses twice. This is a sign of danger."

"Lively was able to clear her mind this morning when the smell first appeared. He made her forget it happened," says Victoria. "She doesn't remember *why* she fears the smell of rotting roses, but it may be only a matter of time before she *does* remember."

"We've been searching for this woman for the last year and have not found her. She is elusive and dangerous."

"Should we warn Lilith?"

"Not yet."

The female closes her eyes. "Then we keep searching for that woman and when we find her, we—eliminate the problem."

THIRTEEN

After we closed Midnight Ink, my mom and dad dropped me off at home and left to go to Hunter's place to talk with him and his dad Gideon. I've only met Hunter's father twice; he's not exactly a recluse but he's very private and reserved. He illustrates children's books and makes a very, very good living at it. Secretly, I think his dad is rich but neither he nor Hunter act snobbish the way some rich people do. Aside from being a werewolf, Hunter is the most normal, easy-going guy I know.

Hunter told me that his father spends a lot of time in his home office working. They live in a charming house on the edge of town very close to the woods. Once a month Gideon goes on an overnight business trip, but that is the only time he leaves his house.

I am anxiously pacing back and forth in my room, wondering if I should just go to Hunter's house myself when the three of them show up a little before 9:00 at night. I can hear them talking in very serious tones as I run down the stairs.

I hug Hunter tightly. "Well," I say, "did you check out what you wanted? Any idea who that big grey wolf was? The one who killed C. Thomas Ringwood's father?"

"No, I still don't know who that grey wolf was but my dad said that she did *not* kill C. Thomas's father. Someone or something else killed Ringwood, Sr."

"She?" I feel a thrill of curiosity. A she-werewolf! Legend has it that they're fiercer than the males. My parents have known a few she-werewolves in their long lives, but I've never seen one.

"Who was this she-werewolf?"

"Gideon says he didn't know her and that she may have traveled over from another pack that summer. He says that it can happen, a werewolf wanting to run in a new area. But, he was adamant that she didn't kill Ringwood, Sr." Hunter takes a step back from me and gestures toward the garden. "Let's go outside. I need nature around me."

All of us go outside and sit on the chairs we have under the big tree, the one I crashed into last night during my maiden flight.

"This whole thing about a huge grey werewolf who looks like me has gotten me thinking. It ties into something that I've felt ever since I began changing into my wolf self. A kind of nagging, muted thought that seems more like memories. Something that was experienced in the past." Hunter shakes his head. "It has to do with running free under a full moon, then a terrible fear. Except, the memories aren't mine and I can't access them because they're not strong enough to come through clearly. They're kind of like memories I inherited through a genetic code. A genetic memory. Remember we learned something about that in our Psych. Class?"

Inherited memories, I remember. It was fascinating and weird at the same time. Fears, sadness, happiness, why we prefer to live in warm or cold climates—all thought by some scientists and neurologists to be inherited from ancestors. It's like generations of birds always returning to a certain area to mate. The memory to fly there is built into their genetic code. It's not a proven science for humans but my dad has said that anyone who is part of the "super" natural world knows about them and strongly believes in that theory.

The wolf was female, but I wonder, is Hunter sure it was a werewolf or could it have been just a large, regular female Canis Lupus? My mom speaks and answers my question. Vampire mind-reading.

"We've pretty much established that she *was* a werewolf, Lilith."

I look at Hunter and see a look in his eyes that I've never seen before. His eyes look sharp and a bit dangerous. He looks as if he is determined to solve this mystery, no matter what he may find out about the wolf who was killed. I've never seen Hunter anything but happy and carefree—this look unnerves me.

"I think the grey she-werewolf that C. Thomas saw that night might have been from a pack that is no longer near Summer Valley, a pack that is related to me somehow. I just have this feeling. Like I said, inherited memories. But my dad refused to say anything else about it. Maybe he ran with them at one time before he met my mother. I don't know—he won't say. What I do know is that he got really agitated when I kept asking questions and just told me to stay away from Ringwood's stables, but that's all. I had to promise him, just like I promised you, Lilith, that I wouldn't go anywhere near there."

"He's just trying to protect you. We all agree that you should stay away from that area," says my mom.

"Hunter," I reach over to where he is sitting and squeeze his hand. "I'm confused. Why does C. Thomas say that his father was killed by that big grey wolf? Did he *see* the attack?"

Before Hunter can answer, my dad interrupts. "I asked Mr. Paget about that. While your mom and Hunter talked to Gideon, I went to see Mr. Paget. He's been around a long time and I suspected he knew about what happened over fifteen years ago. Paget has his sources, his winged messengers he calls them, and they're very reliable.

"He says that the large grey wolf was indeed a she-werewolf. Then he told me that he believes that C. Thomas didn't actually see anything that happened that night, only what he assumed happened. It was foggy and the full moon went in and out of the clouds. Paget's messengers said, when they arrived at the scene, that the werewolf was standing near Ringwood, Sr. who was sitting on the ground. She stood there snarling. C. Thomas shot her with his rifle. The werewolf was wounded but managed to run deep into the forest. His winged friends followed her.

"C. Thomas sent a group of hands after the she-werewolf but they couldn't find any trace of her. When they returned two hours later, followed by Paget's loyal messengers, they found Ringwood, Sr. dead, his son C. Thomas bent over the body screaming that the wolf had killed his father. There was grey fur gripped in his father's hands as if he had tried to fight off the wolf. There were marks on his throat that were assumed to be from a wolf attack. No trace of the she-werewolf, or of any wolf for that matter, was ever found."

"A werewolf will change back when—", Hunter looks at me before continuing. "You know what I mean, Lilith?"

I nod. I do know. If this wolf was killed by C. Thomas, her wolf body would *never* be found. There are three specific times when a werewolf will forcefully make the change back to human form—when it is gravely injured, before a female werewolf gives birth, and at the moment of its death.

"Was a *human* body ever found?"

"No," answers Hunter. "That's the strange part. If he did manage to kill this wolf, her human form would remain and there would've been a body."

"Something killed his father. But the mystery is what."

The four of us talk for a while longer until my parents tell us that they're going to feed. Even though I know they've probably hunted on their way to Hunter's house, they look hollow and translucent, a look that comes with that craving for more powerful blood. I know that they're going to pay a visit to Rudy down at the blood bank. Telling us they'll try to be back later to see me fly, and cautioning me to fly only in our large garden, they disappear in less than a heartbeat.

For a long time, Hunter and I just hold hands and don't talk. We're both lost in our own thoughts. I don't like the fact that C. Thomas Ringwood is posting a reward for a large grey wolf, brought to him alive or dead. I feel chills just thinking about those words. Hunter will be careful, I know, I know—he takes making promises seriously—but there's always the chance that those looking to get the reward money will spread out into the countryside, or even close to our town, looking for the grey wolf that is my Hunter. They can look all they want now, they won't find any wolves, but in a few weeks when the full moon rises again, Hunter could very well become the hunted.

I've heard stories about how some werewolves, who were in danger from local hunters while in wolf-form, had a safe-room installed in their homes where they hid when the effects of the moon made them change. It was awful for them, though. All they could do was pace and pace all night in frustration in that small room—no howling allowed, no precious touch with nature—locked in a self-imposed prison for their own safety. When they reverted back to their human form in the morning they were hollow-eyed with exhaustion and despair. A werewolf needs to run free under the full moon. It's a healthy and critical part of who they are.

There's something odd about the fact that C. Thomas's father was mauled, but not killed, by this wolf who so resembles Hunter. Strange too is the fact that if the wolf didn't kill him, who or what did? What's the motive and what is the reason the kill was blamed on a wolf? Then there's the whole mystery of the werewolf herself. What happened to the werewolf? If she was wounded did she get away? If she died, why wasn't a human body found? It's a puzzle, a mystery and it has to be solved.

Suddenly, the thought of people trying to catch or kill Hunter makes me more angry than afraid. I will not let that happen, I can't. There must be something I can do. I can't just wait around for this issue to get resolved. I need to gather information and gain access to any witnesses, more than likely otherworldly creatures of the night, who saw what happened that night. I can use my powers to be a criminologist in the truest sense of the word.

Hunter is looking at the stars, his brow furrowed, a look of pure concentration on his face. I hold my breath; I don't want to guess what he's thinking about. I'm afraid to ask, but when he turns to face me, he surprises me. He looks at me with that shy, boyish grin that I love and says eagerly. "You know how you and I always talk about becoming criminologists? Remember that you said that one day you'd like us to open our own agency and solve crimes?"

I nod, quickly picking up his train of thought. "I do remember. I think we'd make a great team, especially since we both have powers that enhance our thinking and physical strength not to mention a stronger sixth sense."

"Plus my wolf savvy and your ability to fly. Let's not forget those."

"Definite advantages."

He gives me a sad smile. "You know something Lilith? This thing with C. Thomas Ringwood's father and the grey she-werewolf is our first crime mystery. Something that's of powerful interest to you and me and a case in which we're completely invested because of who we are. This mystery has to be solved! And we may just be the only ones who can solve it."

I'm so relieved that he's not just going to sit back and do nothing.

"You're right. All we have to do is piece together the events of that night along with some crucial clues and witnesses and we can begin to solve it! We'll start the case tomorrow by asking Mr. Paget a few questions."

I love the idea of us working together, having our own agency, even while we're in college next year. That would be incredible! For the first time that night, I smile. Hunter kisses me and then begins to easily climb the old tree.

"Come on up, Lilith! Fly up!"

I do as he asks. I imagine my wings and they immediately appear, soft, black as night, and powerful. With one quick downward beat of my wings I fly straight up and land on the thick tree limb where Hunter is sitting. Then I nose-dive downward, turning at the last second, inches from the earth and soar upward. I feel free and strong. I love my wings!

"We can do anything, Lilith!" shouts Hunter as he climbs to the highest bough of the tree.

And I believe him as I wobbily circle the tree, playing a sort of hide-and-go-seek among the leaf-filled branches with Hunter.

FOURTEEN

"**I** want to use the castle turret as my office. You know how I mentioned that Hunter and I want to go into criminology and all. I mean, I know that we'll be in college next year and that anything official is a long way off but, it'll be good practice for us. Having a private office available where we can work without interruption is something that I really want."

I announce this to the male and female the next day as soon as I see them enter Midnight Ink. They weren't home when I left for school and this was my first chance to speak with them. I asked Hunter to drop me off at the bookstore and let me talk to my parents alone.

"Got it. I'll go get us some snacks. I'll be back soon."

Since Hunter and I had made the decision to solve the crime of Ringwood, Sr.'s murder and the mysterious disappearance of the grey werewolf, my subconscious had hungrily nibbled all night on the question of a quiet, safe place where he and I could work together. Either of our houses was out of the question; we needed quiet and privacy.

During English Lit., while my teacher Mrs. Holder was expounding on the use of figurative language, my wide-awake conscious mind answered the question that had kept me tossing and turning for most of the night—the turret room in Midnight Ink would be the absolutely perfect place. Definitely quiet and private.

Unfortunately, when my mind answered the question, I yelled out, "Yes! Yes! That's it!" and had to grip the desk for fear of levitation. The entire class turned to stare at me and Mrs. Holder dryly remarked that she was happy that I was so excited over the use of imagery, symbolism, and tone in a story, but to please keep my enthusiasm in check. The girl in front of me stage-whispered something about how English Lit. can make "some people orgasmic". I laughed along with everyone else while the teacher tried to get us back on track.

But I was happy. I had a plan.

"Is that okay, Mom, Dad? I mean, I really would like that. It's just sitting there waiting to be used and I've always loved it. And," I rush on breathlessly, "I'll make sure my school work gets done. Actually that room is perfect for studying. Plus, I'll still be able to work down here to help with customers. I won't give that up. Can I use it, please?"

If the male and the female are surprised at my request they don't show it. All my mom does is to ask me what type of PC I want to be installed in the turret.

"I know you love your laptop, but every professional office should have a PC as well. We can get you the same type as the one we have at home if you like. Top of the line."

"Oh Mom, that's great! Hunter can bring his laptop and we'll be all set. Thank you!"

I fling my arms around both of them and hug tightly. Their vamp bodies are cooler than my own, but no way are they cold.

"No problem, Lilith of the Angels," says my dad smiling as he always does when he calls me by the name he gave me the night I was found. "We've never really properly cleaned out that room. I'll bring up some boxes and we can get rid of what you don't need and straighten up the room to make it a real office. It already has two swivel chairs, a sofa, a desk and an old bookcase. We'll order another desk. The turret room will be all yours, Lilith."

The male and female go to the rare book room and I go upstairs and wait for Hunter to return. The turret room is in pretty good shape. The walls need a good dusting but the soft yellow paint on them still looks good. The windows will definitely need to be washed and maybe the wooden frames can be varnished to bring out their deep cherry wood finish but on the whole, the room is perfect.

Lively is seated on the desk near the floor-to-ceiling windows. He's still a Tuxedo black and white cat. Next week will see a change in him. With my enhanced sensitivity to all creatures increasing every day, I'm more in tune with his changes. I wonder what breed of cat he'll look like next?

"You need a name for your agency." His thoughts enter my mind clearly.

"It's not really an agency, not yet, Lively."

He stretches and yawns. "But it will be. You need to think ahead."

"When did you get here, Lively?"

"While you were talking. This room is where I need to be. A criminologist's office needs a resident cat. I can advise you on many things. First thing is, you need a name for your agency."

The fact that I'm mind-talking to a cat is amazing. I have to smile. Professor Reed is right; I value Lively's insight into life more and more each day.

"A name? Wait a minute, Lively. I just want a quiet place to work on this Ringwood murder. Find out what really happened."

"Exactly. You're working to solve a murder case. You have a criminologist agency and it needs a name. I'll think up a great name for you."

Shaking my head at Lively's insistence about naming this place, I walk around the window-enclosed circle of a room. I'm glad I asked if I could use this room as my office. There's a great panoramic view from up here, the town, the outlying woods, everything. I see Hunter approaching on his Vespa from several blocks away, easily taking the two sharp turns that come right before the main street where Midnight Ink is nestled between the park and a law office. He parks his Vespa on the street and comes inside.

I hear him talking downstairs in the main room of the book store with my parents. In a few minutes Hunter and my dad climb the circular stairs to the turret, each carrying two large, empty boxes which they deposit next to the desk. My dad leaves and Hunter silently surveys the room while gently scratching Lively behind his ears.

"Wow, Lilith, this is the best place for us to have our own official office." He points to the floor-to-ceiling windows. "The view is fantastic and there's plenty of room here. Your mom said something about putting another desk in here. This is a great place for Wings & Wolf

Criminologists."

Lively stretches and taps my leg with his paw as if to say, 'See? I told you that you needed a name for this place!' I swear I see a smile on his cute little cat face.

"Wings and Wolf Criminologists? Seriously? Let's not get ahead of ourselves in naming this place just yet. We're not a real agency. Besides, we've got a million things to do first before we become official. Right now, we've got a helluva lot to do before the next full moon arrives. *And* please remember that we're still seniors in high school and that this senior," I tap my forehead, "has to pass Advanced Calculus if she wants to graduate."

"You said you were doing better in that class," says Hunter taking a large bag of chips and two large bottles of iced tea out of one of the boxes he carried up.

"I am, but that final has me stressing out."

"You'll be fine, no worries," says he who is a veritable math whiz. Right, uh-huh, sure. Big sigh.

"Let's get this place cleaned up," I say grabbing a box. "Nothing stays but the furniture for now."

"Okay." He opens the two iced teas and hands me one to me, then opens the bag of chips. "After that we'll have to get started on this whole Ringwood crime mystery puzzle. I'm getting antsy to solve this."

So am I, I think as I begin putting things into a box. Old hole punchers that no one ever really uses anymore, some purple paper whose ink rubs off on my hands, an old Walkman, dried out pens, pencils worn down to almost nothing, a ledger with the names of books and authors written in a spidery script probably leftover from the former owner of the book shop. These I place neatly in one of the boxes.

We work non-stop for three hours, then sit on the floor eating chips and finishing the iced teas. Both of us are lost in our own thoughts. I'm planning to ask Mr. Paget some questions about the Ringwood murder and see if he can shed some more light on what really happened. So many questions form in my mind—I hope I can get answers to most of them.

Hunter has leaned up against the window and closed his eyes. "Hunter?" I whisper. No answer. From his soft breathing I can tell he's fallen asleep. Sighing, I idly glance around the room. Really we've done a pretty good clean-up job here. All we need to do is sweep the floor, dust, and wash the windows. That'll take a couple more hours, but not tonight. We can finish it tomorrow after school.

My eyes dart around the circular room, glancing into corners and that's when I see what looks like a small cardboard box, the size of a jewelry box. Something left over from my childhood days playing princess in the turret?

Quietly, so as to not wake Hunter, I slide my butt over the floor to the corner where the object is lying. Funny that I didn't see it before. I thought I checked every inch of this room. Looking closer, I see that it isn't a box at all. It's a book, maybe three inches by three inches. When I reach for it, the tiny book floats up from the floor and over into my outstretched hand. Lively comes over to investigate, staring at the book intently.

The raised title words, embossed in faded gold leaf on the brown cover, are in a language that I identify as early Italian. *Il Libro degli Incantesimi Perduti*. "The Book of Lost Spells," I say quietly to myself. There's no author's name on the cover. The pages are numbered and hand-written, calligraphy style. Some pages have marks that look like a dagger. What's this book doing here? As far as I know, my parents have never used this room to store old books. Gently opening the cover, I read and translate what is on the first page. It's an introduction in poetry form.

This book is not owned, this book has no home,
It goes wherever most needed,
The spells are old and the magic time-honed,
Take care that all warnings are heeded.

The next page has a list of how to protect yourself when casting a spell, everything from burning a special type of incense to certain colored candles and wearing gemstone amulets. I've never spelled and I don't know anyone who has. It's both fascinating and scary to think about actually casting a spell.

Turning a page, I read another poem.

Take your time an, cast with care,
This book stays as long as you nee, it,
The spells are ancient, the book is rare,
You are urge, to carefully rea, it.

The word *carefully* is underlined in red and at the very bottom of the page, written in large red letters is this statement—

Remember—
Time stan,s still as the spell is cast,
The past is present an, the present is past.

Now that's downright weird and confusing. How can the 'past be present and the present be past'? Curiously, I carefully turn a delicate page and look at the magical spell written there. I turn more pages. All of them have some type of incantation on them, some with ancient symbols or drawings etched around the spell. Some spells have a certain phase of the moon for the best time to cast them. I have no intention of casting any spells but, there has to be a reason that this book just magically appeared. I'm concentrating on one spell, which is embellished with intricate drawings of planets, when I hear Hunter yawn behind me.

"Lilith? I guess I fell asleep. What're looking at over there?"

He gets up and stretches and I quickly hide the book under my shirt and tuck it into the waistband of my shorts. For some reason I can't explain, I feel that the book doesn't want anyone else to know of its existence here—at least for the time being. I get up on my knees and pretend that I'm sweeping something out of the corner.

"Just some cobwebs." I clap my hands together pretending to shake the cobwebs off of them. "We really have to sweep and dust this room before we can call it a proper office. The windows need to be washed too."

"Yeah, you're right. Tomorrow we'll start all that, okay? Today I want to get home while it's still light and make my special chili for my dad." He grins and I smile back. Hunter's chili is kick-ass good. "Maybe he'll be more inclined to answer some questions about that grey female werewolf and the death of C. Thomas Ringwood's father if we're alone after dinner. I just have this weird feeling that he knows more about what happened than he's letting on. Your parents ever keep things from you?"

I push up from my knees and shake my head yes. "Sometimes. I guess there are things parents don't want kids to know. Maybe they think they're protecting us or something."

"How do you feel about that? I mean, do you think we're so fragile emotionally that we need protection from the facts?"

I ponder that question before I answer. "No, it's not that we're fragile or anything—I just think that maybe they feel the time might not be right for us to learn about things that might be bad or upsetting. Perhaps they're waiting for the right time to tell us."

"Maybe. I just wish my dad would understand that it's worse for me to *not* know what happened to that female werewolf. *Imagining* what happened can be worse than actually *knowing* what happened."

I totally agree with Hunter's statement and tell him so. We head to the spiral stairwell but as we're about to leave, something prevents me from walking out the of the room. I can't leave the turret room. I feel a slight pressure against my waist. The book! It won't let me leave. The poem said that "it goes wherever it's needed." Maybe the need is only here in this room. But why? Is it here for me? I don't think I even want to cast a spell. Why would I want to do that?

"You coming, Lilith?" Hunter pauses at the top of the first step.

"Yes, I just forgot my, um, my—keys. Go down, I'll be right there."

I check all around for a place to hide the book but it seems to have a mind of its own. When I remove the book from under my shirt, it floats away from me over to the side of the room and lodges itself in a small opening in the corner window frame. It blends in so perfectly that, even with my new enhanced power of sight, I can't see it.

"Lilith?" Hunter's voice floats up the staircase.

"Coming!" Before I descend the stairs, I take one more glance back to where the book should be. I don't see anything until a small glint of light appears and shows me where the book is hidden. Then, just as quickly as the pinpoint of light appeared, it is gone. No trace of the book.

But I know it's there. Hell's Bells!

FIFTEEN

I remember the first time I drove my car alone. It was last year two days after I passed my road test and got a brand-new license. Just me, my fav songs coming through the speaker system, and the open road. Okay, the road was not so open. I was only driving familiar streets from our house to Midnight Ink. But still, it was just me and the car. It was an exhilarating moment and just the tiniest bit scary. I loved it!

Tonight, I'm preparing for my solo flight. I've always loved when the male and female took me up, up, up into the night sky and we glided from one place to another. I was never afraid because one of them always held me securely in their arms while the other flew close to us, and I knew that I was safe. In the summer we would hover gently over fireflies and watch them light the darkness of the night. I really believed that they were fairies who came out only at night the same way that my parents did. The female, my mom, said that I talked to them and swore that they talked back to me. Childhood fantasies. It is one of my happiest memories.

I'm just as excited at the thought of soaring through the air on my own with no one helping me, but, if I'm honest with myself, I'm more than a little scared. Before tonight, my parents or Hunter were close by during my flying attempts and I didn't feel alone. If I fell or smashed into a tree limb, they were there to help me. When I fly tonight, I will be all alone, there will be nothing between my hovering body and the ground or a tree. Still, I'm determined to do this.

It's 10:30 at night. I'm alone with Lively. Hunter is with his father more than likely trying to find out what Gideon knows about the Ringwood murder. The male and female have gone out to feed, but they gave me strict orders to call for them if I smell that horrible odor of decayed roses or if I felt some type of presence that made me uncomfortable. I haven't mentioned that I intend to fly solo tonight. They think that I'm staying home to study Advanced Calculus.

"We're only a call away. You know how quickly we can come back if you need us," says my dad. Then he picks up Lively, stroking him gently and looking into his cat eyes. The cat stares back, his look inscrutable. Mind communication, Dad? Try as I might, I can't hear what he's saying to Lively. The male has blocked me. Hell's Bells!

"Yes, okay, sure, Dad. I know! You already told me at least ten times." I'm exaggerating but I'm anxious to fly.

The female looks at the male. "Christopher, she can fly in the garden after she's studied." Turning to me, she says, "Lilith, darling, why don't you practice flying in the backyard later? You can perfect your take-off and landing skills and the exercise in the night air will do you good."

I nod and smile thinking that I sure will be practicing in the night air—practicing *real* flying. They kiss me good-bye and their vamp speed takes them out of the house in less time than it takes to draw a breath. See you later, Mom and Dad. You're going to be so proud of me—after you're done being so upset with me for flying solo.

With Lively watching me through the open door, I go outside and summon my wings by envisioning them. They appear in an instant. I stand a few minutes taking some deep breaths and giving myself a pep talk. "You can do this Lilith, you can fly. You *will* fly!"

I gently open my wings and make a sweeping motion. The air rustles with the feathery brush of my wings. Making a quick downward motion, I propel myself into the air until I am at the top of the old oak tree in our yard. I look down at Lively who seems to communicate approval of my take-off technique but cautions me with, "Be very careful." I tell him I will.

Okay, here goes my solo flight. Slowly, I beat my wings up and down and fly higher into the open night sky. Veering left away from tall trees and houses, I head toward the grassy knolls that are just a distance away near the forest. Nice wide-open spaces, nothing to impede my flight.

I glance up and wish I had the courage to fly higher, but, I'm taking this one flight at a time. Tonight my goal is distance; how far I can go from the safety of my home and still feel comfortable. Flying higher is a goal for tomorrow.

The grassy knolls outside of town are the perfect place for me to fly. The area is filled with fireflies flitting from place to place. Seeing them in the grass, their lights winking off and on as I fly just above them, brings me a pleasant link to my childhood and the nighttime flights with the male and female.

The sky is clear and cloudless and I gain more confidence the farther I fly. I even attempt to somersault, careful not to kick my wings with my feet. I am loving this flying power! I still take care to stay safely over the knolls. Then a thought hits me. Hunter lives a short distance from where I'm flying, near the forest. Why not fly over his house just for the fun of it? Maybe he'll be outside or somehow sense that I'm near. I smile at the thought of him staring up toward the sky and seeing me waving down at him while I do a flyover. Maybe it's an ego thing or maybe I just want to tease him a little with a "Hey! Look at me! Look at what I can do!" Whatever the reason, I want him to see me flying in the open, not just in my backyard.

Shifting slightly to the right I fly toward his house, struggling a little from the air friction of the soft night breeze. It's a little like swimming against a slowly rushing current of water. I open my wings wide and try to coast on the undulating air. I hardly have to move my wings at all.

The distinctive red chimney of Hunter's house comes into view as I lazily float on a breeze. I'm preparing to swoop downward toward the house when the soft summer breeze turns into a sudden gust of wind that propels me up and away from where I was headed. Immediately, the air around me feels uncomfortably hot and moist. An unexpected thunderstorm is coming in from the ocean.

I move my wings in hurried up and down motions, trying to get back on track but the wind and the rain are more forceful than I realize. Try as I might, my wings, and my inexperience in using them, are no match for the gusting wind blowing me away from Hunter's house.

"Okay, Lilith. Don't panic," I tell myself in a desperate attempt to stay calm and not call out for my mom and dad. Amsterdam, Rotterdam, damn, damn, damn! The wind forces my wings straight up making me plummet toward the earth. It takes all my strength to force my wings wide open so I can move them down and up in a series of quick beats propelling myself up and away from crash landing on the ground. Concentrating on keeping my wings wide open, I coast wildly on the erratic currents.

The hot wind makes it difficult to get good, deep breaths. I look down and see that the strong gusts of wind have taken me past the lake area. That's a helluva distance from my house. I'm getting scared. I just want to fly back home. Flying solo was a stupid idea. I don't know what I should do. Hell's Bells!

The wind takes me farther and farther out. I look down and see that the terrain is different. No grassy knolls, just thick areas of trees blocking my view of the ground, and, within a clearing, a large house and vast yard from what I can see, surrounded by tall fences. A gloriously new house so far away from civilization. Who lives there I wonder before being blown away from there like a rag doll. The wind whistles and rustles around me.

Mixed in with the sounds of the wind I hear a mournful howl. Must be a dog, a rather large dog by the sound of the howl, frightened by the wind, making that fearful sound. Poor thing. The long, sad howl continues and it is heartbreaking to hear. I hope that poor dog is not alone. Then, a sound, a more distant howl, carried by the wind, fills my ears, a response to the howl that is filled with such intense sadness. I try to figure out where the different howls are located but the rushing sound of the wind makes that impossible.

Abruptly the rain stops and the wind begins to die down. With my wings spread wide as a hawk's I float for a long time. Finally, I get my bearings, circle slowly down, and am able to make a halfway decent landing. Standing once again on terra firma with my wings settled at my sides, I try to calculate the best way to return home. I close my eyes and concentrate hoping my newly enhanced senses also include the sense of direction. In my mind's eye I can see where I have to go—south and then turn west. Okay, I relax, pleased that I seem to have a built-in GPS now. So, quick breather and then I'll be off. Hopefully I'll arrive there before my parents.

I spread my wings and catch a current of air which helps me lift off from the ground. Pumping my wings, I veer to the south and home. A howl full of fear and desperation fills the night. That poor dog. The wind must have really terrified it. As I head home, I hear the answering howl from farther away.

SIXTEEN

My built-in GPS helps me get home at 1:19, twenty minutes before my parents arrive. They appear suddenly in the back yard where I'm sitting pondering my first solo flight away from the safe confines of this yard. I realize it could've been a disaster. I could have been smashed against a tree or one of those lonely looking buildings out in nowhere land. Maybe suffered a concussion or worse. Maybe I'd be knocked out and not even able to summon my parents for help. Amsterdam, Rotterdam, damn, damn, damn!

I still have to learn how to react to wind currents and the possibility of a calm wind changing unexpectedly to a roaring one. I have to learn how to use my magnificent and strong wings in that type of situation. But the fact is that I *was* able to fight the powerful force of the wind and that is actually to my credit. I'm stronger and more determined than I think I am. I just have to make absolutely certain that I'm prepared for any changing activity in the weather and make damn sure that I can handle it more easily than I did tonight.

"Lilith? How'd it go tonight? Easy flying?" asks my dad ruffling my hair. My mom comes over and gives me a kiss. I catch a familiar whiff of that coppery, iron smell of blood on her breath.

"Um, yeah, pretty easy." I'm a poor liar, at least to my parents. Other teens can lie easily and their parents are none the wiser, but having vamp parents, I always have the feeling that when I do lie, they know. Vamps are good at reading minds. Tonight, however, they seem to take my answer as truth. Anyway, I'm not really lying. My flight *was* kind of easy—before the windstorm hit.

My mom looks at the trees in our big backyard. "Looks as if the wind came here as well, Christopher." Turning to me she says, "There was some type of storm coming off the ocean. I didn't realize that it had come this far inland."

"It did get windy and rainy for a while here," I say looking at Lively. He just yawns and begins bathing his face. The female looks at me and smiles. Then she and the male tell me they're going out again and that they'll see me later.

Until I was fifteen my parents never left me home alone. One of them was always here while the other one went out to feed. They also relied a lot on the bottles of blood supplied by Rudy. They were determined to make my childhood as normal as possible and to let me know that they were always here for me. The last two years they've gone out together and I was home alone with my spirit cat Lively. I was always reminded that they were only a call away—and they always were.

My phone buzzes in my pocket. It's Hunter.

"Hunter, how did it go with your dad tonight?"

"Not good. He's still being very evasive about things. I mean. He obviously knows that Ringwood, Sr. was killed one night years ago, but why it was blamed on a wolf, well he says he doesn't know. Says he doesn't know the she-werewolf either." There's pause. "Lilith, he's keeping something from me, some crucial piece of evidence, I just know it."

"I don't know Hunter. Maybe he knows nothing at all about what really happened that night or who that werewolf was other than what he's heard from beings like Mr. Paget."

"When I mentioned the Ringwood place, there was a look in his eyes that I had never seen before. It was a mix of both anger and fear—I really think he knows a whole lot more than he's telling me about that night."

I hear him yawn into the phone. It's late, going for 2:00 AM and we're both tired. I know that flying in that windstorm has left me exhausted. We'll be able to deal with what we refer to as the Ringwood Case tomorrow when we're refreshed from sleep

"Let's pick this conversation up tomorrow after school at Midnight Ink. Neither one of us can think anymore tonight Hunter. Get some sleep."

He yawns again. "You're right. Tomorrow will be better. Anyway, remember that we don't have to be in tomorrow until 10:00 when we have that senior assembly. It's Student Peer Day. I'll be by to pick you up around a quarter to ten."

"Got it. Good-night Hunter. Love you."

"Night Lilith, love you too."

I click off my phone, stand, and stretch. Lively follows me up the stairs and jumps onto my bed to wait for me while I go take a long shower. The wind has left bits of dirt and grit on my skin and in my hair. I grab a pair of sweats and a t-shirt, then fall on top of my nice, soft bed. I fall asleep thinking about the wind, my powerful wings, the distance I traveled to get back home, and that mournful howl carried on the wind. I hope that poor dog is okay.

I have the weirdest dream. I'm sitting in Advanced Calc. taking my final exam before graduation. One look at the paper and I am horrified to see that I have never, *never*, learned any of this. Panicking, I keep thinking that, "I have to pass this, I have to pass this" but I can't seem to get started. I look around the room and see that other students, all faceless, are writing furiously, while I haven't even put my name on the paper yet.

I'm so nervous I begin to levitate out of my seat and grip the desk hard when I see Mr. Mendelsohn look at me. Smiling, he walks over to my desk and takes the exam away from me.

"Wait Mr. Mendelsohn," I protest, "I haven't even begun the test yet. I need to pass this in order to graduate."

"Nonsense Lilith, look! It's already done." He carefully scans the paper. "And the answers are all correct! Wonderful!" He looks piercingly at me. "You *finally* understand."

Mendelsohn shows the joy all math people exhibit when a student finally gets it. I grab the paper out of his hand and look at it. It's completely finished, my name neatly displayed at the top of the page.

"That's not possible," I say confused. "I never wrote down anything! How is this happening?"

"It's magic, Lilith. Magic! You're a magical girl!"

A sudden wind makes a classroom window close with a slam. "A storm is coming," says a faceless student.

"Yes, so I've heard," responds Mr. Mendelsohn, closing the other windows in the room. He stops moving and stands perfectly still, as if he's listening to a sound that no one else can hear. "Someone had better take care of that poor creature. The storm that's coming will only upset it more."

I wake up to find my body floating two feet above my bed. It takes all my concentration to will myself gently back down onto the soft bedding. Lively is sitting on the other side of the bed watching me float down. He's a grey tabby today.

"That was nice. You're learning," he says stretching his front paws out gracefully. "Easy landing."

"Thanks." I sigh, check the digi-clock on my nightstand, and stare at the ceiling. It's just a little after 8:00. I've got plenty of time before Hunter gets here on his Vespa.

Dreams, I once read, can be interpreted in three ways. Some people see them as portents or warnings of possible future danger—in other words, they can give you a head's up on what might happen in the future in your waking life. Others view dreams as giving us clues to better understand what is actually going on in our lives at the present time. Still others believe that a dream is just a dream—a messy mixture of our daily lives, thoughts, hopes, and fears.

My mother has her own take on dreams—she calls it the 'crow in the garden' theory. "Sometimes a crow landing in a garden is just a crow landing in a garden," meaning that if some people see a crow land in their garden, they take it as a sign that something bad will happen when maybe the crow just landed there for no particular reason.

But four things stand out in my dream—the statement, 'You *finally* understand', the comment about me being a magical girl, the coming storm, and the fact that someone should take care of the poor creature, obviously already upset, who will be more upset by the storm.

I think the dream is trying to warn me of something, a type of storm, not necessarily weather-related, that is heading my way. That I can understand. Hunter and I are entering a storm of sorts to find out what happened to Ringwood, Sr. and the grey she-werewolf fifteen years ago. The rest of that dream I'll have to work on and figure out.

Magical girl, poor upset creature—obscure clues there for sure.

SEVENTEEN

I've just finished drying my hair when I hear voices. They're coming from the master bedroom. The male and female must have come home when I had the dryer on full blast and I didn't hear them. It's just a little after 9:00 AM. Why in the world are they staying out way past sunrise? I look at Lively, who I know has read my mind, but he gives me a curious look as if to say, "I don't know why either." He gets up when he sees me head toward the stairs and follows me down to the kitchen where he knows I'll give him breakfast.

"You look really nice, Lilith" says my mom coming up behind me, as I'm buttering a bagel, and giving me a kiss. "I like what you're wearing."

She looks approvingly at my short yellow summer dress and my tan wedge shoes as she opens the fridge and grabs a bottle of Type O blood. Then she comes and stands next to me.

"Senior assembly for Student Peer Day," I say. "We have a couple of guest speakers coming and the principal wants us to look like, as she said it, young adults." I give her a hug.

"Yes, I remember that you told us that last week. It's a good experience for you to mentor other students, especially since you've mentioned that you want to have your own agency to solve crimes." She smiles. "Wings and Wolf I believe someone suggested it be called?"

"Hunter! I can't believe he told you that. It is definitely not official, no way. Hunter's getting way ahead of himself here."

"No matter, darling. Hunter's just showing enthusiasm for something he knows you both want, I guess. Anyway, enjoy the assembly, my love. We'll see you later at Midnight Ink. We might be later than usual today. We're looking at a computer for the turret room. Can you and Hunter handle things until we get there?"

I nod yes. She touches my hair gently and goes up the stairs to the master bedroom where she and my dad will probably sleep until 3:00 this afternoon. I put Lively's bowl, filled with his Kittie Crunchies on the kitchen island and then go sit next to him while I eat my bagel. It's an old habit of mine from when I was a little girl; I told my parents I didn't want Lively to be alone when he ate. "You have a beautiful heart, Lilith of the Angels," smiled my dad when I said that. Since then Lively usually eats with us here or at Midnight Ink.

While I'm in the midst of eating and trying to unravel my dream to make some type of sense of it all, a tap on the kitchen window gets my attention. Hunter. He's early. Opening the kitchen door, I let him in and ask if he's hungry.

"I ate really early but if you've got one of those," he points his chin at my half-eaten bagel, "I will definitely eat it."

I pop a bagel into the toaster and get out the cream cheese and butter before settling back down by Lively. I debate whether I should tell Hunter about my solo flight and the storm but decide that it can wait until later. I do tell him about parts of my dream, the parts where Mr. Mendelsohn says to me, 'You finally understand' and 'You're a magical girl'. Finally, a bit hesitantly, I mention that part about a storm coming.

"A storm, Hunter. That doesn't sound good—storms destroy. You think that dream has any significance in my life or is it just a jumble of my own thoughts?"

The toaster pops suddenly and Hunter takes the bagel and places it on a plate. He carefully butters it and then heavily layers on cream cheese before he answers me. "I think it has significance. It's a look into the future, Lilith. I'd take it seriously and look for signs in your daily life that fit the dream's message."

"You think it's a message. Hmmm. Guess I have to be on the alert then." I sigh. One more thing to think about.

"And listen," Hunter swallows quickly before continuing. "You mentioned that storms destroy. Well, that's not always a bad thing."

"How so?"

"What happens after a storm is important. That's when the clean-up and rebuilding start, Lilith. Sometimes a storm has to wash away what's not good in order to create a clean slate so we can begin something new and better. It's nature at her finest."

"You may be right. The only problem is weathering the storm and surviving. That's the hard part."

With that thought in mind, we put the plates and glasses in the dishwasher. Putting our helmets on, we get on the Vespa and head off to school, the sunshine on our faces falsely letting us think that no storm will ever enter our lives and that no harm can touch us.

As assemblies go, this is one of the best ones I've attended. The two speakers are actually kind of interesting and best of all, wonderfully brief— even with a quick question/answer session, the assembly ends twenty minutes early. To fill up the remaining time, the principal asks the students to 'discuss among yourselves' the importance of what we've learned from this assembly. Hunter and I take this opportunity to discuss the Ringwood case. We go off to the top of the bleachers where we can be alone. I face Hunter and begin.

"Okay, so here's my strategy for later at Midnight Ink. I'm going to talk to Mr. Paget and see what he remembers about the night Ringwood, Sr. was killed. I want to know every little detail, no matter how small, that he can remember."

"How do you know he'll show up at the book store this afternoon?"

"Yesterday, I checked the list of books that are due for delivery today and who ordered them. Paget's name is on the list. He ordered a manuscript. He'll be there."

"That's good. He's a reliable source even if he does tend to go off on a different track sometimes. He can talk for hours about a dozen different things, none of them remotely connected!"

I laugh. Mr. Paget knows a lot and is a wealth of information, but Hunter's right. Many times when you're talking to him about one thing, he suddenly switches over to another topic that has nothing to do with the original conversation. Kind of like a train switching tracks when you least expect it.

"How are you going to keep him there long enough to talk to you?"

"I'm stopping at the pastry shop after school to pick up an order of scones and clotted cream. I know how much Mr. Paget loves his scones. While he's enjoying them, I'll subtly steer the conversation to the Ringwood murder. What about you?"

"I'm going to check old newspaper files from fifteen years ago on my laptop. Maybe there's something on them that might give a strong hint about what happened. Or maybe there will be a small clue that was overlooked in that case. Either way I'm determined to find something out about that night."

An announcement comes over the PA system. "Remember students, when the bell rings, you are to report to your home room for attendance before going to your next class."

"Listen, Hunter. I think it's a good idea if I talk to Mr. Paget alone for a while. Get him comfortable. Just see what info I can get from him."

"Got it. And I'll check the internet. I'm going to check a new site called, Internet Archive Way Back Machine. I tried to check it out this morning in the library but I didn't have time. I'll use our new office." He grins at me. A small chill runs through me. The Book of Lost Spells is hidden there. Will Hunter find it? I shake my head. When I held it, I had the very strong feeling that the book didn't want anyone else to know of its existence. I know that the book, for whatever reason, will only appear to me for now.

Just as the bell rings, Hunter squeezes my hand and steals a quick kiss. Then both of us join the rest of the kids exiting the auditorium and head to our homerooms. I cannot wait to get to Midnight Ink and talk to Mr. Paget.

EIGHTEEN

Mr. Paget is right on time as always. Midnight Ink opens at 4:00 and fifteen minutes later, on-the-dot, Mr. Paget arrives. My parents aren't here yet and Hunter is doing exactly what he said he would be doing—using Newspaper.com, and the other site he mentioned, to check local newspaper stories from fifteen years ago. He's hoping to see what was reported about the Ringwood murder.

I greet Mr. Paget as he walks slowly through the door, his whiskers bristling as he sniffs the air. "Lilith, ah, Lilith. *There* you are but, where is everyone else? My package should have arrived by now. Yes, yes. Your parents said it would come today. Are they in the back room?"

"Actually it's just me and Hunter right now. He's upstairs, um, working on something. My parents will be here soon, though. But, I can get your package Mr. Paget. Come with me and I'll wrap it up for you after you look it over."

"Ah yes, yes. Must look it over, that's right. Is that," he sniffs the air, "is that delicious aroma that I smell scones and clotted cream? Reminds me of my boyhood, yes indeed. You know my mother—."

I stop him before he can begin a long-winded story. "Oh, yes, Mr. Paget. I stopped at the pastry shop on my way here. They wrapped them in foil so they're still warm. Would you like some tea and a scone or two?"

"Yes, yes, Lilith that would be wonderful. Tea and scones! Delightful! Simply delightful!"

"Let's go into the Magicis Scripturam and I'll get your book. Then, while you examine it I'll make the tea."

We go in the back and I look for his parcel among the eight that I had taken earlier from the large delivery box in front of the shop. His package is easy to find—it's the only one marked 'Fragile-Handle with Care'. After giving it to Mr. Paget, I hurry to the electric kettle where the water is already boiling, and get a cup and two paper plates. Then, while Mr. Paget is intently looking at his newest acquisition, a delicate parchment manuscript, I grab a bottle of water and quietly go up the winding staircase to the turret room.

Hunter is so focused on the computer screen that he doesn't turn when I enter the room. "Hunter," I whisper from the doorway, "Mr. Paget is downstairs."

"Lilith? What did you say?"

"I said that Mr. Paget is downstairs. We're going to have tea and scones. I'll save some for you. Come down in about an hour so I can talk to him for a while."

He holds up a finger, a gesture asking me to wait a second. Then Hunter turns in the swivel chair and faces me. "Good. I think I'm onto to something here but I'm not sure. If I *have* found a small clue, maybe later I can ask Mr. Paget about what I've discovered."

"Here." I walk over and hand Hunter the bottle of water. He smiles his thanks and goes back to looking at the screen as I turn to leave. At the doorway, I stop and look toward the small opening in the corner window frame where the Book of Lost Spells has hidden itself. A tiny flash of light sparks there for only a fraction of a second, then quickly fades. It is definitely well-hidden and no one knows about it.

Just me.

Downstairs again, I pour the prepared hot tea into a large mug and set it in front of Mr. Paget. I don't know how he takes his tea so I go to get cream, lemon, honey and sugar and bring all of it, along with napkins and spoons, to where Mr. Paget is sitting, sniffing the air. He happily inhales the delicious aromas in the room as he adds two heaping spoonful of sugar, and a slice of lemon, to his tea.

"Ah, dear Lilith. Scones and clotted cream, a lovely smell, a treat indeed! Thank you, my dear, thank you."

I place the warm scones and clotted cream in the center of the small table. Mr. Paget smiles as he carefully takes one and spoons a generous glob of warm cream onto it. His whiskers bristle with anticipation. "Delicious, delicious, my dear Lilith. This is wonderful!"

"I'm so glad you like it, Mr. Paget." I take a scone.

"Isn't young Hunter joining us, my dear? I would hate for him to miss this lovely teatime."

"He'll be down soon. He's just working on a—paper." I don't want to broach the subject of the Ringwood case just yet. Mr. Paget doesn't need to know about Hunter's research into that night. I want him relaxed and happily sated with scones and tea before I begin to ask him questions.

"Well, we'll just make sure to save him some nice scones then, won't we? A young pup like Hunter is sure to have a healthy appetite."

Young pup. Mr. Paget sees Hunter as a wolf pup. That's interesting since werewolves don't begin to change into their lupine selves until they hit puberty, around twelve or thirteen years old. I smile picturing Hunter as a werewolf puppy. I wonder what Lively would make of that?

"He'll join us shortly, Mr. Paget. I've got some scones and cream here for him." I pat a foil-wrapped box on the table.

"Good, good. Lovely, lovely." Mr. Paget goes back to enjoying his tea and scones. He's looking very relaxed and now just might be the time to ask the questions I carefully prepared in my mind.

"Ummm—Mr. Paget?"

"Yes, my dear?" He delicately wipes his mouth with a napkin and looks at me expectantly.

"You've known me for a long time and I want to talk to you about—"

"About flying? Oh my dear Lilith, how rude of me not to ask how your flying is coming along. I imagine you must be getting to be quite expert, yes, quite expert at it. I, myself, don't fly, but you know my little friends do. So graceful!"

He's misunderstands me. I can't have him go off track or I may never get him to talk about the Ringwood murder.

"No, it's not about flying. I need to ask you some serious questions."

He looks at me confused. "Questions? Serious questions? Oh, dear, please tell me everything is all right with your parents and Hunter. Or Lively? Nothing's wrong is it? Questions, oh my goodness!"

"Everyone is fine, Mr. Paget." He looks relived. I take a breath and plunge right in. "The questions I need to ask you are about the night Mr. Ringwood, Sr. was killed and about the werewolf his son shot. Will you tell me what you know?"

Mr. Paget takes a deep sip of his tea and then looks at the wall for a long time without saying a word. I sit, watching him and waiting.

"Dear Lilith, dear girl," he finally says with a deep sigh. "As I told your father, that was a terrible night, terrible night indeed. Those of us otherworldly creatures who make our home in the forest were quite, quite shaken by what happened. Three of my little friends, my little birds were startled from their nests and came to my window looking for comfort. I let them in and they stayed huddled together in my house until the next morning. Even then, they were afraid to go outside. Terrible, terrible night!" He shudders a little.

"I am so sorry, Mr. Paget." I pat his arm gently. He lowers his head for a second and then sits up straight.

"You must have a good reason for wanting to know about what happened so I will answer your questions as best as I can."

"Thank you Mr. Paget. I do have a good reason, a very good reason to find out what happened. Can you begin from the beginning? Tell me everything about that night that you remember." He nods slowly. "What's the first thing you remember?"

"I remember the exquisite howling."

NINETEEN

"The night started out so peacefully." Mr. Paget sips his tea as he tells me about that night. "There was a fine mist floating in the air and the beautiful moon filled the sky. I was so excited with anticipation, my dear! I knew that the werewolves would soon begin their full-moon run. I loved watching them. They would run for hours! Settled in the topmost room of my house, from that big bay window, I watched them. I never go into the forest at night, oh no, dear Lilith. I prefer to stay snug and safe in my own little home. Daylight is the only time I venture into the dark woods. Once I did leave my house and go there at night, silly of me I know, and I forgot the way back! My little winged friends found me and they—oh dear, what was I talking about, Lilith?"

"You were talking about how excited you were to see the werewolves begin their moon run."

"Oh yes, thank you, thank you, my dear. For me, the full moon is a magical, spiritual time, still is, you know. And the werewolves! They were so graceful as they ran through the forest in and out of the mist. They only ran in the forest and the surrounding fields, never outside of those areas, oh no, never. Outside those perimeters were danger zones where humans lived. They knew they had to avoid those areas. It wasn't like the old days when the werewolves ran free through fields and forests and even some towns. No, now civilization was encroaching on their territory so they knew they had to be careful.

"But the joy of seeing them on their moon run, oh how lovely they all were! The greys, the browns, and those with fur of a pure solid color—the ebonies and the moon-lit white ones, beautiful creatures. Ah, Lilith, I can see them now in my mind's eye! Males and females, all of them spectacular as the undisputed royalty of the night. Every so often, one of them would stop, throw back his or her head, and howl at the moon producing an eerily beautiful sound. Soon that solo voice would be joined by the others and the lovely sound of their howls filled the night with magic and beauty. You see my dear they were acknowledging the moon in all her splendor, for giving them the power of the run, the ability to change from human to wolf. It was an incredible experience to hear them howling."

"Mr. Paget, are you saying that there were werewolf packs that ran in this area as little as fifteen years ago?" I'm surprised. I've never heard my parents mention werewolf packs. Hunter and his father Gideon are the only werewolves I have ever known and Hunter is the only one I've seen in wolf form.

"Oh, yes, dear Lilith, most definitely. What a beautiful sight to behold. I was in awe of these creatures. And, as I said, the area surrounding the forest, the wide open spaces owned by the Ringwood family, was so much larger back then before some of their land was sold and developed for houses. Now, today, we only have the forest and just a little bit of open land surrounding it." He smiles. "Anyway, back then I loved to watch the werewolves on their full- moon runs."

I focus on what he said about the moon-lit white ones. My dad told had said that *"Gideon is a Ghost Wolf—his pelt is pure white, so white it brightly glows."* Could Gideon have run with the pack that night? Is that what he's keeping from Hunter? But, if he is keeping that fact from Hunter, the question is why? Hunter told me that his father didn't even do the moon run with him the first time that Hunter changed into his wolf form. He was thirteen and Gideon, in human form, only walked with him, showing him where the boundaries were. He never remembers any time when his father changed into his own wolf form and ran under the full moon.

I hear a noise and glance at the spiral staircase expecting to see Hunter coming down the stairs but it's only Lively chasing a cat toy down the steps. He looks at me and I understand the look. Lively is communicating that Hunter is still engrossed in whatever he's reading online.

"The night was a mystical, magical night for me, my dear," continues Mr. Paget dreamily, reliving the memory of a pack of werewolves running through the forest where he lives, "and as I said, that fine mist made the running all the more beautifully otherworldly. You know, I remember a book I read about a lost world where running in the mist was—"

He seems lost in a fog of his own and about to go off-track so I interrupt him. "Did you happen to know these werewolves, Mr. Paget? I mean, did you know them personally at all? Their names maybe, or where they lived when they were in human form?"

My interruption seems to make the fog lift and Mr. Paget blinks rapidly, his whiskers bristling as he sniffs the air. The scones and clotted cream.

"Would you like some more tea, Mr. Paget, and another scone?"

"Oh, ah, yes, my dear. So delicious. Make sure you save some for young Hunter. So, so, so, delicious."

I get the kettle and pour more tea for him then place a large scone and a generous scoop of cream, on his plate. I wait while he prepares his tea with sugar and lemon. I wait while he sips his tea and wait while he slowly spoons cream onto the scone and delicately cuts it into smaller pieces. I wait. And I wait and I wait. Finally, I cough discreetly and he looks at me.

"Yes, my dear? You wanted to ask me a question, I believe." He pauses with the mug halfway to his mouth. "Dear me, what were we talking about?"

"Mr. Paget, we were talking about the moon run on that night fifteen years ago when Mr. Ringwood, Sr. was killed. You were talking about the werewolves and how beautiful and strong they were."

"Oh, ah, yes, yes." He sips his tea.

"I asked you if you knew any of those werewolves personally. Their names, where they lived, anything at all."

He shakes his head rapidly. "No, no my dear. Why, as I said, they were royalty! I would never presume to approach any one of them. I am only a humble creature, my dear girl, and I was so in awe of them, so in awe! I admired those noble creatures from afar."

"Okay, Mr. Paget. Now let me ask you about what happened with Ringwood, Sr. and the grey werewolf. Just tell me what you remember."

Mr. Paget pauses for so long I start to think that he's going to go off onto another subject. Then he looks at me, his whiskers quivering, and says, "It wasn't what I saw, my dear. No, no, it's what I heard from my winged messengers, my little friends, the ones who didn't hide in my house. The ones who saw it all. It was horrible, simply horrible. Just—horrible." He closes his eyes and shakes his head.

"Go on, Mr. Paget, please," I say encouragingly. "What did your winged messengers tell you?"

"They told me they saw, oh my dear girl, they said they saw the most awful thing that can happen to werewolf."

TWENTY

"An unexpected fog began to roll in which is rather rare in the forest. Actually very rare indeed. As I said, I always stay in my little house at night—I don't see very well in the dark. Mists in the forest are a natural occurrence—they're usually light but there was something different about this particular mist. It was much, much thicker than normal, and in a matter of minutes, it became a fog and seemed to be all-consuming, covering everything in its path, even the tallest of trees. My beloved forest was like a lost world." He takes another sip of his tea before continuing.

"And Lilith, that all-consuming fog that blanketed the forest was dangerous—not for the creatures of the forest night, but only for the magnificent werewolves. You see my dear Lilith a dense fog, a blanketing fog, affects werewolves in a very strange, but perilous, way. While other night creatures will simply stay where they are and wait it out, the fog causes the werewolf to panic. It sharply distorts their powerful senses of sight and smell. They get confused and they easily lose their way. They get lost traversing the familiar paths and the hidden areas where they run. This confusion can lead them into the dangerous territory where—," here he pauses, cautiously looks around, and says in a low voice, "oh, dear me, where *humans* live."

If the fog was so thick, then how were his winged messengers able to see anything that really happened? I ask this of Mr. Paget.

"It was after the fog began to roll out that my feathered friends saw what happened. The fog was beginning to dissipate, to fade away if you will, when the horrible event took place."

"What happened during the fog?"

"That fog, that dreadful, dreadful fog was madness, pandemonium, for the werewolves. I could hear howls coming from out of that fog, howls so different from when they had howled at the moon earlier in the night. Their howls sounded as if they were in distress and lost and indeed they were. They were lost, lost in that fog! Some of the howls sounded as if a few of the wolves were far away from where they should have been. Far away and lost, oh dear!, lost in the danger area where the humans live."

Mr. Paget slumps back in his chair and stares at the wall. He's reliving that night and what happened to that grey werewolf. I let him sit there and gather his thoughts. I feel so sorry for this gentle creature who loves nothing more than to read ancient books, tend his garden, and care for the winged messengers he calls his friends. My heart goes out to him. Gently I encourage him to finish the story.

"Ah, yes, of course. The werewolves were lost and their howls were heartrending to hear. But then, the fog began to lift and there was the sound of running near my house. I knew that the wolves were coming back from the deepest part of the forest. Carefully I ventured outside my door and watched them up close. They were safe!

"Just as I was feeling relieved that they had escaped unharmed, I heard a howl coming from outside the safe areas. A howl of desperation, of pure fear. One of the werewolves must have traveled too far in the fog and was now alone with no pack for protection. There were other sounds as well, there were voices! They were distant but I still heard them. Sounds of men's voices. I heard someone shouting, 'He's been attacked. My father's been attacked! That wolf mauled him!' and more shouts of 'Over there! Can you see it? Find that damned wolf.' That was C. Thomas, Ringwood, Sr.'s son. My winged messengers told me that C. Thomas was a strange man. Why he hated wolves, I don't know, but he did, oh yes, he did."

I digest this information for future reference and then say, "Go on, Mr. Paget. Please continue."

"Oh, yes, yes, of course. I heard a howl of fear and then, oh dear, and then, a shot followed by another desperate howl. Another shot, a whimper, and—silence."

Shots? Guns? Summer Valley is a relatively safe town, the kind where parents want to come and raise their children. Who needs a gun? Hunting is not permitted around here—the forest where Hunter lives with his dad and where Mr. Paget has a small cottage, is on a protected preserve. The fact that C. Thomas Ringwood had a gun to shoot that poor werewolf is a total surprise to me. I look at Mr. Paget who has put his head in his hands as if the memory of that sound was too awful to relive.

"Go on Mr. Paget, please."

He raises his head and continues. "For several agonizing minutes I heard nothing more. I was beside myself with worry. I listened carefully and then I felt it." He stops and closes his eyes.

"Felt what, Mr. Paget?" I urge. We're getting somewhere with this story. I need to know what happened.

"A huge shape had run past me in the fog, back toward the sound of the shot. It went by me so fast and it was still fairly foggy so I was unable to truly see it. However, I knew that it was a werewolf and that it was a male by its scent. In all modesty, my dear Lilith, one of my powers, besides that of healing, is my sense of smell. It is strong and accurate."

I pat his hand again. His sense of smell is truly powerful.

"I was amazed and afraid for that werewolf. He was running toward danger and possibly death. That wolf was going back to save the werewolf who had been shot. The leader of that wolf pack was going to try to save one of his own. Yes, yes, indeed, one of his own. Oh, dear! I was frightened for them both."

"And the fog! The fog which had begun to fade a bit seemed to be returning. It was not as thick as before, but it was hard to see anything clearly. There were shouts of 'Where is it? Where is it? Can you see it?' Oh, it was awful to hear what was happening and not be able to help!"

"I waited and waited to see if the werewolves who were in danger would somehow escape and pass by my house, but they never came. I went back inside my house and bolted the doors. During the night, after the fog had lifted completely, I saw lights beyond the forest edge and heard the voices of men who were still searching for something or someone. I did not sleep that long night. I waited for daylight to end the terrible night."

I'm anxious to hear the rest of the story but I look at Mr. Paget sitting there, utterly exhausted just by retelling the events of that night, and say gently, "Mr. Paget, would you like to take a few minutes to just sit and rest? You don't have to finish the story just yet."

He stirs slightly and shakes his head. "No, dear Lilith, it's very kind of you to suggest that I rest, but no. Let me finish and tell you all I know about that tragic night."

I pour yet another mugful of tea for him and sit down to hear the rest of the story.

"In the morning, my winged messengers came. They had spent the foggy night in their nests in the forest and they had heard and seen what had occurred with the werewolf. They told me all that had happened. It was so dreadful to hear, my dear girl, so awful.

"A large she-werewolf, disoriented by the fog had wandered onto the property of the Ringwood riding stables. She got as far as the edge of the front lawn of the Ringwood house where a silent alarm was triggered. In her fear she didn't know where she was going. She knocked down Old Ringwood, Sr. who was taking his usual late night walk. She struggled against him in fear and then a strange thing happened. I don't know if it was the effects of the fog or something else but, the she-werewolf stopped struggling and looked at the old man for a long time. My winged friends say that she looked deeply into the old man's eyes almost as if *she* knew him and *he* knew her, both unafraid. In fact, one of my messengers said that the man appeared to try to comfort her by stroking her head and speaking to her. Very strange, very strange indeed!

"C. Thomas Ringwood arrived to see his father sitting on the ground and the she-werewolf standing near him. She was snarling. C. Thomas shot that poor werewolf twice. She howled in pain and ran into a forest thicket for cover. When his hands came, C. Thomas told them that he would stay with Ringwood, Sr, and ordered them to go into the thicket to make absolutely certain that the wolf was dead. My little friends, my winged messengers were so brave! They followed the men into the thicket. But when the area was searched, she was nowhere to be found.

"The stable hands went deeper into the forest to see if they could spot her, but they never found the she-werewolf. There simply was no sign of her. Eventually they gave up the hunt and returned to the scene of the attack. My little messengers followed them. There they found C. Thomas kneeling over his father. Clutched in his father's hand was a tuft of thick grey fur from the werewolf. Ringwood, Sr. was dead."

"Did Ringwood or his son think that it was a werewolf who attacked him?"

"Oh, no, my dear. Most humans don't believe werewolves really exist. To them it's all myth and legend, not real at all. Truthfully, they don't believe that *we* exist, we creatures of a, shall I say, different make-up? Otherworldly creatures like your parents, young Hunter, and you and me. No, humans do not believe in us. And that is an advantage to our kind. Some call us supernatural but we prefer the word otherworldly." He looks directly in my eyes. "Do you know why we're called otherworldly, Lilith?"

I shake my head no and he continues. "Because even though we *exist* in this world our distinct differences, powers so to speak, make us not really a part of it. So, inside ourselves and our homes, we are in a world of our own, otherworldly so to speak."

"What happened to the werewolf, Mr. Paget?" I ask almost in a whisper.

He shakes his head. "Ah, Lilith, dear Lilith, that's the saddest part of this story. Much later in the night, my winged messengers finally found her, hidden in a deep ravine near a stream. They told me that the large male I had seen going back through the fog to find the injured werewolf, did indeed find her and led her there. This large male watched in deep sadness as her poor body tried to change back to her human form, as is the normal course for a werewolf who is gravely injured and believes it is dying. But, she couldn't make the change. Something inside her had stopped her from becoming human again. She lay there, a severely injured werewolf, with the male lying next to her, guarding her from any further danger. My feathered friends led me to where they had last seen that poor creature. They thought that perhaps I could help her." He pauses and smiles sadly at me. "The birds of the forest know that I am knowledgeable in healing potions. My small power as an otherworldly healer allows me to help my fellow creatures."

I pat his hand gently, encouraging him to continue. Mr. Paget wipes his eyes. "When we got to the stream, no one was there. Neither werewolf was there. They had disappeared."

"And the wolf pack? What happened to the wolf pack?"

"After that night, I never saw them again. It is as if they never existed except in my mind. But I know they did exist and so do my winged messengers. Where they are fifteen years later, I have no idea. They are lost to us. I only know that I miss them. Now, the only werewolf with whom I am acquainted is young Hunter."

For a long time neither of us speak. My mind is filled with the visions told to me by Mr. Paget. The glorious run of a pack of werewolves, something I can only imagine. How wonderful it must have been to actually see them doing a full-moon run! The howling at the moon, the beauty of what Mr. Paget referred to as royalty. The dreadful fog that disoriented the werewolves and led to a tragic mystery. My enhanced senses of inner vision try to imagine it all as if I had been there myself. A werewolf who can't change back to human form, a pack that is no longer in the area, a tragedy that somehow could involve Hunter. But how? What is it about that grey female werewolf? A glance at Mr. Paget, who's sitting with his head down and staring at his hands, tells me that he's lost in his sad memories of the night.

I sense Hunter at the top of the stairs, then watch him come down them two at a time. I wonder how much, if any, he heard about that night but I decide he's heard nothing. The expression on his face lets me know that he's eager to tell me something, some important info he found online in the newspaper archives. I shake my head slightly and nod toward Mr. Paget. He gets my message—Mr. Paget needs a distraction, a mood-lifter so to speak. Hunter pretends that he's just come down for a snack.

"Hey, Mr. P., how are you?" He comes over to the table. "Scones! I am *starving*," he says grabbing a plate and spoon. Lifting the foil from the bakery container, he carefully scoops clotted cream onto two scones and places them on a plate. Grabbing a bottle of the cold tea, he sits down and begins to eat. "These are great, Lilith. What do you think, Mr. Paget, sir? Sir?"

Mr. Paget raises his head. For one moment he looks lost, as if he's in some type of dream. Then he nods his head and says, "Young Hunter."

"How are you Mr. Paget? Have you had some of these scones? They are unbelievable!"

"Oh, ah, scones? Oh, scones, yes, delicious, delicious."

Hunter's enthusiasm gets through to Mr. Paget and he smiles and nods his head. In a few minutes, Hunter gently leads him into a conversation about flying and Mr. Paget begins to talk about the art of flight, bird versus other creatures.

I mouth a silent thank-you to Hunter and leave the table to get a cold bottle of iced tea.

TWENTY-ONE

It's just after 6:30 PM when Mr. Paget leaves with a bag containing the rest of the scones and clotted cream. Hunter took my hint about distracting a sad-looking Mr. Paget and not a word was said about Ringwood or the grey she-werewolf.

The male and female haven't shown up yet and it is just Hunter and me alone in Midnight Ink. Neither of us is hungry. Scones and clotted cream are still settling in our stomachs as we sit and discuss my talk with Mr. Paget. I tell him what I was told, hoping I do justice to Mr. Paget's eloquent description of the beautiful werewolves doing their moon run.

"It must've been quite a spectacle to watch all those werewolves. What I wouldn't give to have been able to run with them!"

"Are you concerned about the fog affecting werewolves that strange way?" I ask a bit worried about Hunter if a rare fog ever does come up on a full moon night. "It's a scary thought."

He shakes his head. "It sounds scary!" He looks at my concerned face. "Don't worry, Lilith. I check the weather report on my phone for the days of the full moon each month. That wasn't available fifteen years ago."

Hunter grabs my hand and pulls me to my feet. "Come with me." He has something he found online that he wants to show me, so we go upstairs to the turret room. Sitting in front of Hunter's laptop I watch as his fingers click on the keyboard and bring up an archived article about the wolf attack from fifteen years ago.

WOLF ATTACK KILLS PROMINENT CITIZEN, BITES ON THROAT WERE FATAL screams the headline in big bold letters. The article goes on to detail the story as told by C. Thomas Ringwood. *"This wolf, a large, grey wolf, came out of nowhere and viciously attacked and killed my father. It must be found and killed."*

Included in the article are old, smudged-looking black and white pictures of the scene of the attack after the fog had lifted. Large paw prints are visible in the dirt as well as signs of a struggle made by a human body. Hunter clicks the pictures forward. Someone leaked pictures of the body of Ringwood, Sr. on a slab in the county morgue before the M.E. could clean the marks. I shake my head in disbelief. There's always some person who wants to make a few bucks and will do something like this.

Hunter zooms on the picture and waits for my reaction. I bend forward for a good look as the quality of the picture isn't the best. A dead body on a slab with what appears to be bite marks on the throat. I'm no stranger to pictures of dead bodies—I've seen them in my Criminal Justice class as part of the lessons in forensics. I don't know how I'd feel seeing a dead body in person, but I can look at this picture in a detached manner.

"Look really closely, Lilith. Look at the marks around the throat. What do you see?"

Hunter zooms in one last time and I look closely at Ringwood's throat. Marks are visible and at first glance, they would seem to be the cause of death. Then there are the scratch marks from the wolf's claws—long, bloody scratches on Ringwood's arms. I take the cursor from Hunter and move it slowly over the marks on the body, enlarging each one at a time. Definitely signs of contact between human and wolf. But there's something about the bite marks on the neck, something that doesn't fit with the cause of death. What is it that I'm not seeing? My otherworldly eyes, able to see things more clearly as my powers become stronger each day, look closer. There's something very strange about those wounds. But what?

While Hunter sends the newspaper file to our phones, I get up and stretch. It's been a long day. I walk over to the windows and look out on the familiar street. It's a very peaceful view and I stand there watching the usual hustle and bustle of people going about the end of their day. It's still a relatively small town which is one reason the male and female brought me here to live.

I feel a slight vibration and glance over at Hunter. He's still checking online for more info on the Ringwood murder and doesn't seem to notice anything at all. I do though, and when I feel it again, I instinctively know what it is. My attention is drawn to that little Book of Lost Spells that's hidden in that small opening in the corner window frame. For some strange reason, I feel as if it is acknowledging my presence here, as if it wants me to know that it recognizes me, and only me in this room. It's at once a comforting feeling and a slightly frightening one. What does that book want with me anyway? The line in the first poem in that book read, "*It goes wherever most needed*". Why does it seem to feel that I need it? Oh, wow, now I'm giving human thoughts and feelings to a book! Magical it may be but it is not capable of thinking—or is it?

My phone alerts me that the files Hunter sent have been received and as I look out the window again, I see the male and female walking, like normal people across the street. I have to smile at how well they blend in. Then the chimes sound as they open the front door. Sending a thought to the Book of Lost Spells to stay hidden, I tell Hunter my parents have just come in and that I'm going downstairs to see them.

"Got it," he says closing his laptop with a satisfied click and standing up. "Let's go tell them what we found." He bounds down the stairs as I lag behind. A small glint from the book's hiding place seems to wink at me as I glance back before going down the circular stairwell. My quasi-normal life is turning more magical as the days go by.

The male and female listen carefully to all that I'm telling them about Mr. Paget's narrative concerning the night C. Thomas's father was killed. They are equally as attentive when Hunter shows them the pictures of the marks on the body from his phone along with the newspaper article. With their vamp eyes, they study the pictures. I know that they can see much more in-depth details than either one of us no matter hard Hunter or I look at the pics.

"Those wounds weren't made by a werewolf or any otherworldly creature," says my mother. "See this one here and this one?" She points to two wounds near the man's throat. "They're not teeth marks. A werewolf's bite is more savage and ragged, tearing the throats of their victims to shreds. This is nothing like that at all."

My dad agrees. "These wounds were made to look deeper, but they're too uniform, too perfect."

While Hunter calls his dad, Gideon, to tell him he's still at Midnight Ink, and my parents discuss the pictures and the article, I excuse myself and go to order take-out—a large peppers and onions pizza for Hunter and me and two very rare burgers for my parents. It's getting late and the fullness of the scones have pretty much worn off.

Hunter comes back to the table shaking his head. "That's weird."

"What's weird?" I ask counting the money my mom handed me for the take-out.

"I just called my dad's cell phone. He didn't pick up right away and when he did he sounded—strange."

"Strange? How?"

"I can't describe it really. I mean, my wolf sense picked up on something but I can't figure it out. There were noises, like, an animal noise, a whining sound almost."

"Maybe he's outside. You do live on the edge of a forest."

"That's the strange part. I asked him what he was doing and he hesitated, then said he was finishing up his latest book. He said he was in his study."

"Open windows maybe. The forest can get noisy."

"No, Lilith. I think he was somewhere else but didn't want me to know."

"That doesn't sound like your dad. Where do you think he was?"

"I have no idea but—why wouldn't he tell me where he really was?"

It does sound a bit strange that Gideon wouldn't want his son to know where he was, but I don't want Hunter to worry about that tonight. He's got enough on his mind about this Ringwood case.

"Seriously, you're over-thinking this, Hunter. I'm betting he had a window open and was probably standing near it when you two were talking."

"I don't know, maybe. I guess it's possible."

I don't really think Hunter's over-thinking it. I've learned that vamp sense, werewolf sense, and my own burgeoning magical sense, is nothing to dismiss. Why would Gideon lie to Hunter about where he was anyway?

After we finish eating, or in the case of my parents, sucking the blood from the almost raw burgers which neither Hunter nor I find unusual, it's almost 11:00. I'm wiped out physically but mentally my mind is going a hundred miles a minute. We have an actual case to follow and solve. That's exciting. I have a secret Book of Lost Spells and I have no idea why it appeared to me. I'm concerned that Gideon Hollis Hopper wasn't truthful to his son Hunter. I'm getting more concerned about the fact that my parents are keeping strange hours for vampires and not letting me know why. I'm dying to try out another solo flight and, topping off all that, I have a Calc. test tomorrow. Mystery, magic, math—my life.

Hunter's giving me a ride home and, as we walk to where he's parked his Vespa, I marvel at how quiet and peaceful this town seems. The whole area, really. The forest that borders the area, the small lake where I swam as a little girl, the houses and the charming little businesses and shops—all of it deceptively peaceful. Deceptive because underneath it all is a danger to those of us who are different. Hunter and Gideon, my parents, gentle Mr. Paget, the elfin-like and so wise Professor A.J. Reed, and me.

The humans who live around here don't know there are vampires and werewolves and otherworldly creatures in their midst. Creatures who go about their everyday lives just like everyone else, not harming anyone, but who stand a terrible chance of being harmed themselves if they are ever found out. Being harmed just for being different.

TWENTY-TWO

There's a buzz at the picnic tables outside of the cafeteria. Kids are excitedly gossiping over their lunches about the wolf search parties being organized by C. Thomas Ringwood. I listen in without saying a word. There's always the possibility that I'll overhear something crucial that might give us info about how to work this case. I hug myself and smile. I know this is a serious situation and all, but I have to say that I am so excited about it—our first real case!

Hunter comes over to the table where I'm sitting and the other kids obligingly move over as he squeezes in beside me. One thing about Hunter—even though he's a pretty solitary person he is well-liked by just about everyone, students and faculty alike. I don't do too badly myself although in my case, while everyone is nice and pleasant to me, I'm pretty much left to myself. That's okay. I'm kind of a loner.

After a half hour, kids begin getting up, some to walk around the area before the bell rings for afternoon classes, some to go lay out on the grass and get some sun. When we're alone, we share what we've heard the other students say.

"So," begins Hunter, "I heard that C. Thomas wanted to form a group hunt with up to twenty-five people. He wanted them to scour the whole forest. The good thing is that he needed to get a permit for that and that's not a possibility. Hunting is banned in Summer Valley."

"Whew! Thank goodness," I say.

"Yeah, but, listen, he can still do it in a sneaky way. Just him and the people who work for him. That's not good. What did *you* hear?"

"Just stories about the reward money and how to get it. Some of our classmates are really just so naïve about what it would take to actually earn that money. The danger of not knowing the forest, the risks to themselves—no one is really thinking it through."

"Creatures like us can smell things like danger or fear and be on guard, but it seems that the scent of money seems to have the opposite effect on humans," he nods toward a group kids talking animatedly, "making them act kind of recklessly. They have no idea what could happen in those woods."

We're silent for a few minutes and then I ask, "Hunter? This may sound crazy, but, do you think there's any chance that the male werewolf, the one Mr. Paget said went back to help the big grey female, might somehow still be around? I know you said that you've never seen other werewolves when you do the moon run but, if they're not here, they have to have gone somewhere. What if they simply left this particular forest area but are nearby in another forest?"

"Well, didn't Mr. Paget say that he doesn't know where they went? That they just—disappeared? And it is over a decade later, who knows where they might be now."

"If Mr. Paget doesn't know, maybe someone else does. Remember what we learned in science about how some species, like the wolf and mountain lion, will suddenly appear in a new area? We can check online and see if wolf populations not too far from here suddenly increased fifteen years ago or if a pack of wolves unexpectedly appeared in a new area. It happens a lot with some species. For most wolves it's because of better hunting, but for the werewolves, well maybe they found another forest for the full-moon runs and maybe animal behaviorists believe that a new, larger species of wolves just entered a new hunting ground. It's worth checking out some old science journals online."

"You might be on to something Lilith. I never even thought about that." He leans over and kisses me. "You're brilliant, you know that? Just absolutely brilliant!"

I smile and kiss him back. I have a very good idea of how we're going to be spending our time in Midnight Ink after school. Old science journals, here we come.

July, 2003. "After an absence of *deca*des, the wolves have returne* to Shasta County an* we at the Society for the Preservation of Nature an* Natural Inhabitants, are *elighte*. The California Department of Fish an* Wil*life (CDFW) has confirme* that a group of a*ult wolves, (grey, ebony, sable-brown, an* pure white), seem to be inhabiting the northernmost reaches of the state in our own Shasta County. A lone cani* was first caught on camera in May an* June, prompting the CDFW to *eploy a**itional cameras, which photographe* the members of the pack. The group, more than likely *escen*ants of the original wolves, has been appropriately name* the Shasta Pack."

It took us almost an hour to find the article buried in the archives of the small press magazine, *Nature Sightings*, but when we did, it was as if we had found gold. The byline states the article was written by a woman named Deidre Pace.

Finding her is going to be significantly harder than finding the article because, outside of a few other articles written for this little-known nature magazine, there is not a whole lot of information about her. In this day and age when almost everyone has some type of an online footprint, we find nothing. The only contact info for the magazine Nature Sightings is an email, no phone numbers, no address, nothing. The website for the Society for the Preservation of Nature and Natural Inhabitants has not been updated since 2011.

"Okay," I say turning away from the new PC my parents have installed in the turret room and facing Hunter, "let's do this. You email the magazine and I'll call the number that's on the site for the society. If the site is still up, someone is paying a yearly fee for it, so they must still be active. But, before we do, let's take a break. My neck and back are cramped from sitting here at the desk."

Both of us get up to stretch and then head over to the windows and gaze down at the street while we drink cold tea.

"Are you flying tonight?"

"I have to! It's been two nights now that I haven't gone flying and I miss it. Not only that, I need to practice."

Hunter nods and tells me that the first two times he did a full-moon run were difficult because he had had to wait twenty-eight days between runs. "It's not a question of forgetting—I mean, there's muscle memory involved in what you and I do—it's more a need to practice what you already know and to perfect it." With his eyes focused on the park across the street, he says, "And, I have to ask, Lilith, but, have you gone flying alone, outside of your back yard? You don't have to tell me if you don't want to. But I know that when I was supposed to stay close to home on my third run, I didn't. When my dad was asleep, I snuck out of the area and ran farther than I was supposed to run. It was exhilarating and scary at the same time, but I loved doing it."

I laugh and nudge Hunter slightly in the ribs. "How'd you know I did a solo flight?"

"Because, I know you, Lilith Angel and I know that you'd try the solo flight as soon as you could." He laughs and nudges me back." So, tell me— how *was* it?"

"Hunter, it was wonderful! Glorious and, like you said, scary." I go on to tell him all about my flight, how I saw the chimney on his house and wanted to do a lazy fly-over but a sudden wind carried me away from there and farther than I wanted to go. I tell him how terrified I was especially when my wings were blown straight upward and I was falling to the ground. Finally, I tell him about the howling dog and how mournfully desperate it sounded.

"It was so sad, Hunter. Just heart-wrenching."

"Probably afraid of a coming storm and that wind." He pauses, "Do your parents know that you flew alone?"

"I don't think so, I don't really know. Hard to tell what they might know because, truthfully, they're acting a bit weird lately, staying out past sunrise, saying mysterious things like they have 'a few things to take care of', and 'some special things need our attention'. And they're being even more protective of me than usual. Did Gideon know about *your* solo run?"

"I think he did even though he never said anything to me about it. He's pretty savvy so I think that, yes, he did know."

I tell him I believe the male and female know about my solo flight too but, for whatever reason, they've chosen not to mention it to me. "Anyway, enough of a break—we have somewhat of a lead on this case so let's see what we can find out."

TWENTY-THREE

Midnight Ink is busier than usual today and that means that one of us has to be downstairs at all times. Hunter takes his laptop down to the main room and I stay in the turret room to use my PC. We're going to take half-hour shifts.

Finding the owner of the domain is easier than I'd hoped. It's registered for the Society for the Preservation of Nature and Natural Inhabitants by the same woman who wrote the article, Deidre Pace. Big help there. I go back to the site and look at the contact numbers for the society. It's worth a try. The site might not be updated but maybe the person who used to run it has kept the same phone numbers.

I try the first one with no luck. Three rings and then the message that *this number is no longer in service* is heard. I stare out the windows in frustration for a few minutes. Maybe I'm hoping for too much. It's been fifteen years and people move on. Sighing, I turn back to the screen and key the second number shown into my cell phone. One ring, two rings, three rings, four rings—my thumb hovers over the disconnect button on my phone.

"Hello?" A woman's voice. "Hello?" I'm so surprised that for a second I can't answer. Then I find my own voice.

"Yes, hello. My name is Lilith Angel and I'm looking for a Deidre Pace."

"Who is this?"

"My name is Lilith Angel and I'm looking for Deidre Pace. She wrote the article in Nature Sightings magazine. The 2003 article about wolves returning to Shasta County?" There's a long pause and for a minute I think the woman has hung up. "Hello? Are you still there?"

"I'm here. That article was written a long time ago. Why are you interested in it?"

I take a deep breath and let it out slowly. "I'm a student in an environmental science class and I'd like to interview the woman who wrote it. I, um, I'm doing a term paper on animals returning to natural habitats. This article says that the wolves returned to Shasta County and that's of interest for my term paper."

Another long pause, then, "I'm Deidre Pace."

"Ms. Pace, I would very much like to speak with you about the article you wrote. I'm a— keen observer of wolf behavior," I say thinking to myself how true my statement really is. I certainly am an observer of Hunter's behavior.

"How did you find the article?"

"On the internet," I say truthfully. "I keyed in wolves and habitat."

"And my article came up? I'm surprised it's still there."

"Nothing is ever lost or forgotten on the internet, Ms. Pace. It's there, ad infinitum, really forever. And may I say add that your article is very good. I'd like to know more about these wolves. Can I—is it possible for me to interview you? Are you still in Shasta County?"

She doesn't say anything for quite some time but I know she's there because I can hear her fiddling with her keyboard. Finally, she says, "Yes, I've lived here for over thirty years. I assume that you're in California. Where are you calling from?"

"Summer Valley."

"That's a pretty fair distance from Shasta County. A long way to come for an interview."

I pull up a map on my screen. It's two hundred forty miles from Summer Valley to Shasta County and the estimated time, according to the map's directions, say it is a one-hour-twenty-minute drive. I wish that I could fly there but over two-hundred miles is a bit chancy for someone who has only just learned the basics of flying. I think about how the wind nearly took me into a crash landing a few nights ago. Flying two hundred forty miles is a risky venture. A sudden weather upset could well push me out over the Pacific Ocean or send me crashing into rugged hillsides. I sigh deeply. Not an option. I'm still not skilled enough in flying techniques.

I weigh the possibility of a phone interview but immediately discard that idea. I want to see the area where the werewolves, if they are *indeed* werewolves *and* the same ones who used to run free here, are located. I quickly key in colleges in Shasta County and decide to outright lie. This opportunity is too good to miss. Those wolves may very well be the Lost Pack of werewolves who once ran on full moon nights right here in Summer Valley.

"I'm supposed to have a tour of Lake College in Shasta County this weekend. I can stop by wherever you are while I'm up there."

"What are you interested in taking?"

What? Hell's Bells! I quickly look up the course descriptions at Lake College and settle on one. Swallowing hard I say, "Animal Behavior and

Environmental Studies."

"Lake College is limited to associate degrees. Are you only looking to get an associate degree?"

Amsterdam, Rotterdam, damn, damn, damn! This is taking too long. My knees hit the underside of the desk as my body levitates. I concentrate on relaxing. "Um, oh no, but the program at Lake College is supposed to be, um, one of the best, um, in the country. It'll get me started and I'll finish up at one of the many universities in California."

"Interesting. A type of environmental protection degree, hmmm. Very good. Well, you are lucky. I'm only about fifteen minutes from the college. When would you like to do the interview?"

"Are you available Saturday, um, around 11:00?" I cross my fingers and lie again. "The tour is at 9:00 and shouldn't be more than an hour and a half."

To my surprise and relief, she says Saturday morning around 11:30 AM will be the best time for her. "Does that fit into your schedule? I have a work meeting with the Society for the Preservation of Nature and Natural Inhabitants in the afternoon."

"Oh, that's works fine for me, Ms. Pace," I say a little too eagerly. "

"You must really be interested in wildlife to have that early a tour! I'll see you at 11:30 then." She gives me her address and hangs up. Yes! A lead that may actually pan out for Hunter and me.

A glance at the time on my computer screen tells me I should go down and relieve Hunter but somehow I remain sitting at the desk and thinking about meeting Deidre Pace. We'd have to go by car—even if I wanted to fly, Hunter can't. The male and female bought me a car which they use at times when they want to appear human like going to back-to-school nights, shopping with me for clothes, and other human-related activities. Okay, so we'll take the car. No problem.

With a quick glance at the place where the mysterious Book of Lost

Spells is hiding itself, I get up to go downstairs. I haven't told anyone about the book yet, I feel as if it truly wants to remain my secret and I'm good with that. Maybe someday when I need it, really need it, I'll tell Hunter. For now, the secret is mine alone.

TWENTY-FOUR

The male and female are very good about me taking the car on Saturday and driving two-hundred forty miles to Shasta County to find out if the wolves who suddenly appeared there fifteen years ago are the werewolves who used to run in the forests here in Summer Valley. Actually they're too good, too accommodating for this request. I have a feeling that they will be monitoring me every mile of the drive with their vamp senses.

Hunter and I will take turns driving and we'll make at least one pit stop. We're going to leave early on Saturday morning around 7:00 so we'll have time to find our way without any problems. The car's GPS has us taking I-80 E to CA-32, and then branching off onto some unpaved roads. It's the unpaved roads part of the journey that bothers me. Unpaved means rural and that means basically being out in uninhabited country, possibly miles from what I consider civilization. To me civilization means a pizzeria and shopping mall within a short distance of home. Maybe it's a good thing if my vamp parents monitor this trip even if it can be annoying.

But all that is two days away and tonight I'm flying away from my home ground. My parents have decided to visit Gideon and tell him about my and Hunter's little sojourn. At Hunter's request, they're using the lie about a college tour as the reason for our trip. No mention of Shasta Valley is made.

"I don't want my dad to know that I'm searching for the werewolves who used to live here. I hate to lie but—."

"Sometimes, a lie is the only way to ease into what we truly want," says the female. "No worries, Hunter. We're good with this."

Then the male told me it would be perfectly okay to practice my flying skills at Hunter's house. "Just be aware that there are more trees here than in our back yard, darling," says the female. For some reason my parents are more protective of me than ever. I have no idea why. I ask Hunter about it and he seems to think that it has to do with me flying.

"It's the same thing I went through when I began my first solo full-moon run away from that small area of forest near my house. Just like my dad was worried about me running alone, your parents are worried about you flying solo."

"I guess," I sigh, "but it's annoying. I mean, I'll be turning eighteen years old this summer and going to college next year. I don't want constant surveillance."

Hunter smiles at me sympathetically. "Yeah, well whether we want it or not, we've got parents who are kind of overprotective. It's worse because they're not like other kids' parents—*ours* have powers."

The night is warm with just the lightest of breezes when my strong, beautiful ebony wings lift me up from the ground and have me float gently on the breeze for a few minutes. Then I power them up, waving them in a down and upward motion and practice making turns. Wide circles, tight circles, turning and turning. As I fly, I find that I am in another world, a world where there might be danger but also incredible beauty. Zooming up toward the night sky with its brilliant stars, soaring gracefully with wings outstretched, hovering over the tops of the trees just on the edge of Hunter's property, I feel powerful. I'm glad to see that Hunter is observing my flight with obvious awe.

I practice landing several times making sure that my knees are slightly bent, and that I balance on the balls of my feet, allowing my wings to gently ease back down before I stand up straight. My wings are immaculate, shining with a soft, rich glow—they don't seem to need any type of care like brushing or washing. Maybe they're self-cleaning or something. In any case, they are perfect.

"Don't will them away, Lilith," says Hunter, which is something I usually do with my wings after I've landed. "You look so different, like a mysterious winged creature from another world." He takes several pictures of me with his cell phone before I move from my landing spot. "Look. Look at yourself, Lilith Angel. You really *o look like an angel," he says softly.

I take his phone and look through the pictures he's taken. It's me all right, but a different me, someone out of a movie or a fantasy comic. My long reddish wind-blown hair is hanging past my shoulders and the sleeveless tank top, leggings, and sneakers, all in a mossy black, seem to blend perfectly with my wings. The whole effect is one of a life-sized fairy who has decided to visit the world of the humans, an angel come to earth. "Lilith of the Angels," I say to myself. "I really *am* Lilith of the Angels."

Driving my car to Shasta County is freeing. I am more than thrilled to be on my own with Hunter who considers this an adventure and a possible connection to the mysterious murder of Ringwood, Sr. My parents, and Gideon who came to our house with Hunter to wish us a safe trip, wave to us as we get in the car and begin the journey to Shasta County. My dad made sure that the GPS was working properly before I keyed in the address of Deidre Pace, hit start, and began the road guidance.

"Make sure to charge your phones with the charger I put in the car," says my mom, holding Lively who has now morphed into a calico cat. He's beautiful and he mind-sends me a message to be careful and not do anything dangerous. I nod my okay to him.

I take the wheel first until we get halfway there and make a pit stop at a small gas station for water, snacks, and a chance to stretch our legs. Then Hunter takes over and as we talk I look out at the road in front of us and see a hawk, gracefully floating on an updraft. I get a sudden urge to fly. How wonderful it would be to fly out here over the open terrain and under this blue, cloudless sky. My eyes follow the hawk as it seems to be effortlessly suspended in the air, wings spread wide.

Hunter glances over at me and then up at the sky. "I know how you feel, Lilith."

"Feel? About what?"

"You want to fly. You see that hawk up there just doing what comes natural to any winged creature and you want to be up there too. I know how it feels. I can't wait for my full-moon runs. Sometimes my blood races and I feel such an urge to make the change to my wolf self. Waiting for the full moon fills me with such longing sometimes."

I touch his hand lightly. "Hell's Bells! I never wanted any powers. All my life I've only wanted to be normal. I mean, even though my parents are vamps, my life was pretty typical. Levitating, not so typical but still, my life was fairly normal. But, now that I've got these powers, I understand what Professor Reed meant."

"Which is?"

"Having them, the flying and all, *is* normal for *me*."

"I guess everyone is normal in their own way, Lilith," says Hunter as he turns off a dirt road and onto a newly paved street.

The GPS tells us that we'll be at our destination in less than twelve minutes. I think about the questions that I want to ask this woman Deidre Pace. Hopefully, these wolves are the same ones who ran free during the full-moon runs that so enthralled Mr. Paget. Fingers crossed.

Deidre Pace lives in a lovely, old house with a large, fenced-in front yard. As we pull up in front of the house, three large dogs who resemble German Shepherds come running from the back yard and look at us curiously through the slats of the fence. They're beautiful animals with wolf-like markings and a high intelligent look on their faces. We open the door and get out. It's almost 11:30 AM, the time Ms. Pace set to meet me.

The dogs bark in unison as we walk toward the gate. Hunter smiles and whistles to them. As a werewolf, he's connecting with his fellow canines. They stop barking and put their front paws on top of the fence, emitting a low whining sound of kinship. They know. All animals can sense one of their own kind, I've been told. Hunter walks right up to them and extends his hand which they sniff. Then he begins to pet each one as they compete with each other to be nearest him as if they see Hunter as the alpha wolf. I wonder what they'll think of me. I'm not a wolf or werewolf, just—kind of human. But, as I approach, they seem to be okay with me as well. I pet their soft luxurious fur.

"They like you," says a voice. I lift up my head and see that a woman is standing outside the doorway of the house. She's tall, slender, with short white hair and an open smile, wearing old jeans and a faded loose shirt. She calls the dogs to her as I open the gate and step through. Immediately the dogs go and lie down at her feet, gazing up adoringly at her.

"Shepherds, right?" I ask.

"Two shepherds, Brett and Henry. Artemis here—she's a large husky-wolf mix."

"They're beautiful."

"Intelligent and beautiful. They're my babies." She takes some treats out of her pocket and gives one to each animal. "I'm Deidre Pace. You must be Lilith Angel, yes? The person who wants to interview me about the wolf article."

I tell her that I am indeed that Lilith Angel and introduce Hunter. "I just have a few questions so I won't take a lot of your time."

"I've got a couple of hours free today. That should be enough time for an interview. By the way, how'd your trip to the college go?"

I swallow hard and lie easily. "Good, yeah, really well. Hunter might want to go there too, right Hunter?"

"Uh, ye-s-s, right." He looks at me a bit startled as he answers. It's harder for Hunter to lie, I guess.

"Hmmm, interesting. Well, come into the backyard. I've got some lemonade in a pitcher out back. We'll sit and talk there."

And with that, Ms. Pace turns toward the side of her house followed by her dogs, and Hunter and me, two otherworldly creatures on a quest to find a pack of werewolves.

TWENTY-FIVE

"So when did you develop an interest in wolf behavior, Lilith?"

After handing both Hunter and me tall glasses of lemonade, Deidre Pace sits back in a low slung Adirondack wooden chair, her magnificent dogs lying comfortably at her feet, and asks her question. I answer truthfully that I became interested a little over a year ago. No lie—my interest was piqued when I began dating my favorite All-American werewolf. Hunter's fingers brush mine gently.

She scrutinizes me as I tell her that wolves hold a certain fascination for me and I am particularly interested in why certain packs of wolves will leave an area that was their natural habitat and then suddenly and, unexpectedly, return years later.

"There are many reasons why they leave, Lilith. Laws allowing hunting to thin out the packs, hunters who take advantage of that to excess.

Ranchers who fear that the wolf will decimate a herd of cattle, and of course poachers. Once a wolf pack begins to lose numbers, the remaining animals seek newer grounds. But they seem to have a homing instinct similar to all migrating animals that brings them back to their original grounds, even many years later. A need for familiar grounds that is passed down from generation to generation."

"Are the wolves who returned to Shasta County, from a pack that was known to have originally been from here?" Hunter asks.

"Now that's interesting that you asked. I would assume yes, given what I know about the homing instinct, but there was a debate about that very question among animal behaviorists. Were they actually descended from the same pack that had disappeared? These wolves are bigger, *much bigger* than the wolves who were here many years ago. Pictures of wolves native to Shasta County from years ago compared to pictures of the ones here today clearly show the difference. Of course, as I wrote in the article, these are more than likely the descendants of the original pack, but the size of them remains a debatable topic."

"Maybe better hunting grounds, abundance of prey? Better nutrition has been shown to increase size in future generations of mammals," says Hunter.

Deidre Pace acknowledges this statement with an approving glance at Hunter. "All of that was, of course, a solid possibility. But, there were other reasons to question if these wolves were from the original pack." She looks out at the mountains in the distance for a few minutes. "You know, when I wrote this article, the only thing I was really interested in was the fact that there were wolves in the county again. Nature seemed balanced once more, settled and the way it was meant to be before we humans came into the picture and disrupted it all.

"I watch them, I go out into the valley where they live and I sit on a boulder and observe them. I keep track of their behavior in my notebook.

They frolic and run like the wind. They're beautiful and so majestically royal-looking."

Her words are so similar to what Mr. Paget said about the werewolves he saw, "*All of them spectacular as the undisputed royalty of the night*".

"But, there is something different about these wolves, something I can't exactly put my finger on. I'm happy that they're here of course, I love to watch them, it's a dream for an animal behaviorist. It's just that they're somehow—different—and I can't explain how. None of the other behaviorists can explain it either. They're just—different. Now this may sound weird but, it's almost as if they, these wolves, well there's no other way to say it, almost as if this new generation of wolves has *human intelligence*."

"That's an interesting theory," says Hunter smiling.

"It is, isn't it? On the nights that I observe them, I like to think they're communicating with me as well as with nature. They love the night time. Seeing them then, in the beauty of nature is a rare gift."

Seeing them, night time. Her words spark a thought. We're in rural territory here with wide, open spaces and, I'm sure, very little light. She can't use any artificial lighting because it would disturb the natural activities of the animals here. "Ms. Pace, do you have a specific time of the month when you observe them? You know, when you can *really* see them? I'm assuming you don't use artificial light." From the corner of my eye I see Hunter look at me—he knows what I'm asking.

"Yes, I usually do my observations on nights when the moon is full. You're right about not using artificial lighting—I never would use light that isn't natural. We have lots of stars out here, but most times they're obscured by the clouds hovering over the mountains. So, the nights when the moon is at its brightest are the best time to observe the wolves. Wolves are crepuscular."

Hunter looks at me with a 'huh?' look. Yay, words! My specialty! I smile and explain. "Crepuscular, comes from the Latin word crepusculum meaning twilight. Animals who are crepuscular come out at twilight making them most active after dusk."

"Yes," says Deidre Pace. "True creatures of the night, especially when the moon is full."

Ms. Pace has agreed to show us where the wolf pack runs, cautioning us that we probably won't see them. "It's too bad you won't be here for the full moon. Have you ever heard a wolf howl at the moon? It's unearthly!" This time it's Hunter's turn to smile. Howling at the moon is *his* specialty. How I love when he howls at the moon!

Her dogs walk in front of us sometimes straying to chase a rabbit or other small creatures. I'm happy to see that they catch nothing. It's all playing, no preying. I ask if she takes the dogs with her when she goes out at night to observe the wolves.

"Oh, no. I'm afraid that they would take off after the wolves and since the wolves are wild, my babies might get injured. But, you know something? On the nights when I leave the house for my observations during the full moon, they seem strangely alert, as if the inherited memories that all animals possess makes them hyper-aware of their heritage at that time of the month." Hunter nudges me and nods. Inherited memories.

"Ms. Pace? Have you ever known wolves to attack or kill for no reason?"

"You mean other creatures? No, not unless there's a good reason and the only good reason would be if they felt threatened or cornered or they were protecting their babies." She walks carefully around a group of rocks. "These wolves here seem friendly. That may sound strange but there have been times when I was out here observing them and one or two would come and sit a few feet away from me. I have a habit of putting out buckets of water when the weather is too hot and I like to think that they were thanking me. Silly I know but still—."

Not silly to me. All creatures respond to kindness.

The terrain we walk is rough and there're groves of trees, several mini-forests, actually. She takes us over to the boulder where she sits on nights that she observes the wolves. The only sounds we hear are the sounds of insects and birds. I ask questions about wolf behavior, habitats, food supplies and put it all on my iPad.

After I run out of questions, we sit back and just look around at the majestic, raw beauty of where we are. This place is perfect for full-moon runs. Looking at the mountains and the plains I feel a twinge in my shoulder blades where my wings appear. The longing to fly is getting stronger in me.

"This is my spot," says Deidre Pace. "It's the perfect place to watch and video them when they run out of the woods and across the plains."

"Videoed? You've videoed them then." I'm excited.

"Yes, of course. I record their movements, the sound of their howls, and then, when I'm done for the night, I go back to my home and put all I've compiled into my computer along with some specific scientific notes about my observations."

Her dogs sit down on the soft earth, but there's a vigilance about them. Their otherworldly lupine relatives have been near and they can smell their scent. I hear Hunter inhale deeply. The dogs aren't the only ones who sense the fact that the werewolves been here. Have been here recently, too, less than three weeks ago.

"The wolves seem to be prospering here. I've seen two very young wolves. Not pups exactly, but, young. I haven't ever seen their pups and that's probably because the momma wolf is very cautious and protective."

She doesn't see the pups because a female werewolf will change into human form to give birth to her pup who enters the world as a human itself. They won't begin to change to their wolf form until they're in adolescence and that's when she sees them—as young wolves.

Here they live as wolves but where do the werewolves live when they're in human form? They have to have regular homes when they're not doing a full-moon run, living like normal people, as Gideon and Hunter do.

"Are there any houses or people living nearby this area?" Ms. Pace looks at me curiously. "I mean," I say quickly, "it's a beautiful area and I would think that many people would like to live around here."

"Well, the country is lovely here. There are some ranches and farms around our small town and there are homes on the edge of this particular area." She points off into the distance where we can just see some rooftops of houses. They seem separated from the farms and ranches.

"I guess all the houses around here are old."

We get up and dust ourselves off. Deidre Pace has invited us to have lunch at her house. "Shasta Valley is an old community founded in, oh I think it was 1840. There are a lot of original houses here, seems that they were certainly built to last a long time. But those houses I pointed out to you? They were built less than fifteen years ago. The houses are a rustic style, very country-like. I believe whoever had them built wanted them to fit in with the rest of the area homes and that's very nice of them. Shasta Valley should be preserved just as it was when it was first settled and the newer buildings should appear as if they are part of the original architectural style."

I look at Hunter. Fitting in, blending in, that's what Professor A.J. Reed told me that otherworldly creatures do. Building houses that resembled the older ones already in Shasta Valley is more about blending in than just respecting the look of the area.

Deidre tells us that after lunch she will show us pictures she has of both the old and the new wolf packs. With her dogs leading the way we walk back toward her house leaving behind the valley and forested area where I believe the werewolves run.

After a lunch of turkey and ham and cheese sandwiches washed down with more lemonade, we sit at the table while Deidre Pace shows us pictures of the original wolves taken over fifty years ago. When she excuses herself to go to her home office and we're alone, Hunter whispers to me, "These are Canis Lupus, regular wolves, not werewolves. They're big wolves but nowhere near the size of an adult werewolf."

He's right. They're wolves, beautiful creatures but definitely not werewolves. I turn as Ms. Pace comes back to the room. "Beautiful weren't they? Too bad they're in black and white. Now let me show you what my hi-resolution camera, a Sony Alpha A 6000, caught of the newer wolves who came into Shasta County fifteen years ago. These pics are in color. Wolves are a breath-taking sight in nature and being able to capture all their magnificence on camera is a gift." She hands me a large manila envelope.

The pictures are definitely of werewolves. They're large, perfectly proportioned creatures. The colors of their fur are just as Mr. Paget described them to me. Brighter, warmer, richer than their distant cousins the Canis Lupus. How lucky Mr. Paget was to have seen them up close!

We're comparing the old black and white photos to the new ones in full color when Deirdre

says, "I'm sorry to cut this interview short, Lilith, Hunter—I have to leave in a few minutes. But," she smiles at me, "since I can see that you really do have an interest in wolf behavior, I have a real treat for you. You want to see these wolves in action, right? Well, I've got videos of them running in the moonlight and I downloaded them on to a flash drive for you. I would love to sit here and watch them with you but this meeting of the society is very important. Here." She hands me a flash drive. "Watch them when you get home. You'll be amazed at the raw beauty of these wolves. Watch for the beautiful alpha-male. His fur seems to catch all the glow of the full moon's light. It's amazing. Take this too. It's my cell number in case you have another question or two. You can text me and I'll get back to you."

I've seen Hunter run and he's a combination of both grace and strength. I can't wait to see these werewolves running. I thank Deidre Pace for the interview, lunch, and the flash drive. She walks us out to my car, her dogs following.

Before he gets in the car, Hunter gets down on the ground with the dogs and each one sits before him, their heads on outstretched front paws. It's their acknowledgement of his wolf essence. He scratches the head of each dog in turn, hugging them close. After he's done, I pet each dog, then squat down looking into the eyes of the husky-wolf mix. Her eyes are blue and she looks back at me knowingly, maybe recognizing that there's something different and otherworldly about me, too. When we stand up, the dogs roll over in front of us exposing their bellies, a sign that they feel safe with us.

"You two certainly have a way with my babies," says Deidre handing me a paper bag with sandwiches and cans of lemonade for our trip back home. "I've never seen them act like this with anyone they just met. They're usually aloof and wary of strangers."

"Hunter's kind of the dog whisperer and, I guess, they just automatically know that I'm an animal lover."

"Well, that's a good thing if you're going to become animal behaviorists and work in environmental studies. You seem to have the right stuff for the field. Keep me posted about what courses you're going to take and if I can, I'll advise you on them. And, oh yes, let me know what you think of the videos after you watch them."

"I sure will. Thanks again for everything. It's been a good day."

We say our good-byes and, before getting in my car, I text the male and female while Hunter texts Gideon letting them know all's well. Hunter takes the wheel and we pull onto the road. It *has* been a good day filled with hope and the possibility that the old wolf packs that Mr. Paget so admired have found a new home. I can't wait to see the videos. But first there's something I want to do.

I want to see those newer homes Deidre Pace told us about, the ones she said were built only fifteen years ago.

TWENTY-SIX

I soar and circle the forest and Shasta Valley. The view is incredible. Hunter is seated on the highest rock he can find as he watches me fly. I zoom close to him, high enough so that I avoid the rocks, close enough to see the happy smile on his face. I land gracefully on the strong limb of an old tree. As I watch in awe, Hunter makes the change to his wolf form. The process is both terrifying and beautiful—powerful and majestic. He throws back his head and howls lustily at the midnight sky, a sky emblazoned with millions of stars.

Hearing his howl my body levitates with joy and my ebony wings lift me higher and higher until I catch a warm current of air and float almost motionless, my wingspan hawk-like in appearance. Below me Hunter begins to run, faster, faster as I float above him. I look up toward the heavens. The starry night winks down at me. Looking at the stars I know that I'm looking into the past, as even the closest star light is 4.5 light years away and others are billions of light years distant from us. How incredible to look at a star and be able to see into the past!

But something isn't right, something is very wrong. How did Hunter become a werewolf? There's no full moon tonight. I scan the sky—there's no moon at all! Suddenly I hear Hunter howl, but the howl is different. It's a howl of pain. And then I hear my name. From his wolf's mouth he calls for me to help him.

"Lilith, Lilith, help me! I can't change back! I can't make the switch!"

Quickly I zoom down. Hunter is lying down with his head on his enormous paws, his sides heaving with the tremendous effort to change back into human form. I see his eyes changing from wolf to human in brief spurts. He's in agony, I can feel it.

"Lilith!"

I have to help him!

"Lilith!"

I don't know how to help him!

"Lilith?"

He's stuck in wolf form and I can't—

"Lilith! Wake up. You're having some type of nightmare."

Startled, I open my eyes. My car is parked on the side of the road and Hunter's hand is on my shoulder, shaking me lightly. "You okay Lilith? You were talking about something and you seemed terrified. Must have been some nightmare."

"When did I doze off?"

"About a half hour ago."

"Hell's Bells, I'm sorry Hunter. I meant to stay awake and keep you company. It's kind of desolate out here."

"That's okay. I intend to take a nap when it's your turn to drive." He touches my face gently. "But that was one helluva nightmare, Lilith. Do you remember it?" He uncaps a bottle of water and hands it to me. I nod yes as I bring the bottle to my lips.

"At first, everything was wonderful. I was flying over the Shasta Valley and you were watching me." I say guzzling the cold water. "Then suddenly, it turned horrible, Hunter. I noticed that there were millions of stars in the sky. You changed into a werewolf which didn't make sense because there was no full moon. There was no moon at all! And then, you couldn't change back into human form. You called for me to help you but I didn't know how."

Hunter is silent for a moment as he gathers me into his arms. "It's just a bad dream, Lilith. Your subconscious is remembering what Mr. Paget told you about the grey she-werewolf not being able to make the change back into human form. You're just mixing all that up with you, me, and the werewolf pictures we saw today."

I look out of the windshield at some houses off in the distance on this unpaved road. "Where are we?"

"You told me that you wanted to see that new development of houses that was built fifteen years ago. According to the GPS, and the direction we were facing when Ms. Pace pointed to the houses, this road leads to that area."

The houses possibly built by werewolves looking to find a new place to live. They're the ones that Deidre pointed out to us when we were sitting on that rock and talking about the wolves. The new houses built to look as if they have been there since the 1840s.

I sit upright and open the passenger side door. Stepping out I stretch and then bend slowly from the waist, going forward until my hands are lying flat on the dusty ground. My muscles, especially those in my back, feel tight and cramped. When I straighten up I look up the road toward the houses. I feel a thrill of excitement and that new itch between my shoulder blades. One possible clue to the whereabouts of what Hunter and I have started referring to as the Lost Pack.

"How long before we get to that development?"

Hunter gets out of the car and stretches and I hear his neck crack. "GPS says less than twenty minutes."

"Okay, let's take a ten-minute break, eat a sandwich, drink some lemonade, and go."

"Um, okay. Just a sec." He looks out over the road and disappears behind some wide boulders.

I open the driver's side door and say in his direction. "And let's find a gas station with a restroom. You may be able to pee by the side of the road, but I can't."

Hunter laughs as he gets into the passenger side. "Just marking the territory." I throw a sandwich at him which he deftly catches and then we both laugh. Sandwiches, lemonade, and a gas station. Life's simple pleasures.

The houses are set back from the road, close to the forest. I park the car a short distance from the new development and we get out. There are a few people outside their homes doing things like gardening, washing their cars, taking in groceries—all the usual things you would see people doing on a Saturday. Fitting in. Hiding in plain sight. No difference detected except one. These homes are not near any of the other homes in the area. Close to the forest and away from the town, just like Hunter's house and that of Mr. Paget. Far enough away to have the privacy necessary for beings who are otherworldly.

Hunter takes my hand and we wander along the road until we come to a pretty little cul-du-sac that has a basketball net and a trampoline set. The area, a short distance from the house, ends where the forest begins. There are trees and flowering bushes that hide the path that leads directly to the forest.

"Hi. Are you two lost?" a voice calls out. We stop and turn. A woman and man are walking over to us.

"No, we were visiting a friend not far from here," I say. Not exactly a lie, Deidre Pace could become a friend. "We stopped before heading back home and saw these houses. Then we saw the forest and we're just admiring the beauty of it. It's so lush."

"Oh it certainly is. One of the reasons we love the area so much."

"It's not a problem, is it?" asks Hunter looking at the couple with a smile. I see his eyes are looking directly at the male who holds his ground and smiles back.

"Oh, no, no problem. This is kind of private property, though," says the man surreptitiously sniffing the air in Hunter's direction. "We're sort of like a gated community, but without gates. Our kids play here and we all hold this piece of property in common. Legally it's for the people who live in these homes." He gestures toward the houses.

"But the forest isn't part of that common property, right?" I ask.

"No," says the woman smiling as she eyes both of us in a cautious manner. "Just be careful if you walk in there. Tree limbs and hidden tree roots can trip you up. But, please take a walk and see our lovely forest. It really is spectacular."

"Animals I guess, too, right?" I look directly into the woman's eyes. She doesn't blink, just gazes back calmly.

"Well, all forests *o* have animals. That's where they make their homes, that's where they live. But, most animals are shy creatures around humans. I doubt you'll see more than squirrels, rabbits, and birds and those only at a distance."

Thanking her, Hunter and I begin to walk toward a path between two large trees.

"Where are you both from?" The man is standing slightly apart from the woman and speaking to Hunter. I look at him. His eyes are fascinating with a clear, fearless gaze.

"Summer Valley. We have a beautiful forested area too."

The man says nothing but I notice his eyes squint a little as he sniffs the air again, and there's a slight, wistful smile on his face. "Summer Valley. That's a bit far from here."

"You know the town?" I ask.

"Yes, I know it. Pretty area."

The woman says something to the man that I can't quite hear and then tells us to have a good day. The green forest canopy covers us as we walk the path. It's humid and warm. As we walk my ever-expanding sixth sense tells me we've been conversing with werewolves in their human form.

And I could tell they sensed the same thing about Hunter.

TWENTY-SEVEN

"They know that I'm a werewolf," says Hunter confirming what I was just thinking. I squeeze his hand.

"It's them, Hunter, the Lost Pack. I really believe we've found the Lost Pack."

"Me too. They have to be from the Lost Pack. It can't be coincidence." He shakes his head. "But, Lilith, even if they know that I'm a werewolf, how do we connect? I mean, I can't just blurt out, Hey, hi, I know who you are and why you left Summer Valley fifteen years ago, and oh, by the way, whatever happened to the injured she-werewolf and the male who stayed by her side? I mean how do we let them know why we showed up here?"

The path is worn smooth by use, a perfect track for animals scurrying back and forth. I can see faint images of paw prints, some small from rabbits, squirrels, and chipmunks, other larger canine prints. I stop, lean against a tree and gaze down the path. "I don't think that we can let them know the real reason we're here. They sense the wolf in you and the man did react when you said we were from Summer Valley. I know that they're curious about you. Right now we're just observing them and they're checking us out as well."

"Maybe you're right. I guess I'm just anxious to find out what happened to that she-werewolf and her mate. Plus, all this stuff with Ringwood has gotten me uptight. Did you know that my dad doesn't want me to do the full moon run next time? He says it's better if I keep a low profile for a few months. That means that I'd have to stay in a room when the change comes over me. That's crazy. I mean, I've heard stories about werewolves who do that and none of them are pleasant."

I clutch his hand tighter. I can't bear to think of Hunter locked up in a room every night of the full moon. We have got to crack this case soon. How I don't know. I watch a bird, startled from its perch by our approaching footsteps, fly from one tree to another. The desire to fly is becoming stronger and stronger in me.

We continue walking through the woods until the path seems to end and it becomes just a maze of trees, then we turn around and follow the path back toward the houses. There are several adults, about eight or more, standing near the basketball court along with some children. All heads turn as we come out of the forest. A basketball comes rolling toward us and Hunter neatly picks it up. Then he aims it, expertly making a perfect half-court basket to the delight of the kids there.

"Nice shot," says the man we had met before. "Impressed our daughter. You play?" He and the woman walk toward us.

"Yeah, well, a little. I kind of like basketball but running is my real passion," says Hunter.

The man looks at him appraisingly. "You're built like a runner. I'm a runner too. Did you like the forest?"

"It *is* beautiful," I answer as he and Hunter size each other up, one werewolf to another. "Right, Hunter?" I tug on his hand slightly and take a step toward where the car is parked.

"Um, yeah, yes, really beautiful."

"Your name is Hunter?"

"Yes, sir," says my young werewolf politely, "Hunter Hollis Hopper from Summer Valley."

Hunter has told him his full name in a bid to see his reaction and, it works. The name registers on the man's face. It's crystal clear that he knows the name well and perhaps once ran with Hunter's dad, Gideon.

"I'm Lilith Angel, also from Summer Valley. Well, it was nice meeting you. We have a long drive ahead of us so we'll be going now."

I wave at the kids and tug Hunter's hand more strongly. There's a moment of silence broken by a little girl calling for her mommy and daddy to come and watch her shoot a basket. The woman turns toward the child and tells her they'll be there in a minute. Then she looks me full in the eyes, taking my measure before she warmly smiles at me.

"Have a safe ride back to—Summer Valley. Come back any time. By the way, my name is Lara and this is my husband Hugh." Lara nods at us and Hugh extends his hand first to Hunter and then to me.

"You're welcome here, Hunter Hollis Hopper and," he turns to look at me with those piercing eyes, "you're welcome as well, Lilith Angel."

There's going to be a lot to talk about on the trip back home, I think as I slide behind the wheel of the car. A whole lot to discuss.

"I've never met another werewolf before." Hunter is lying almost prone in the passenger seat with his feet resting against the dashboard. "I have to take this all in slowly and really concentrate on it, Lilith. I met, *we met*, other werewolves. It's—it's a lot to get my brain around. They're my kind, I'm not alone."

"Not a lone wolf anymore?" I kind of joke because Hunter looks so serious and overwhelmed. He glances at me then closes his eyes.

"Aren't you just a little bit curious to find others like you who can fly? I mean, I always knew there were other werewolves, I've heard about them and read about them, but a pack, a group of werewolves doing the full-moon run together was never a part of my life. This is big to me."

I think about what he's just said. Truthfully, I haven't really given any thought to there being other creatures like me who can fly, let alone finding them. I'm fine being a loner. But then, maybe it's in Hunter's genes to want to be part of a pack. Maybe it's a wolf thing, who knows? As for me, I really like flying solo.

We drive for another hour before getting out to stretch at a small country type restaurant. A cheeseburger for me, a veggie burger for Hunter, and fries, along with cold ice teas refresh us. In the women's bathroom, I brush my teeth and pull my hair back into a ponytail. We should be home in less than thirty minutes. I sigh as I return to the table where Hunter is going over the check. We've really accomplished a lot on this trip, more than we bargained for anyway. I thought it would just be an interview with the person who wrote the wolf article. That was interesting in itself but meeting the man and women who we truly believe are from the Lost Pack was the real gem of our trip. As Hunter said, it's a lot to process.

The bill comes to twenty-four dollars and I insist that Hunter take half of the money from me.

"Come on, Lilith, you and your parents are always buying me dinner when I work late at Midnight Ink. Let me pay for this and treat you."

"Nope, not until we're rolling in money from our criminology agency," I tease grabbing the bill and the thirty dollars from his hand. "Then you can buy me the most expensive dinner in the world. I'm counting on it." I pay the bill, give Hunter my half of the amount, which he reluctantly accepts, and leave a six- dollar tip.

"Your turn to drive," Hunter say running to the car. "I'm taking a nap on the way home."

TWENTY-EIGHT

Midnight Ink is still open when we arrive back in Summer Valley. Of course my parents' vamp senses let them know we're back and the female is already outside by the open door. Having parents who are vampires means two things—one, they are always quick to protect you, and two, the idea of privacy is somewhat limited.

When I started getting serious about Hunter I had to tell my mom and dad to please back off and let Hunter and me have some private time. I mean, how many teen girls want their parents sensing them kissing and, um, otherwise *being* with their boyfriends? To give them credit, they promised to put a lock on reading my thoughts and turn off their protective radar where I'm concerned if I promised to be responsible about the *being with Hunter* part and to always let them know if I was going to be late coming home. A deal was struck between us.

"Darling! How was the trip? Successful I hope." She grabs both of us into a hug. The male does the same.

Seeing my parents has me bursting with excitement about what we may have discovered.

"Mom, Dad, I think, I *really* believe that Hunter and I found the pack of werewolves who left here fifteen years ago. We think we found the Lost Pack."

"Lost Pack?"

"Uh-huh, that's what we named them."

"Interesting," says my dad. "The Case of the Lost Pack. I like it."

"Dad! That sounds so lawyer-ish, like something out of a novel by John Grisham. I'm not going to be a lawyer."

"No," he says putting his arm around my shoulders as we walk into the book shop, "but you have it in you to become a good investigative criminologist. If, that is, what you want to be."

Gideon is in the back of the book shop and Hunter goes to hug his dad. I notice that Gideon is a shy man, reticent and reserved about showing affection. Not at all like my parents who have no problems showering me with affection. Talk about cold vampires is so untrue. They're the emotionally warmest creatures I know. I say hi to Gideon and we talk about the trip. I'm careful not to mention the werewolves of Shasta Valley and I make up a story about visiting the college.

"You only went to the college? You didn't sightsee in Shasta County then."

"Nope, not enough time, Mr. Hopper. The tour was extensive."

Gideon seems relieved at my answer. I catch the female and male looking at me approvingly and remember something very important that I was told about lying when I was a child.

A puppy had jumped out of a car window hoping to follow its owner who had gone into a store next door to Midnight Ink. Another car came by and accidentally hit the pup who lay lifeless in the street. We were outside of the shop and saw it all. The owner, who ran to the pup, was practically hysterical. The driver stopped his car in the middle of the street and ran over as well.

"Do something daddy!" I sobbed as the female held me close. "You can save him! Please, daddy!"

A look passed between my parents and then the male went out to the street where the woman was screaming, "He's dead, oh my God, he's dead!"

Kneeling down near the lifeless puppy, the male gently laid his jacket under the dog's head, rubbed his body, then bent close to his mouth. Anyone looking at the scene would assume that the male was listening for a sound of breathing from the lifeless dog, but I knew what he was doing and I watched closely, holding my breath.

The male bit his own tongue and let droplets of his blood drip into the dog's mouth. In just a few seconds, the dog came back to life and began wagging his tail. He whined gently and licked the male's face. Through my tears I saw it all. I was ten years old and even at that young an age, I understood that the powerful blood from my parents could heal wounds and even restore life. I was so happy that my father had brought that puppy back to life.

"You saved him, oh my God, you saved him," said the owner cradling the puppy in her arms. "How did you do it?"

The male simply said that the dog was only stunned and that he had done nothing at all but try to make the dog comfortable. He then told the woman to take her dog to the vet to make sure there were no broken bones. I knew there would be no broken bones—the blood would have healed them too.

"You made him alive again, daddy!" I jumped into his arms and he carried me inside Midnight Ink. Once inside, I touched his face and looked in his eyes. "Daddy? I'm happy you saved that poor puppy but why did you tell the lady a lie about what you did to save him? My teacher told us that it's bad to lie. Why didn't you tell her the truth about the blood drops?"

He sat me down on a high bookcase so that we were face to face and smiled at me. "The thing about lying is this—there are good lies and bad lies. Bad lies are the ones that hurt people and we never want to hurt anyone, right? That's the bad lie that your teacher told you about." I nodded my head solemnly. "But," he continued, "here's a secret that you must never tell anyone. A *good* lie helps people, Lilith. Always remember that."

And I did. I never lie to hurt someone.

After an hour or so of small talk, Gideon takes his leave of us, telling us that he has a deadline to meet for an illustration he's been working on for another book. I promise to drive Hunter back home later. My parents look out at the darkened street and say that they'll see me at home later.

"We hate to leave you darlings, but we need to go out," says my mom. I nod. No problem. They look pale and luminescent. The hunger is upon them. They need to feed.

I kiss them both and Hunter hugs them. "We'll be fine. Don't worry," I tell them. "See you at home." Truthfully I can't wait until Hunter and I are alone. I'm dying to plug in the flash drive Deidre Pace gave me and watch the wolves run.

The male and the female disappear quickly and Hunter and I run upstairs to the turret room and power up the computer. I plug in the flash drive and we watch Deidre Pace make a few comments about the wolves returning to Shasta Valley and how this is the first of the videos of them that she hopes to turn into a documentary. Then the screen goes blank for a few seconds until a scene appears that shows a camera pan around the area—the mountains in the distance, the full moon in the sky, and the open area that connects to the forest.

For a long while, all we see is the empty area and hear Ms. Pace talking about the habits of nocturnal animals. A few times she pans up to the full moon which looks larger and more imposing over the empty plains. Then we hear it. A full-throated howl that touches some ancient cord within me. I glance at Hunter and see that his breathing has quickened and he's mesmerized by that sound, his wolf-sense responding to a sound as old as time.

Soon that single deep, long howl is followed by a full chorus of howls. It's thrilling and frightening. I can understand why the werewolf was feared in ancient times. The sound is one of power and unbridled strength. Out of the forest come the werewolves, males and females—all large, intimidating animals. Perfect creatures of the night engaged in an ancient tradition—the full-moon run.

The rich colors of their pelts flash before our eyes as they begin to assemble. They stand proudly howling at the moon and then stop and direct their attention to the forest opening. The camera pans from the howling wolves to the opening where a very large werewolf stands in shadow. The alpha-male.

He throws back his head and howls long and loud while the other werewolves seem to bow before him. Proudly and powerfully, he walks toward the pack. As he comes out of shadow I can see him clearly. His fur is white. *So pure white that it brightly glows.* A Ghost Wolf.

Hunter's father Gideon.

TWENTY-NINE

"It can't be," I think. "Can it?" Gideon running with the pack. *Leaving* the Lost Pack.

I say nothing to Hunter but think of everything that Mr. Paget had told me about the night the grey werewolf was shot. Was the male werewolf, who went back to help her, Gideon, in his wolf form? Is it possible that he led the Lost Pack to another location to keep them safe and still runs with them even now? And, supposing this werewolf in the video *is* the werewolf who went back to help the grey werewolf, then where is *she?*

"My dad would love to see this video. Too bad I can't show it to him. It's really a shame that he doesn't run anymore. Maybe seeing this would give him the push to run again."

I face Hunter straight-on. "Do you know why he doesn't run anymore,

Hunter? I mean, is there a specific reason he stopped doing the moon runs, even with you, his son?"

"I told you, Lilith. He stopped running after my mom died. They ran together and I guess he lost his desire to run after she was no longer with us."

"Hunter, think carefully. Do you remember any werewolves from your childhood? Anyone at all?"

"That's kind of a strange question, Lilith. I mean, I know my dad is a werewolf and my mom was one. You mean other werewolves, like relatives or friends of my dad? No, I don't ever remember anyone else who was a werewolf. There was someone who baby-sat me sometimes. She was an otherworldly being, but she wasn't a werewolf. Why?"

"Gideon stopped doing the moon run when you were just two-years-old. That's when your mom died." A look of pain crosses his face and I touch his hand lightly to comfort him. Growing up without a mother has to be hard. "But, before she died, your parents did the moon run together, right?"

He squeezes my hand, acknowledging my comfort and says, "Well, yeah, but I don't understand what you're trying to get at."

"You were a child but you must have seen both your parents change into their wolf forms during the full moon. It's just something they do like, you know, like putting on a coat or jacket. You must have seen them go off to the run."

"I guess I did. Why?"

"What color was their fur?"

"Color? I don't—."

"Just try to remember. Is it possible that your dad is a white werewolf, the kind that's known as a Ghost-Wolf?"

"You mean like that werewolf in the video we just watched? I don't know. Why?"

"It means that if that white werewolf *is* Gideon, he knows about the Shasta pack and has run with them."

Hunter looks at me strangely. "No, that's crazy. It can't be him."

"I can't explain it, Hunter. It's just a theory. Maybe the wolf in the video isn't him at all."

"Maybe. But if it is, why—"

"If he didn't tell you, maybe it was to protect you."

"I guess." He closes his eyes in frustration. "But don't you think that I'm getting just a little too old to protect? I'll be in college next year. I don't need to be kept in the dark about what's gone on in the past and what's happening now."

Suddenly, a soft glow, and a barely audible humming sound comes from where the ancient Book of Lost Spells has hidden itself and catches my attention. It seems as if it signaling me, like it wants me to notice it even though Hunter is in the room. Then, as suddenly as it began, it fades.

"I can't seem to remember anything about my parents back then, Lilith," says Hunter opening his eyes. "It's as if my mind is blocked. Too bad there isn't a way to go back in time so I can see them again as they were in wolf form." He sighs deeply. "I'm going to get a bag of chips and some water from downstairs for us. Be right back."

Back in time. I remember the words written in poetry form in the Book of Lost Spells.

Time stan•s still as the spell is cast,

The past is present an• the present is past.

"The past and the present can merge." I turn around and see Lively, who is now a brown and grey tabby sitting by the window.

"When did you get here?" I ask.

"A few minutes ago. I was visiting an old man to whom I once belonged when he was a little boy. Seeing me again made him happy. He needed my visit."

I pick him up and snuggle him. I love that he visits his past owners although, I muse, no one really ever *owns* a cat. The cat picks the human with whom they want to live. But, he goes back to let them know that although he may be gone from their lives, he's okay. Lively allows me to pet him for a few minutes then jumps down to go back to the window.

"Excuse me, you just said that the past and the present can merge. What exactly does that mean?"

Lively puts his front paws out and arches his body in a complete stretch, his back legs and tail reaching as far as they can go. Then he begins to bathe his face. "Lively? What does that mean?"

"It means that a person in the present can visit past events and someone in the past can visit the present. It's complicated but that's what it means. I think that you can figure it out."

"You knew about the Book of Lost Spells?"

"Of course. Your secret is safe with me." He gracefully moves a paw over his face. "And, you should remember that a spell is, after all, only words."

Words. Okay. Words are safe, I had told Professor A.J. Reed. *"Yes,"* she had responded, *"but they're also powerful."* That power has to apply to casting spells. Spells contain words and, despite potions and candles, it is really the words themselves that make the spell potent.

A glow from the hiding place of the Book of Lost Spells catches my attention again. It doesn't stop its glow even when Hunter re-enters the turret room. He turns and stares at the soft light. It's as if the book wants Hunter to know it's here.

"Um, Lilith? There's something happening over there." He points to the where the Book of Lost Spells has materialized and is floating motionless in the air.

I make a quick decision. I have to tell him about its existence, what it is, why I think it came to me to use, and what I think I should do. Maybe there's a spell in the book that can help us begin to solve this mystery of the werewolves and the murder of Ringwood fifteen years ago. Hunter needs to see the past. We both do.

"Hunter? We need to talk."

"We need to talk about something that may help us solve the mystery of the wounded werewolf and the murder of C. Thomas Ringwood's father. Hunter?" He's is staring transfixed at the softly glowing book suspended in mid-air.

"Hunter!" I grab his arm and make him face me. "Look at me and I'll explain everything, okay?"

He turns back to the book and points. "Um, yeah, sure, but—*can* you really explain *that*?" As we watch, the book floats slowly through the air, circling the entire turret room before landing softly on my outstretched hand. The glow grows fainter and fainter until it's just a pinpoint of light flickering around the edges of the book. The expression on Hunter's face is a mixture of awe and confusion.

I hold the book lightly in my hand. "It's a book, Hunter. Simply, or well not so simply, a book. A really ancient magical one to be exact."

"Does it, you know the book, does it have a—*title*?" Hunter appears to relax a bit but keeps his eyes on the book in my hand. For someone who turns into a werewolf, a creature who would scare most humans to death, Hunter belies the myth that werewolves fear nothing.

"It does have a title. *Il Libro egli Incantesimi Perduti,* the Book of Lost Spells."

"Okay. Lost spells, huh? So, have you cast any spells with it or what?"

"Hunter, let's go sit down and, as I said, I'll explain everything to you."

We walk over to the desk where I place the still gently flickering book between us. I tell him about how the book appeared to me and how I had the feeling that I had to keep its existence secret. "I didn't tell my parents or call Professor A.J. Reed about it. I had a strong feeling that it was my secret to keep. But now, I think that it wants you to know about it too."

I take Hunter's hand and gingerly place both our hands on the book. There is a small shimmying feeling from the book, similar to one a cell phone makes when it's on vibrate. When we take our hands away, the cover opens to the first page.

"And it just appeared to you? It must know about your new powers."

"That, and the fact that I'm probably part-witch. My mom believes that I am."

Hunter looks at me closely and begins to nod. "Yeah, I can believe it. You have that witchy look about you, now that I think about it. And that's one of the things that makes you beautiful."

He smiles and seems more relaxed around the magical book.

A witchy look, huh? I like that. "Remember that you said it was too bad that you couldn't go back in time and see your parents as werewolves again? Well, this book may be able to help us do just that. I don't know for sure and, truthfully, I'm almost afraid to find out. I'll read the next few pages and you'll understand better what I mean." I pause after I read the part about time standing still.

Remember—

Time stands still as the spell is cast,

The past is present and the present is past.

"This doesn't make a lot of sense, Lilith. Can time really stand still? Scientists and physicists have debated that for centuries and no one can say for sure one way or the other."

"Lively says that the past and the present can merge. That we can be in the present and visit the past and be in the past, and see the present. I know it sounds weird but maybe, with the help of a spell in that book, it's possible. Anyway," I sigh, "let's eat something and think about how we want to proceed with this."

Leaving the book on the desk, we go to sit on comfortable chairs by our favorite place near the curved windows. I grab a small box of cat treats and place them on a paper plate and Lively jumps off the sill to come eat them.

Hunter gently rubs Lively's head. I open the large bag of chips and we both grab a handful for ourselves. Time, time, time. What have I learned about time theories in physics class? Just speculation about time and travel which didn't seem real to me at all. But there's something else, something in the dark recesses of my mind about time. We munch chips and sip water both of us lost in our own thoughts. Finally, when I find myself nodding off, I tell Hunter we need to call it a night. Tomorrow is Sunday, and no school, so we can work on this in the morning. The excitement of our find in Shasta Valley, the driving, and the late hour cloud my brain even more. I look at the clock. It's after 11:00 and we're both exhausted.

"Okay. We'll both be able to think more clearly after a good night's sleep." Hunter stretches and yawns. "Hey! Where's the book?"

I get up and look at the desk. It's gone. For a moment exhaustion makes me panic. Where did it go? Then I laugh at myself. It must sense that we're leaving and has gone back to its hiding place. I look over to the small opening in the corner window frame. A tiny pinpoint of light winks back at me. Lively is gently pawing at it. "Over there," I point out the light to Hunter. "That's where it stays." He shakes his head impressed. As we watch, the pinpoint of light slowly disappears.

We go down the stairs and out into the street where my car is parked. Lively follows us and jumps into the back seat. I drive Hunter home and am glad to see that the porch lights are on and Gideon is sitting outside with his laptop. He waves to me and stands up waiting to greet his son.

"Drive safely, Lilith. See you tomorrow, around 10:30?" Hunter pulls me into a warm hug and kisses me sleepily then turns and pets Lively before opening the door

"Yup, 10:30 is perfect. See you then. Good-night."

We drive off toward home, a girl with untried witchy powers and the ability to fly, whose boyfriend is a werewolf, and whose cat is a ghost. Driving home to parents who just happen to be vampires. I'm so tired that I start giggling. If this is normal for me, then all I can say is that I am happy with it all. Life is just fine.

I hope.

THIRTY

A clear and concise brain-wave awakens me at exactly 3:12 in the morning. Despite thinking that I'd have a hard time sleeping because, exhausted or not, my mind was going faster than the speed of light, I drop off to slumber-land immediately after hitting my bed. The brain-wave that woke me up had only two, but highly significant and important, words—Block Universe. Those two words jolt me awake just before dawn and I sit up in bed so suddenly that I dislodge a deeply sleeping Lively from my stomach where he had decided to camp out last night.

The Block Universe! Of course! It's a theory that states that nothing in the universe is located only in any one single time frame. We are in a temporarily scattered condition. According to this theory, nothing and no one vanishes forever—they only exist in different parts of space-time, especially past and present. These different parts can be accessed if you know how to do it.

I remember reading about it in a comic book at Midnight Ink when I was about twelve years-old. That was my super-hero period. The Block Universe theory was a storyline in one of the comics and I was fascinated by the thought of it. I imagined going back in time to when the male and female found me and seeing my baby-self from the vantage point of being a know-it-all pre-teen.

This is something that I should be able to access with the Book of Lost Spells. There *has* to be a spell in that book that can show Hunter and me the past at a specific time. I lie back on my pillow and think of what I want to do. I know that I want to, *have to*, do this on my own and that means that I can't tell my parents. I hate keeping things from my parents, but this is something that I feel has to be done by me without anyone's help.

"You're absolutely right darling. You must do this on your own." The female's voice says quietly inside my mind.

"Mom!" I jump out of bed and run down the stairs where I find the female in the hall calmly sipping blood from a Baccarat wineglass. She's been reading my thoughts. "I thought we agreed that you'd put a lock on reading my thoughts," I say flustered, thinking of all the times Hunter and I get just a bit carried away when we're kissing. Arousal, Professor Reed called it.

"That we did, darling, but, there are times when a parent has to snoop to make sure a child is safe." With her lips closed, she runs her tongue over her teeth before giving me a smile. "But, the lock is on almost all the time, so don't worry about us snooping on you and Hunter."

"What about when we went to Shasta Valley? I was pretty sure you would be reading my thoughts to make sure I was okay."

"We were—aware. That's different than reading your thoughts. No snooping, just highly aware in case you needed our help. In other words, if you called out or we strongly felt that there was imminent danger, then we would come to you."

I sigh. Okay, no snooping when I'm with Hunter. I believe her. Neither of my parents has ever lied to me. "Where's dad?"

"He's on the patio, gazing at the stars. They seem to be brighter tonight, more so than usual."

"You guys are home early," I say walking toward the patio where I see the male sitting in a lounger holding the same type of wine glass as the female.

"Come look at the stars with me, Lilith," says my dad. "The sky is incredibly clear tonight."

My parents are both right—the stars look phenomenal and so close to us in a sky completely unblemished by any clouds. I sit down in a lounger and gaze upwards for a few minutes. "Mom, Dad, how long have you known about the Book of Lost Spells.

The female comes over and sits on the arm of the lounger. "We only sensed that a special and powerful magical item was coming to you. We didn't know it was a book until you mentioned it just now."

"I don't get it. Less than ten minutes ago you said that this was something I should do on my own. You knew about the book—you read my thoughts!"

"No, darling, I simply got a feeling of awareness. I felt that you were trying to convince yourself to do something on your own, something that had to do with magic. I responded to that feeling."

"So—you guys *isn't* know about this book of lost ancient spells at all?"

Both of them shake their heads no and the male says, "You can tell us about it if you wish. Maybe we can shed some light on its origins."

Staring upward at the stars, I begin to tell them about the Book of Lost Spells and how it came to me. I tell them how it hides itself in the window frame when I leave the room, and how it has just allowed Hunter to see it.

"I think it wants to help us solve this mystery about the night Ringwood was killed." I then tell them about the Block Universe theory and am not at all surprised that they both are totally aware of it.

"That theory has been around for centuries, well at least for the last three hundred years, darling. We've always known about it, but we never had any need to test its existence."

My dad nods at my mom. "Truthfully, I've never known any creature, human or otherwise who tested that theory." He looks at me. "Do you think this book will allow us to see it? If I can hold it, I might be able to know where it came from and how far back in time it goes. It's very interesting that it chose you."

I nod. Why it chose me is still a mystery in and of itself. "I thought I might be able take the theory that we exist in a Block Universe and use a spell from the book to help me go back to the night Ringwood, Sr. was killed. I want to take Hunter with me."

My mom sighs. "You'd need a strong spell to do that."

I sit forward eagerly. "Do you think it can work, a spell I mean, and take us back fifteen years ago?"

"If it's the right spell and if it's properly cast, darling. From what I know of magical spells, they can be tricky. One little thing missed, or a mispronounced word, can change the entire action of the spell."

"You're right, Victoria. She would have to be very careful with spells."

I sit gazing at the beautiful heavens and the constellations, deep in thought about the Block Universe theory when I hear my name called. "Lilith? Care for a flight? It's a wonderful way to relax and to recharge your thoughts. This night is magical, Lilith. Let that magic work for you."

The male and female have risen from their chairs and are floating effortlessly a few feet above the ground near the biggest tree in our yard. I stand up, and as I do, I feel that lovely twitch of my wings beginning to manifest. In a few seconds my ebony wings spread delicately to my sides and, swooping them up and down, I rise into the night. A current of air ripples past and I turn, catching it and riding it upward. I glance at the sky and feel as if I'm one with all the mystery of the night. My parents join me, gracefully being borne on the air currents, one on either side of me. Into the night we go.

I let go of any thoughts of Ringwood or the Block Universe theory. My mind is concentrating on the feel of my wings, the rush of soft air against my face, and the utter peacefulness of flying in a star-filled night. No distractions, nothing but the joy I feel as I swoop and soar on powerful wings.

THIRTY-ONE

Okay, so my dad was right. Flying last night has recharged my thoughts. They're clearer and more precise. I awoke around 9:15 the next morning. After having flown for a few hours I came back home to get some sleep and I feel great. A plan has taken solid form in my mind and I am ready to talk to Hunter and put that plan into action.

I've also decided to see if the book will appear to my parents the same as it did to Hunter. Maybe, if the male can somehow discern the history of this book, it might help me know its power and the best way to use it.

After a shower and telling my parents to come to the shop around noon, I run out the door to wait for Hunter. Lively is lying on his cat perch in the open bay window in front, watching birds and squirrels in the front yard. The sun is up and the world looks beautiful and clean. I sigh and take a deep breath and—gag. A smell of rotting roses hits me full blast.

I stand up and sniff the air around me, looking for a possible source like a compost heap or uncovered trash cans. The smell doesn't seem to be coming from just one area, though. It seems to surround me. The yard is empty of animal life, no birds or squirrels. What's going on? Lively scratches at the window screen and I turn my attention to him. His green eyes shimmer, looking right into mine for several minutes. "Hunter's here," he says in my mind and I turn to see my werewolf boyfriend come around the corner on his Vespa. I shake my head trying to remember what I was thinking of—something to do with, what? Oh well. Waving at Hunter I walk down to the edge of the walkway, kiss those sweet lips of his, then climb onto the Vespa, eager to tell him my plan. I think about my budding witchy powers and hope that I can use them to cast a perfect spell for both Hunter and me.

"Stop for coffee and doughnuts on the way, Hunter. We're going to need energy for what I have in mind."

Speaking of powers, witchy or otherwise, I *never* underestimate the power of food.

Midnight Ink is closed on Sundays so there won't be any interruptions from any customers. Taking Hunter upstairs to the turret room, I put coffee and doughnuts on a small table near the majestic floor-to-ceiling windows and sit down across from him. I made sure that I took a couple of bottles of that dark red liquid my parents crave out of the 'fridge and left it to warm on the counter in the back of the book shop. They'll drink any blood in a pinch but, they prefer it body temperature.

The Book of Lost Spells makes its presence known by the tiniest pinprick of light coming from the hiding place. At least it is still allowing

Hunter to know it's there and that's good. Hopefully, it will allow my parents access as well.

Hunter devours four doughnuts to my two—Mr. Paget is right when he said that a young pup like Hunter has a healthy appetite. I sip my coffee, light with one-third cream, put down my half-finished apple-crumb doughnut, and begin.

"So, this is where we are. The Block Universe theory. Have you ever heard of it?" Hunter nods, his mouth full of Boston crème. "Good. Well, if that theory holds true, it means that we're not just in one place at one time, we're really scattered across a time line where all periods of time are ever-present. Our past and present can merge together and I think that if I can cast a spell that will take us back to the night the she-werewolf was shot and disappeared, we have a better than good chance of solving the mystery of Ringwood's murder. We can see how the two werewolves somehow managed to escape, where they went, and also who killed Ringwood and tried to make it look as if he died from a wolf attack." I take a deep breath. When I have something important to say, I just let it come out rapid-fire, no slowing down for me.

Hunter grabs his coffee to wash down the doughnut before he can speak. "Do you think that you're powerful enough to cast a spell? This is a big deal, Lilith. I don't mean that you're not up to doing it but, you're new to all this. You've always said that, despite the fact your parents are vampires and your boyfriend is a werewolf, all you wanted was to be boringly normal." He levels a concerned look at me. "I guess what I'm really asking you is are you ready to do something that is so totally *not* normal."

I don't blame him for being concerned. I did always say that I wanted to be boringly normal but, over the past month, that has changed. And to be completely truthful, I'm beginning to enjoy this new normal which includes the power of flight. These are gifts to be treasured and used well. I return Hunter's look with conviction in my eyes.

"This *is* normal for me and I am determined to use whatever gifts or powers that I have and to use them for good. I've come to realize that I don't want to be like everyone else. I think I just saw boringly normal as a kind of safe way of living, but I'm beginning to see that's not what I want. Flying taught me that it's good to try new experiences even if they do have some type of risk. I don't want to live my life covered in bubble wrap. My parents are vampires, you are a werewolf, and I am so different from other high school students than I'd ever thought I would be. You, my parents, creatures like Mr. Paget, the power of flight, all of it is a part of my life and I am happy with every part of it. I may still have a lot to learn, but I will learn all that I can. This is me, Hunter Hollis Hopper, take it or leave it. You might just have a witch as your girlfriend, so beware."

Hunter gets up and comes over to where I'm sitting. He pulls me to my feet and hugs me tightly then spins us around in a circle. "You are the absolute best and I will be happy and proud to have a witch as my girlfriend. Lilith, I love you"

"I love you too," I say overcome with emotion and beginning to levitate from Hunter's warm hug. I wrap my arms around him tightly and concentrate on keeping my feet on the floor. We stay like that for a long while.

"Knock, knock," calls the female's distinctive soft-as-wind-chimes voice. "Are we— interrupting?"

Hunter holds my hand as we face my parents. "Do you know that you've got the best daughter in the whole wide world?!"

"Oh we've known that for a very long time now, Hunter," says my dad with mock seriousness. "When did *you* find out?"

"Lilith just told me that she doesn't want to be boringly normal anymore. She's embracing her real self. Powers and all!"

"Is that true, darling?" says my mom looking at me. I nod solemnly. It is true. "I want to be the real me that I was meant to be."

"I'm happy to hear that," she says smiling. "And let me say that you've always been the best daughter in the world, powers notwithstanding. But we're excited that you are accepting your true self."

"What, if I may ask, brought this on, Lilith?" My dad looks serious.

"I think that I just realized what Professor Reed told me was true. Who I am, and what powers or gifts I possess, is perfectly normal for me. So—in that respect, I'm as normal as any other creature."

"Good. All your mother and I ask is that you use your powers wisely and for good. Be cautious and keep your powers a secret." He looks around the room. "Now, let's see if your hidden book with the ancient spells will manifest itself for us."

THIRTY-TWO

It appears from its hiding place as a dim glow that becomes brighter and brighter as it floats slowly around the room. The Book of Lost Spells circles the room twice before coming to rest on my outstretched hand. I hear Hunter's quick in-drawn breath and see the vampire eyes of the male and female glitter an inhuman crystal-clear bright.

The book gently floats from my hand and over to the desk where it settles and opens to the first page. My parents and Hunter lean forward as I translate the words out loud.

This book is not owne, *this book has no home,*
*It goes wherever most nee*e*,*
The spells are ol an* the magic time-hone*,*
*Take care that all warnings are hee*e*.*

"This book came specifically to Lilith for a reason," the female says turning to the male. "That's a sure sign that it wants her to use any spells in it that she deems are necessary."

The male puts a hand forward and the book doesn't move. I hold my breath. Slowly he places his fingers on the binding and closes his eyes. The Book of Lost Spells seems to accept him. I expel my breath in a rush. Very gently his fingers move over the book's open page. A deep sigh escapes from him. Opening his eyes, he stares at the book. "Somewhere around 1270, the Late Middle Ages." Removing his hand from the book, he looks at me. "It's over seven-hundred years old, Lilith and it has come to you."

No one says anything for the longest time. Over seven-hundred years old! Four-hundred years older than my vampire parents. A book of spells from the time of Dante, the man who first wrote in the common language of the people instead of writing in Latin as other authors did.

The female touches the book and glances sharply at the male. A look passes between them, one of absolute caution. She nods slowly. "There is a great power in this small book, Lilith. A great deal of power. You have to be very careful in how you use it."

Taking the book, I turn a few pages. "Here's the part that refers to time. 'The past is present and the present is past'. Somehow the fact that it indicates that time is merged made me remember the Block Universe theory. Do you think I can cast a spell that takes Hunter and me back in time?"

"You must find the correct spell first, darling. It must be *absolutely exact* for what you want it to do. Then you must follow the instructions in both words and actions. There is no second chance, no do-over, with a powerful spell such as the one you will be attempting."

"But," says the male, "you are the only one who can do this. It came to you and it will only respond to your spell-casting. Whatever, or whoever, sent it to you seems to feel that you need it now. I think we need to leave you alone with the book." The book glows brighter, seeming to show acknowledgement that what he says is true. It's up to me if I want to use it and that is a little bit frightening.

"Okay, I guess I need to go through the book carefully and find the right spell." I pause as I think of something. "But—since Hunter is going to go back in time with me, do you think he can stay here?"

The female shakes her head. "What I've heard about spell-casting, finding the correct spell is a solitary task. Find the correct one first, darling. We'll be downstairs with Hunter. And remember two things—you may not be able to find the best spell today and if you do, you may have to wait for the most auspicious time to use it. We'll leave you alone for now."

Hunter and my parents hug me then go down the stairs to Midnight Ink. I'm alone with the book which is still emitting a soft glow. A humming sound seems to fill the air directly above it and as I look around the room, a feeling of determination comes over me.

It's time to test my witchy powers.

It would be so wonderful if this book had an index or table of contents but it doesn't—the spells don't even seem to be in any type of order. Even though each spell has a title, they seem to have been written haphazardly when the need arose for a specific issue. Some are even written in the margins of the pages. There're love spells mixed in with spells for good crops and spells for rain. The book may be small but the spells seem to be many. Every time that I come across the word 'time' I stop and read the spell carefully.

I sigh deeply in frustration. I'm so used to Googling a topic to get instant information that going through this book, page by page seems daunting. But, I also have to grudgingly admit that it's also kind of charming. Technology definitely has its place in the modern world, but there's something that's really stimulating to the brain in having to search through a book to find what you need.

I eat two more doughnuts and down a half bottle of water while I search. Lively appears on the window seat by the center window. He greets me with a chirping sound and comes over to rub against my leg. I absent-mindedly put my hand down to pet him. "Lively, I'm frustrated. It will take me forever to find the spell I need. Any suggestions?"

He stretches and yawns before answering. "Magic takes time."

"No kidding! That's not a lot of help, Lively."

"What do you imagine when you think of witches, Lilith?"

"Umm, brooms," I say absent-mindedly turning pages and reading spells. "Pointed hats, cauldrons. Warts? All that silly exaggeration."

Lively jumps up onto the desk. "All of those are stereotypes. Think again. What do witches always seem to have with them in pictures and stories? What's the one constant, always by a witch's side?"

"I don't know, Lively, I don't have time for guessing games. I have to concentrate on finding something in this book."

He places a paw on the book's pages causing me to look at him. "The one constant in a witch's life is her creature companion. And most times, that creature is a—cat!"

A cat. Right, witches always seem to have cats with them. They were companions to witches and, in times past, definitely served a health-related purpose by keeping houses free of rodents. And besides all that they were then, as now, beloved pets.

"Your point in telling me this information?" I sit back and close my eyes.

"*I* am *your* companion. *I* sleep on *your* bed, you're the one who feeds me most of the time. I'm your cat. If you are a fledgling witch, even only part witch, it seems to be logical that I can help you with spells."

I think about what he's saying. It's true that witches have always seemed to have a cat with them when they were spelling. In fairy tales and myths, the witch and the cat were always together, a magical pair. That fact may be one of the key factors witches used to find, and cast, the right spell. I open my eyes and looks at Lively who is gently flicking his tail from side to side. "Okay. Then help me find my way through this mess of spells. Can you do that?"

"I can and I will."

"Good. Then, let's get started."

I turn each page of the book carefully and thoroughly read the spells written on them. Lively sits on the desk beside the book, his eyes following as I turn the pages. Finally, he places a paw on one page and I look at the word Shadowcat. Interesting that it has the word 'cat' in the title. I look at Lively who is calmly grooming himself.

SHADOWCAT-a spell for passing through time and space. Like all of the spells in the book, it's in the form of a poem. The first part describes the spell.

The Shadowcat walks in the dark,
Moving slowly, leaving no mark,
In shadowy waves and languid pace,
It guides you safely 'twixt time and space.
You are here and also there,
The times have begun to share,
Shadowcat will show the way,
Day is night and night is day.
A warning given to understand,
You are a guest in Shadowland,
What happens you are only to see,
No changes can be made by thee.

Then come the spell's instructions which I'm cautioned to 'read well, heed well'.

A place of darkness has begun,
Darkness prevails until it's done,

Anoint a can•le, small an• blue,
Light your wish, it will come true,
Keep the can•le close to your heart,
So that you may return from where you start.
Your stay is short, within this spell,
Four hours only, use them well.
The tolling of a bell soun•s, lou• an• clear,
Thirty minutes to return from there to here.
Make haste returning wor•s to say,
Make haste or in sha•ows you will stay,
Hee• the soun• an• hee• it well,
Begin your return at the toll of the bell.

Next to the word 'bell', is a hand-drawn dagger, the same type of dagger that I've seen on other pages. I guess who ever drew the daggers wanted the reader to know that certain spells were more powerful than others in the book. It makes sense—a spell that allows traveling through the mists of time *woul•* be extremely powerful. I continue to read.

In clothing •ark this spell is cast,
In present the caster can see the past,
Speak the •ate, the time, the place,
To travel through the mists of space,
A cup of water for a journey fair,
Sha•owcat will appear to gui•e you there,
Once water is •runk, a bon• is ma•e,
Be thee as one with Sha•owcat's sha•e.
Repeat these wor•s three times three,
'I am the sha•ow; the sha•ow is me'.

The page shimmers brightly as if it wants to get my attention and tell me that I have found the spell I need. I look at Lively again and his eyes seem to glow. This has to be is the spell I need. But it seems too easy, too simple. Can it really be that easy? I mean, my mom cautioned me that one little thing that I might miss could make the spell misfire so to speak. Am I missing something? I think the spell simply allows me, and of course

Hunter, to walk in the shadows back and forth between the past and the present. That has to be it. It's just a simple leave and return.

"Thank you, Lively!" I hug him gently. "How many other witches have you known?"

"Many, but, you're the first half-witch I know. This is a challenge."

I hug him again and go back to the Shadowcat spell. Lively sits on the desk, quietly bathing his face with his paws.

THIRTY-THREE

After reading it over 3 times to make sure that it really is the one I need, I take a picture of the spell with my phone. The book seems to flicker erratically when I take the picture as if it is startled by something so very modern and unknown to its origins. I let my head fall onto the back of the chair. My mom said that spells are tricky, that I should be careful. Is there a catch, an unknown sign somewhere in the spell that I'm missing? Staring at the ceiling, I mentally review the words and what else I will need for the spell. A small blue candle, dark clothes. Okay, no problem there but, the spell says that 'a place of darkness has begun'. Does that mean the place where I'm going to cast the spell must be a dark area without any light? Should the spell be cast by the dark of the moon? Or does it mean that I'm entering a dark, unknown place as I cast the spell?

And that part about the water. I am assuming the Shadowcat drinks it, but the spell doesn't necessarily specify *who* drinks it. Am I supposed to drink it? Are we *both* supposed to drink it in a gesture of oneness or something? I shrug and stretch my arms over my head, breathing deeply. Whatever it is, I've got to try to do my best with whatever the book is offering me.

Lively picks up a piece of old ribbon that's lying on the desk and lays it down on the opened book. A book mark. I arrange the ribbon so that it is sticking up over the page and the Book of Lost Spells gently closes. Then it rises slowly in the air and drifts over to where it hides itself. I pick up Lively and carry him downstairs to where my parents and Hunter are waiting.

All three look up expectantly as I enter the room. "I found it," I say depositing Lively onto the small table where Mr. Paget and I had scones and tea.

"A spell that lets us see the past?" asks Hunter, excited. "You found it? Lilith! That's great!"

I want to sound brave and confident so I say, "Yes, I'm pretty sure that it's a spell that I can cast easily. I mean, it seems simple enough."

"It may look easy, Lilith, but it may not be as simple to cast as you might believe," says the male. "Spells, as your mother says, are not always easy."

"I know, Dad. I understand, but," I drop my head and whisper, "I *have* to do this."

"Be careful, Lilith, that's all we ask. Take caution seriously."

"I will, Dad, I promise."

"Be absolutely certain of this spell and your power to cast it."

"Okay," I say, "I promised, didn't I?" I sound nasty, I know, but I'm tired and I feel as if I'm being treated like a child.

"But, darling, are you sure that you truly know how to do this? Have you read the instructions well?"

"Yes, I did read them very carefully."

"Every little detail, what object to use, what to say, the timing. The danger of not doing the spell properly is too—"

I put up my hand and interrupt her. Some hidden angst that lives in the heart of every teen, that powerful need to rebel against parents and adults in general, rears its head. Why can't they see that I'm almost an adult and that I have to learn to use my powers as I see fit?

"Mom, seriously, I know what you said about magical spells being tricky and that something that is missed, or if I don't pronounce a word correctly, might change the action of the spell, but I read it over *really* well, several times and I feel as if I can do this." I look from one parent to another. "I'm not a little girl anymore. I'll be eighteen soon. Why can't you just trust that I can cast this spell without making me feel as if you don't have faith in me and in my powers?"

"Darling, we *do* have faith in you," my mom comes to me and I grudgingly allow her to put her arms around me. I hide the fact that I'm more afraid than I let on. This is all new to me and, powers or not, I'm still a seventeen-year-old girl who has never in all her life done anything remotely like this. I don't even know if I *can* do this, but something inside of me knows that I have to try. I lay my head on her shoulder. "I can do this, Mom. I *have* to do it or at the very least, try my best to cast this spell."

My dad walks over to us and lifts my face gently in his hands. "We believe in you, Lilith, we're just concerned because we love you. But, you're right—you're not a little girl anymore and we have to trust that you can use your powers wisely and cautiously." He kisses me lightly on my forehead and puts his arms around both of us.

"Okay, then. Now I have to decide the right time to cast the spell." I ease out of the group hug and face them. "Let's go sit down and I'll tell you what the spell says to do."

I recite all the info about casting the Shadowcat spell and show them the picture of the spell on my phone. We debate the words 'a place of darkness has begun' and all four of us come to a consensus that it is best to cover all bases, meaning that the spell should be cast at the dark of the moon, in a dark area with no other visible light except for the blue candle.

"There are about six more days until a new moon appears," says Hunter, whose whole being is in perfect synch with the phases of that nightly orb. "Today is Sunday so the darkest part of the moon will be Friday."

"Yes, the darkest time before the sliver of new moon appears," says my dad, and my mom nods slowly.

Hunter seems uneasy. "There's something I want to ask you. Something that I'm concerned could happen."

I look at him expectantly. "What are you worried about? I think I've thought of everything."

"The full moon."

"Huh?" I'm confused.

"That date fifteen years ago when the werewolves ran? Even though there will be no moon visible here in the present, there *has* to have been a full moon for the date we're going to in the past. When we go back, I don't know if that full moon will affect me—if it will make me change. Then what?"

My dad interrupts. "I don't think you have to worry about the full moon in the past. It might affect you a little but you have to understand that, even though you're still flesh and blood, to the past you are only shadowy visitors. And, remember that fifteen years ago, you were a child, not capable of making the change as you are today," says the male. "The person you are now didn't exist fifteen years ago."

"True," says my mom. "I believe he's right, Hunter. In the past, you are there and not there, if that makes any sense to you. Essentially, the child in the past is the real you while you are only a shade."

I hear Hunter sigh with relief. I smile at him. What my parents say makes sense, I guess. Although the truth is that the idea of being a shadow, a shade as my mom calls it, is a little strange. But, whatever we will become as we go back in time is irrelevant at this point. This mystery has to be solved. There are things that have to be done to prepare for Friday. I turn to the female.

"Mom? I have to get a small blue candle."

"Easy enough to find. I may have some in the back." The female smiles, her white fangs visible. She only allows them to show when she's stressed and I know she's worried about me casting this spell. I decide to distract her by asking questions.

"But, how do I anoint it? I mean, what's the usual way to anoint a candle?"

"With a natural oil, I think. Actually, Mr. Paget might know about that. He has anointed candles for healing. Let me ask him what he would use."

I hesitate just for a moment then say, "He should know what I'm going to do. He was there fifteen years ago when it happened. I'd like him to know."

"Right," agrees Hunter. "It's okay to tell Mr. Paget, but, listen, the only person that should not know anything about all this is my dad. I don't want him to know."

The male and the female nod in agreement. Not a word will be mentioned to Gideon.

"What do you think the cup of water signifies?"

"That would be an offering," the female says quickly. "Water is seen as a blessing in some cultures and a necessary item for travel. Since no creature can survive without it, offering water is a gift more precious than gold."

"Will any cup do? Does it have to be a special type of cup?"

"I have an old cup made of bronze that Mr. Paget gave me. It's ancient and I believe that it has been anointed. Use that."

"Do I offer the cup of water to this Shadowcat? Do we both drink from it?"

"Only the Shadowcat will drink it," says the male. "It's a gift you offer the creature who is taking you into the shadows. It's a type of payment of goodwill."

We dissect the words in the spell over and over again until I feel as if they have been permanently imprinted in my brain. Then comes the decision of when the best time will be for casting. The male and female think that Friday, Midnight is the most auspicious time because the moon will be in complete darkness. Hunter agrees and I see his body twitch slightly with moon memories.

"Be extra alert to the sound of the bell that the spell instructions mention. I'm concerned about that. Wear your watch. Your time is limited for a reason," says my mom. "Once the bell tolls, you will have only thirty minutes to begin your return. If you can't come back within those thirty minutes, well, we have no way of knowing if you'll become part of the shadows permanently." Her face looks exceptionally pale and gaunt. I've never seen her look like this.

"Your mother is right, my Lilith of the Angels. Don't be so distracted by all that you will be seeing that you fail to hear that bell." He pauses. "You know the words that allow you and Hunter to return, right?"

"Uh-huh." Taking it all in, I sigh deeply. Hell's Bells! Spell-casting is more complex than I realized. "I'll be very alert to the sound of the bell, don't worry about that and I memorized all the words."

The male and female still look concerned and I hug each one tightly. "Okay," I say. "Midnight, this Friday it is. I've got a whole week to think about this spell and how to cast it just right. Right now, I'm starving. Let's go to our house and I'll order a pizza." I look at my parents who look paler than usual. Stress can do that to vamps. They need blood and soon. "Are you two going out to feed?" I ask concerned. "There's some raw chop meat in the 'fridge."

"No, darling, that's fine. We'll join you and Hunter after we make a stop at Rudy's. I think that, tonight, we both need something a bit— stronger. We won't be long."

Hunter and I head to the door and a soft whish of air tells us that my parents have already left to go visit Rudy at the blood bank. Hunter grips my hand.

"So, mushroom and extra cheese?"

I laugh. No matter how serious life gets, a guy with a healthy appetite, even if he is a werewolf, makes everything seem—well—normal.

THIRTY-FOUR

"Higher, Lilith, higher. Okay, that's perfect," shouts Hunter watching me fly upward into the calm night. There's no wind on the ground but up here at the top of the old tree in my backyard, there's a perfect updraft for my wings. I stretch them out to their full glorious length and coast lazily in the air.

My parents came home after their stop at the blood bank and now they're seated on lounges sipping the scarlet red liquid, supplied by Rudy. Their normally translucent skin is flushed giving them a soft warm glow. Rudy must have had some strong type O available for them. Lively is lazily watching me from his perch on a lounger, his tail flipping slowly back and forth.

I fly around the backyard and circle to the top of the tall fence where I land lightly on my feet. Crouching forward I catch the female's eye. "I'm going to fly a bit away from here, just to test my navigation." I expect either one of them to say no and tell me I'm not ready yet but they surprise me.

"You probably need to stretch those wings, Lilith. Go ahead." says my dad.

"Yes, darling, fly a little distance away."

Hunter tells me he's going home and asks if I can follow him from above. "Just halfway to my house, Lilith. I love to see you fly." Turning to my parents he says, "I'll go off-road and avoid the streets."

I look at my parents again and they both nod yes. Maybe the fact that my eighteenth birthday is coming soon has them deciding to give me more freedom or maybe it's because I will be casting my first spell in five days and they want me to feel in charge of what I do. Either way, it's a good feeling to fly outside of the safe confines of this yard.

I follow high above Hunter's Vespa as he travels off-road and away from the regular paved streets, keeping his word to my parents. Though it's late, it's better to avoid having anyone see me flying. How could that be explained to those who know nothing of the Otherworld?

I have to say that I'm more confident in my flying techniques. Rising into the night with a few quick thrusts of my wings, learning to sense, and then to catch, the air currents and ride them. Making a landing by bending my knees and balancing on the balls of my feet. It's really a lot like driving a car but so much more fun!

Halfway to Hunter's house, he stops, gets off the Vespa, and waits for me to land which I do a bit ungracefully. My ankle twists slightly as I hit a small unseen hole in the ground, but otherwise a safe landing.

"You look so beautiful with those wings. They make you seem invincible, like someone out of those mythologies we read in Lit. You're perfect. Wouldn't it be great if you could use your wings when we do the back-in-time bit this Friday?"

"I don't think I'll be able to use them. I mean, we're just observing. The spell says that we're there only to see what happened back then and that we can't change anything."

Big sigh. "I know. I guess I'm just romanticizing it, like in those epic poems we had to read. This *is* kind of like an epic poem, you know. You. Me. Actually back in time. That seems almost unreal."

I fold my wings against my sides and snuggle into Hunter's arms. He lightly embraces the soft feathers of my wings and kisses me gently. "See you tomorrow morning for school?" I nod yes and kiss him again. "Be careful flying back," he says mounting the motorbike.

"You be careful too."

Spreading my wings, I catch an updraft and rise swiftly into the night sky. Turning toward home, I hear the puttering sound of the motorbike and turn my head to watch Hunter head home. The night is quiet with warm smells of a summer to come. I fly in the direction of my backyard amidst the warm breeze that gently rushes through my wings.

Five days until I attempt to cast the Shadowcat spell, only five short days. I need to re-read the spell as many times as I can before Midnight, Friday.

Why is it that time seems to drag when you are waiting for something fun or good to happen—a birthday, a prom, a day at the beach—but seems to rush forward dizzyingly when you are hesitant about something you fear? The five days before what I call Zero-Hour Midnight seem to be rushing by. It's already Wednesday and I'm sitting in a study hall reading the spell on my phone for the umpteenth time that day. I've been reading it every day since I discovered it in that Book of Lost Spells. The words swim before my tired eyes. Even though I feel as if the words are imprinted in my brain, I want to make sure that I didn't miss or misunderstand anything crucial. I think back to yesterday afternoon when we spoke with Mr. Paget at Midnight Ink and told him what I was planning to do.

"You and young Hunter? Going into the shadows?" he asked, his nose worriedly sniffing the air and making his whiskers quiver.

"Yes, Mr. Paget. I'm going to cast a spell called the Shadowcat. We need to go back to that night, fifteen years ago, when C. Thomas Ringwood's father was supposedly killed by that she- werewolf."

"Ah, my dear, to traverse in the shadows is something I've only read about in those wonderful old books your parents procure for me, but I have heard it said that it is only in the shadows that we may see what others, even my worthy winged messengers, may have missed seeing. Traveling into the shadows fills me with anxiety, much anxiety. Please be very, very careful, sweet Lilith."

I assured him that I would be careful and then asked him if he remembered anything else about that night or about Ringwood, Sr.

"My dear, now let me think, let me think. Oh, it was a terrible night! I think that I've told you everything I remembered. But," he pats my hand, "if there is something else that comes back to me about that night I will be sure to write it down, yes, must write it down so I don't forget, and then I can tell you." I thanked him and he left shortly afterward, carrying an ancient book he had ordered.

I look for Hunter at lunchtime and find him standing with a group of kids all talking excitedly.

"Money in the bank!" shouts a boy who I recognize as the one who borrowed my notes in Calculus class. "Anyone who brings in the wolf, alive or dead, is getting a load of cash."

"Who'd bring in a wolf alive? Why take the risk?" asks a girl I know from the Photography Club. "Better to just kill it and be safe. You'll still get your money."

Amsterdam, Rotterdam, damn, damn, damn! A chill goes through me as I hear some of the students cheer her words. These are kids I've known for years, some of them since kindergarten. Their bloodlust for money is frightening and disgusting. I look at Hunter who is saying nothing, just standing there listening to all the comments without blinking an eye. How he can do that is beyond my comprehension. But, maybe, he's doing the right thing. By simply listening and not saying anything he can find out what's going on and know how to be prepared for any danger. I walk over and join the group.

A scruffy boy who has been in trouble at school for minor vandalism to the gym lockers and desks, and who would rather cheat on tests than actually do his own work, is speaking to those closest to him. "We're not just going to search in the forest. Hell no! We're going much farther than the Ringwood property. If there's a wolf anywhere for miles around there, we'll find it. And, look, about this reward Ringwood is offering. I mean, I can get a gun."

The mention of the word *gun* makes most of the kids assembled here look uncomfortable. School shootings are branded into my generation's mind and the idea of someone in our school actually being able to get a gun is a frightening thought.

"Think about it," continues the boy. "Ten thousand dollars! I figure if three of us go together to kill this wolf, we'll get four thousand each. Great payday, huh?" He directs this question to a girl to his right.

The girl crosses her arms over her chest. "Wow, you must've skipped elementary school the day they were teaching division in math class. The payday as you put it, divided between three people is exactly three thousand, three hundred, thirty-three dollars and thirty -three cents, you idiot."

"Yeah, so you in?" he said unperturbed by her comment about his lack of math skills.

"No way. Too dangerous to be around an idiot like you carrying a gun. You're a certifiable nutcase. Besides, I want no part in killing any creature. That's just plain cruel."

"She's right," says a boy standing behind the girl. "It's not right to take a life, any life. There's no hunting allowed in this area. And I heard that the local police are talking to C. Thomas about his stupid ad and will be taking steps to stop anyone from hunting. Anyway, guns aren't legal here."

"Who said anything about *legal*?" smirks the idiot, dragging out the word. "There are a lot of ways to get a gun you know."

The bell signaling that lunch is over rings and we begin to disperse for afternoon classes. I grab Hunter's hand and we walk back to the senior hallway. "This is getting more serious by the day, Hunter. Now we've got idiots who want to get guns to hunt the grey wolf who just happens to be you!"

"Don't worry. Hopefully we'll have this whole mystery solved before the next full moon."

We stop at my locker. "I have this feeling that there's more to the story than we know."

"How so?"

"Remember that Mr. Paget said the she-werewolf stopped and looked into Ringwood, Sr.'s eyes? That's odd. No offense, but, most people, confronted with *any* type of wolf, would have freaked out having a wolf staring at them. Mr. Paget suggested that Ringwood was unafraid of her."

"No offense taken. But you're right. What's the story there? Why wasn't he afraid and why did she stop and look at him like she somehow knew him?" He looks off toward the field and the bleachers. "And Lilith? I've been thinking a lot about what you said about Gideon being the Ghost Wolf in the video. Another sort of unclear memory keeps trying to come into my thoughts. I think I *to* remember my dad's fur being white, and, like you said, a soft kind of glowing white. Do you really think the werewolf in the video is my dad and that he once ran under the full moon here in Summer Valley?"

"Yes, I do." Walking to class, we have to let it go. Later, we'll talk about all that—and we'll talk about Friday night.

THIRTY-FIVE

Friday has come. The day I've both dreaded and looked forward to is here. At 11:00 PM, Hunter and I, both dressed in dark colors, are outside Midnight Ink, waiting for my parents to arrive. The 'Closed' sign has been in the window since 4:00 because I wanted time to think through everything that I needed to do without interruption. I breathe in the warm, sweet air before we go in to begin the spell. Hunter is carrying an overnight bag. His father, Gideon, thinks Hunter is staying at my house tonight because we're working on a school project together. Oh, Gideon, if you only knew what a *major* project we'll be working on this night! This is no assignment ever given out at school.

Getting through the day at school was a weird mixture of looking at the clock, alternately hoping that time would fly and I'd get to cast the spell and then, panicking and willing time to go as slowly as possible. Whatever.

Time it seems will go its usual way of minutes and hours no matter how much we may want it to slow down or speed up.

A tap on the window lets me know that the male and female have magically appeared inside the book shop. Their sudden appearances amaze even me sometimes. Opening the door, I see Lively sitting to the right of the entrance calmly licking a paw. He's an all-black cat today.

"Been visiting someone?" I bend and caress his soft fur.

"An elderly woman who was feeling sad today. I lived with her when she was a little girl. Seeing me made her happy."

I bend down to pick him up, burying my face in his fur and walk toward the back room, the Magicis Scripturam filled with all our ancient scrolls and books. I sense a power coming from the room, a power that I never felt before. It instills a sense of confidence in me and that is something I definitely need right now.

"Lilith, darling? I have the objects you will need to cast the spell." My mom hands me a small blue candle, a candle lighter, a bronze cup, and a bottle of water. "Mr. Paget says that the cup was anointed quite some time ago but he suggests that you anoint it again just to be safe. He's bringing a small vial of pure oil for you to use. He should be here any minute."

Just as she says that there's a timid knock on the door and my dad goes to answer it. Mr. Paget comes into Midnight Ink, his whiskers bristling as he sniffs the air. In his hands is an ordinary glass vial with a yellow-gold liquid.

"Ah, Lilith, dear, brave Lilith—and our young pup Hunter!" He looks at my parents and nods his head solemnly. "All here, all here, I see. Oh, my dear Lilith, what an exciting endeavor you are attempting. To travel between present and past, to be able to see the full-moon run of the magnificent werewolves! You will see what I saw and you will then understand what I felt. I hope you will be able to find out what happened to the she-werewolf. Her fate, oh dear, her fate has always been on my mind.

The thought of her and the male who went back for her have never left me. No, never left me."

His eyes mist over and a tear makes its way down his cheek. I place my hand on Mr. Paget's arm. "I'll do my best to find out, Mr. Paget. I intend to come back with the knowledge of all that happened that night."

Wiping away the tear, he hands me the small, stoppered glass vial. "Here, my dear. Pure olive oil, to anoint your magical objects. This oil is quite old, yes, quite old my dear, and it will definitely cleanse your objects. For the cup, you just simply anoint the outer part. The oil should not touch the water you will pour into the cup."

The old clock on the bank a block away chimes the half hour. I look at my watch. 11:30. Only a half hour to Midnight. "It's almost time, Lilith," Hunter smiles at me encouragingly. I take the vial, candle, cup, lighter, and bottle and walk toward the stairs that lead to the turret room. My journey, whatever it will be, and wherever it may lead, is about to begin.

My parents hug me tightly and then go wait in a corner of the turret room, near the window. Waiting with them is Mr. Paget who sits quietly in a chair, Lively in his lap. The one streetlight down the street from Midnight Ink has mysteriously gone dark—I know my parents have done something to stop it from staying lit. I am grateful for their vamp mind power. It should truly be the dark of the moon and there should be no light save for a soft glow once I light the blue candle.

To make absolutely certain that we'll be in darkness, Hunter and I stand in a corner far from the windows. I settle the cup, the water bottle, and the candle and lighter on a small table where I've placed the mysterious Book of Lost Spells. It is opened to the Shadowcat spell.

Opening the vial from Mr. Paget, I moisten my fingers with some of the oil and carefully anoint the bottom and sides of the bronze cup, then fill it with water. With more of the precious oil, I anoint the candle. My heart is racing and I feel myself levitate a little. Taking a deep breath, I will myself to stay calm and to focus on what I have to do next. Place the cup on the floor, light the candle and—cast the spell.

The long end of the lighter emits a quick bright flame as I touch it to the wick of the candle. I read the Shadowcat spell moving my eyes slowly over the words written there so long ago. Who created this spell? Did they write it for themselves or someone else? My shoulder blades twitch slightly almost as if my wings want to spring open. I can't let *that* happen. I shake my head. No time to worry about who or why. It's time for the spell to be cast.

Grabbing Hunter's hand with my left hand and holding the candle close to my heart with my right one, I speak the date, the time, the place I need to see. Then, taking a deep breath I say the magical words that will bring the Shadowcat and will thrust us into the shadows. Three times three, nine times in all, I repeat the words of the spell—

'I am the shadow; the shadow is me'.

As soon as I finish saying the words for the ninth time, everything familiar changes. Where the turret room was, is now just swirls of greyish-blue mists. We're alone. The Shadowcat appears, larger than an ordinary house cat. I cannot tell what color it is. All I see is its shadowy image.

Sitting on a mist-filled path it faces us, its eyes glowing with an otherworldly intentness. I offer the cup of water and watch as the Shadowcat bows its head and takes a few laps. Then, raising its head proudly, it beckons us, turns and begins to slowly travel the path.

Blending easily with the shadows, the ghostly image walks confidently in the mists. Hunter and I hesitantly following. We seem to become shadows ourselves, ethereal, blending with the wisps of shadow. Even though I know that we're walking, putting one foot in front of the other, it feels as if we're simply gliding along the soft ground. I don't even know if it is a solid dirt ground or just swirls of mists in the shape of a real path. Everything is real and unreal at the same time. Time seems to pause as we travel back more than fifteen years to the last time the werewolves ran in the forest here.

Within the mists there seem to be shadows both in front of, and behind, us, moving in the direction the Shadowcat is going. Yet others come toward us, passing by in silence returning to the beginning of the path. It seems as if the Block Universe theory of the merging of past and present is a kind of ghostly highway with shadowy travelers. I can't help but wonder who these shadows are. Human? Otherworldly creatures? Or maybe a mix of half-human and half-otherworldly like Hunter and like me—all searching for something in a different time zone.

The Shadowcat stops at the edge of where the path turns. "I've been here, Lilith," Hunter says softly. "It's the forest where I ran. And look!" He silently points to a shadowy image a short distance away. I strain to make out what the image is and suddenly I know. The shape, the size, the location—it's Hunter's house, no mistake about it. What a weird feeling to be here, fifteen years in the past! Hunter would be two years-old here. Giddily I wonder if we went toward the house, would Hunter come upon a shadow who is his two-year-old self?

A movement from the Shadowcat alerts us that we are moving forward. The path is taking us into the forest itself and the branches of the ghost-like trees seem like arms reaching down for us as we move deeper into the woods. The shadows here are darker, an inky greyish black. I feel like Little Red Riding Hood entering the forest about to encounter the wolf. I stop and laugh at that thought. That's why I'm here with Hunter. I did come here to encounter wolves—*werewolves*!

The Shadowcat stops at the edge of a thicket, it raises its head and I look into eyes that gleam golden in its shadow face. It appears to fade away into the mists but we know it's there by its glowing eyes. The silence in this shadow world seems all-consuming.

"Now what?" asks Hunter.

I shake my head. "I don't know. I guess we have to wait to see what happens."

It seems as if we wait for hours when suddenly a sound so primitive fills the area around us that it makes the hair on my neck prickle. I've heard Hunter howl but this is howl is raw and ancient, visceral and frightening. I can understand why all creatures feared the sound.

"Listen, Lilith! Listen!" Hunter is standing beside me and I can hear his breath coming in rapid gusts. He is reacting to that primal sound, his body resonating with his wolf side.

A full shadow of a moon shines through the trees overhead and for one moment I fear that, despite what my parents said, Hunter *will* change into a werewolf, no matter if we're only shadows and not flesh and blood in this time. But as I watch him carefully, I see that he's still Hunter in his human form, just reacting to that eerie call and not the power of the full moon.

The howl is answered by others who join in one after the other until there is a chorus of those saluting that celestial body that creates the wild change in them. As I listen, I fully understand why Mr. Paget said that the he remembered the 'exquisite howling'. It *is* exquisite, unlike anything I've ever heard, a pack of werewolves literally singing to the moon. I feel a slight tremor on the path where we're standing.

Out of the misty night a pack of werewolves appears. Hunter and I stand breathless and in awe as we watch the majestic werewolves run past us doing a full-moon run. Seeing them running powerfully through the forested area, stopping every so often to howl and pay homage to the power of the full moon, is an awesome experience. Neither one of us moves. Hunter's hand in mine feels as if an electric current is pulsing through it. His eyes are fiery and alive with a wildness I've never seen before. My boyfriend, the gentle, easy-going Hunter Hollis Hopper, is showing the power of the wolf who lives inside him.

The werewolves run in and out of the shadows and we can see their perfect coats. All colors as Mr. Paget said—those with fur of a pure solid color—browns, ebonies, greys, and the moon-lit white ones. And then, in the shadowy distance, I see them. A large grey werewolf running in tandem with a larger white one. They seem to be the leaders of this pack of werewolves, alpha-male and alpha-female.

The two run with absolute joy, always together, nuzzling and gently nipping each other as they run. They're still in shadows and I can't see clearly. They stop near us and the grey turns to face the white wolf who lifts his head to the moon and emits a long, haunting howl. The grey follows the howl with one of her own.

The shadows fade and I am able to look closely at the pair. The unblemished white pelt of the alpha-male glows and shimmers. He lowers his head and looks in our direction. I know he doesn't really see us, we're shadows, but his wolf-sense may have him alerted to the presence of otherworldly changes. His eyes seem to bore into where we are and I hear Hunter gasp.

THIRTY-SIX

"Is that my *dad*? The alpha-male werewolf who led the Summer Valley pack was my father, Gideon Hollis Hopper?"

"I really believe it is him.

"But he never told me anything about it. Why did he keep this a secret?"

"Sometimes our parents only tell us what they want us to know or what we need to hear at a certain time," I say remembering what the male told me about bad lies vs good lies. "

We watch the grey and white werewolves turn and run deeper into the forest but, before we can follow them, a fog arises slowly from the earth beneath our feet. Swirling masses gather quickly, blanketing the forest in a matter of seconds. Mr. Paget described it well.

As the fog thickens, the howls of the werewolves take on a different tone. Unsure, confused, they are calling to each other for guidance out of the fog. For them the forest appears distorted. Werewolves running everywhere in confusion. We walk forward trying to see where the white and grey ones went. Because we're only shadows, we are not affected—we can see through the thickness of the fog and what we see is chaos. Werewolves running in all directions, desperate howls of frustration as the fog increases their skewed perception of their surroundings

"Lilith! Over there!" Hunter has spotted the grey she-werewolf running alone.

My heart pounds in my ears. This is our chance to see what really happened that long ago night. I look around for Mr. Paget's winged messengers and think I see their forms hidden in the branches of the trees. We follow the grey as she runs in frenzied circles. I hear her labored breathing and see the fear in her eyes. Then I recognize the area where she's running—the grounds of the Ringwood Riding Club—and I see a man who appears to be in his eighties standing alone in the fog. As Hunter and I watch, the she-werewolf runs smack into the man knocking him down. Her mouth is open like that of someone who is running a hard race and her teeth graze the paper-thin skin on the old man's throat causing it to bleed. Deep enough to cause bleeding, not deep enough to cause death. Her claws grip his arms in an effort to steady herself, leaving long scratches. The wounds match those of the pictures we saw online of the body in the morgue.

Both man and werewolf seem startled, and then, we see something strange happen. The she-werewolf looks at the man as if she recognizes him. He puts his hand out to gently stroke her head, clutching her thick soft fur in his hand, and we hear, "Shhh, it's all right girl. Only a fog." She seems to relax for a brief moment before the sound of a shouting voice startles her.

"Where are you? Are there wolves out here? What are you doing?"

As C. Thomas approaches, the she-werewolf stands protectively by the side of Ringwood, Sr. and snarls dangerously at his son. Quickly C. Thomas Ringwood raises a rifle and fires, hitting her in her side. Her howl of pain is horrible to hear. We hear his father say, "Stop! Leave her be!" but C. Thomas just curses and shoots again. This time her whimper is piteous as she runs in a panic toward a deep thicket. The alpha-female of the pack is the one who was shot!

As Ringwood, Sr. struggles to get up, C. Thomas viciously pushes him back down onto the ground. The elderly man lies there silent, too stunned to move or speak. "He's been attacked! My father's been attacked. I saw it happen! That wolf mauled him, tried to kill him! I shot it and it ran away to that thicket over there."

We watch five people, two women and three men, all hands at the Ringwood Riding Club, come to where Ringwood, Sr. is lying on the ground. C. Thomas Ringwood, kneels down by his father.

"Should we call an ambulance?" one of the hands asks after seeing the blood streaks on the old man's throat. Ringwood, Sr. moves his lips but no words come out.

"I'll deal with that," says C. Thomas angrily. "I have to stay here with my father. You go find that wolf! It went over there! There! Can you see it?"

"But C. Thomas, maybe one of us should—"

C. Thomas Ringwood vehemently shakes his head no. "Didn't you hear me? I said I'd deal with this. Find that damned wolf. Kill it now!"

His hands run off toward the thicket. The elderly man stares up at his son in a mixture of defiance and fear. C. Thomas Ringwood examines the marks on his father's throat. Surely he can see that the marks aren't life-threatening and that his father is more than likely just shaken up from the wolf running into him. Suddenly C. Thomas smiles and it makes me uneasy. Something is so wrong here. Getting to his feet, he walks toward the direction of the thicket and shouts for his hands to keep looking for the wolf.

Walking back to where his father is lying on the ground, he looks all around to make sure that he is alone before kneeling next to him again and leaning close to his face. Taking a small bottle out of his pocket we hear him say in a low voice, "It's all mine now, old man. I was saving this for tomorrow night, was going to sprinkle it over that apple pie you love so much, but this is a golden opportunity for me, old man. That damned wolf you love so much will be the cause of your death and no one will know any different."

A faint sweet scent seems to drift on the air. We watch as he forces his father's mouth open and pours the contents of the bottle into it. It looks as if he's forcing something dry and crushed into his mouth. Before our horrified eyes, the old man struggles and seems to be having a seizure.

Ringwood, Sr. thrashes about on the forest floor, C. Thomas holds him down, cursing under his breath while looking over his shoulder to see if anyone is coming. Hunter and I both instinctively move forward, but some unseen force holds us back reminding us that we are only shadows here and have no power to change the past. There is nothing we can do but watch, but it is terrible to see this cruelty and not be able to stop it.

The old man struggles rather fiercely for someone his age, but his son is too strong and soon he is lying there unmoving and silent. Hells Bells! Then, taking out a knife, C. Thomas carefully cuts deeply into the light marks made by the werewolf's teeth. The way the blood spurts from the neck, I know he has just cut into an artery. C. Thomas Ringwood sits back on his heels and stares at the man he has just killed, his own father.

From the corner of my eye, I see a movement, a sudden inky blur. I nudge Hunter and gesture toward it. The injured grey she-werewolf. She's deep in the shadows but she seems to be looking in the direction of C. Thomas, who has noticed her as well. I hear him curse again. He grabs his rifle but, at the sound of approaching footsteps, he quickly places the rifle on the ground and bends over his father's body. When I look back toward where the inky blur was, it is gone, swallowed up by the shadows.

"We couldn't find it, C. Thomas," says one of the returning hands. "Could've sworn we tracked it back here to you. Don't know how it got away." He looks at the elderly man. "Your father. All that blood! Is he—."

"Dead, yes." He bows his head as if he is overcome with grief, the phony creep.

"Tom, I'm sorry."

"That damned wolf did more damage than I realized. Must've bit the carotid artery. Bled to death. Died in my arms. Couldn't even get to call for an ambulance. Right after you left, I-I couldn't stop the bleeding." C. Thomas picks a tuft of fur from his father's hand and looks at it. "That damned grey wolf killed my father. I want these woods cleared of that scum. This week, during the day, we'll search and clear out all those wolves. I'll find where they're hiding. Right now, I've got to get my father back to the house. Don't want him out here at the mercy of those wolves. Help me carry his—body."

As they carry the body away, the Shadowcat reappears in front of us. Its eyes gleam as it turns toward the forest and it beckons us to follow. We're going to find the injured she-werewolf and the male who went back to help her. I grab Hunter's hand as we follow our guide to a hidden ravine with a stream near it.

The large white male werewolf is standing in the ravine sheltering the body of the whimpering grey she-werewolf. He is so gentle and loving. She moans softly in pain. He moves slowly to her side and we see an extraordinary sight. Her body is convulsing and her eyes eerily change from wolf to human and back again. In her fear she is trying to change back to her human form. It is heart-breaking. I hear Hunter whisper, "No, oh no." As much as it hurts me to watch, it hurts Hunter so much more.

The male werewolf nudges her, trying to get her on her feet. Slowly and groggily she stands, her eyes still flashing from wolf to human and back again. After scanning the area outside the ravine to make sure there are no humans there, the male gets her to walk with him. The fog has lifted a little more and the eyes of the she-werewolf look toward us. I know she sees us as shadows only but the pain in her eyes haunt me. We watch them lope slowly off toward the path and, the Shadowcat at our side, we follow.

The path is a long one, hidden but well-trod by the werewolves on their full-moon runs. We seem to be on it forever. Where is he taking this injured werewolf? Finally, he leads her toward a small wooden house. It's far from the forest and very well hidden although it is close to a large open area. I know this place but can't remember why. As they disappear into the old house, we find that we can't follow. Again, some unseen force is keeping us from moving forward reminding us that we cannot help her because to do so would make changes to the past.

A long lonely howl cuts through the mists and my heart aches. I see tears in Hunter's eyes. It is a howl of grief and sadness. That poor injured werewolf! We stand there for a long time waiting to see if any humans approach but none come. Neither does the male werewolf leave that small house.

We wait, neither of us speaking, each lost in our own thoughts. What is happening to that poor werewolf, stuck in a form that is trying to change back and can't. I stand still and silent watching the house where the werewolves have gone and wishing I could somehow help them.

THIRTY-SEVEN

The bonging sound of an old-fashioned school bell startles me. *The tolling of a bell sounds, loud and clear, you must return from there to here.* I look at my watch. Out of the four hours we've been here we only have thirty minutes left. Our time here must be almost over. Those hours flew by and, even though we've seen a lot, it seems as if we just got here.

The Shadowcat casts its haunting eyes on me and turns back to the path. Though I hate to leave here without knowing what has happened to the wounded she-werewolf, I'm also kind of anxious to get back to our own time. This place, with all its eerie beauty and mystery, is still a scary place to be. Surreal to see images from the past when you're from the present.

As we take the path back to where we started, Hunter tells me that his mind and body resonate with the werewolves. "The pull of the wolf spirit, the pain felt for the injured wolf is physical, visceral, Lilith. The connection here, to this time, to this place is stronger than I imagined it would be. I'm in awe of what we've seen. I'm anxious to get back and let your parents and Mr. Paget know what really happened on that night so many years ago."

"So am I. Will you tell Gideon about all this?"

"Not until we've done some more work on it. Then, I think it would be good for both you and me to talk to him. Invite him to Midnight Ink and just—tell him what we've found out. He'll probably be ticked off as hell about my not telling him I traveled to the past with you, but, since I think he hasn't been truthful to me about a lot of things, that makes us even."

I look at Hunter carefully, envisioning him being in his wolf form. "That large grey she-werewolf? I understand why C. Thomas was so freaked out by seeing you on his property. You *o resemble her, Hunter. She has to be related to you by blood."

He nods. "I felt that too. A cousin, an aunt. There's a connection, physical, mental, foggy memories, everything."

I hesitate to ask the question but feel as if I have to know what Hunter thinks. "Hunter, what do you think happened to the grey werewolf? Do you think Ringwood and his hands found her?"

"No, I think he assumed that she died from her wounds and never went to look further. That bastard!"

"Then—did she survive her wounds?"

"That's a question I'm afraid to answer. If she did, she's wouldn't be—right. We both saw her trying to change and she couldn't. If she survived, it would be to live in a horrible state, in constant flux between human and wolf."

I touch his hand. "We did find out that *she* did not kill Ringwood, Sr. We know his son did, but, that's something that we have to prove. It's a problem. No one else saw him do that and we can't tell authorities we know who killed a man fifteen years ago because we used the Block

Universe to go back in time to find his killer. They'd think we're crazy."

"Yeah, that is a problem. Our first murder case, huh?" A howl carries through the mists from a long distance away. Pain, sadness, despair. He gives me a wistful smile. "Wish we could find out what happened to the grey werewolf, though."

"Me, too. Who knows? After we get this Ringwood case out of the way, maybe we can work on finding out what happened to her. We have no choice now but to walk on toward the place where our journey began."

At the edge of the forest where we had entered, the Shadowcat levels us with those glowing eyes for the last time then bows its head, disappearing into the mists. Glancing at my watch again, I see that we've only got twenty minutes left to our time here. I hold the candle close to my heart and quickly say the words of the spell nine times. "I am the shadow; the shadow is me." And—

Nothing happens. We're still in the shadowland. I take a deep breath. I probably said it wrong, slurred a word as I rushed through it because I'm so eager to get back to my own time. Okay, okay. Maybe I have to slow down. So I repeat it once again, three times three. "I am the shadow; the shadow is me.

Nothing.

Hunter looks at me, his face showing just the slightest bit of concern. "Everything, um, you know, okay?"

Nodding yes, I take another deep breath and close my eyes in concentration, saying the words of the spell, slowly and clearly. When I open my eyes, I let out a small sound of surprise. We're still here among the shadows. It's not working! Why isn't the spell working?

"Lilith? The words, I mean, is there a chance that you, I don't know, maybe mispronounced something?"

"Hell's Bells, Hunter! No! No way. I practiced this over and over again all week. Besides it worked to get us *here*. I don't know why it isn't working to send us *back*."

"Okay, got it." Hunter smiles at me, trying to give me encouragement but I see the worry deepening on his face. "Try it again, Lilith. Really, really slowly and really, really clearly. They're just words, even if they are magical, and you are the word expert, remember?"

I nod, take a deep breath and center myself with calmness, the way Professor A.J. Reed taught me. Slowly I articulate each syllable.

"I. Am. The. Sha-dow. The. Sha-dow. Is. Me."

Nothing.

I search my mind, repeating the words of the spell, even the instructions, over again. What am I doing wrong? Why isn't the spell to return working? Did I forget something? No, no, I shake my head. I was very specific about learning the spell. What is going on here?! I'm doing everything right, aren't I? Unless—I struggle to think what I might have missed. In my mind's eye I see the words, the scribbles and drawings on the sides of the pages, and what else? The—dagger!

"The dagger, it's the dagger!"

"What dagger? What are you saying? Are you talking about a real dagger?"

"No, no. The *drawing* of a dagger next to the last word of the spell in the Book of Lost Spells. It's ancient."

Hunter takes my hand and forces me to look at him. "I don't understand. What do you mean 'it's ancient'? What does this have to do with us still being here in the past?"

"The drawing of a dagger. I thought it was simply a sign that meant the spell was powerful. But that's *not* what it means at all. I think it might be a marker ancient writers used to show that there was an addition to what had been written. I think it's what they used as an asterisk."

"An asterisk? Makes sense. I guess they had them back then. How does this affect the spell not working right now?"

"There might be an addition to the spell that I missed because it was probably on a page in the back of the book. You know, like when we see an asterisk by a line in a poem in Lit. class? Usually the asterisk leads us to the back of the book where we can find the definition by page number and line."

"Okay, I understand what you mean about asterisks, but what does that have to do with this spell?"

"It could mean that that dagger symbol was telling me that there was more to the spell on the back page. It's means that it's more than likely the part of the spell that I didn't read! It could be the part of the spell that returns us to the present."

"And?"

"*Ani*, if I can't figure out the words to return, it may mean that we'll be stuck here as shadows forever." I look around the shades of grey and black that make up this shadowland. "I have to," I breathe deeply to calm myself and look at Hunter, "I have to try to think of what words need to be said for us to return. It has to be somewhere in the spell itself."

My hands are shaking and I feel sick to my stomach. Stuck here forever! Am I being dramatic, overly frightened? Prof. Reed's voice seems to echo in my head.

"You're braver than you think you are, Lilith. Much, much braver."

But am I really? I sit down on the misty path and try hard to think about what I have to do. Amsterdam, Rotterdam, damn, damn, damn! Fear is blocking my mind. I can't seem to think straight! Fear and emotion blocks powers, Professor Reed had told me. She's so right.

Let's hope that she's also right about me be braver than I think I am.

"Victoria, look."

The Book of Lost Spells is turning its pages rapidly, opening and closing its cover several times before staying open on the page where the Shadowcat spell is written. The dagger next to the last word of the spell shines brightly with a golden light as if alerting those in the room to some danger.

"Oh, dear, oh dear!" says Mr. Paget fearfully, covering his eyes with his hands. "Something is wrong—I can feel it."

"It wants our attention for some reason, Christopher."

As they watch, the book flips suddenly to the last page. Leaning close to the book, the male and female look at the page, easily translating the early Italian with their vampire minds.

"It looks like part of the spell Lilith used to walk in the shadows," says the female, "but—there's something different here. And look," she points at a mark on the page, "see this symbol of a dagger? It's also shining, the same as the dagger on the page with the Shadowcat spell. They're connected. Professor A.J. Reed once told me that this mark is used by witches to let others of their kind know that there is an additional part to a spell. Spells were refined through the years as witches added more words to a spell to strengthen it. Any spell that contains a second part has a sort of asterisk next to it. When Lilith showed the spell to us on her phone, why did fail I to notice this? This page shows the words to the second part of the spell Lilith cast and it is crucial."

"Crucial in what way? Is our child in danger?" The male stands suddenly, his eyes a blue fire glow reflecting a sense of unknown danger.

She nods her head, blood tears at the corners of her eyes. "She may well be. Lilith only used the first part, the part that allowed her *to enter* the shadows. The words that are written here are the words that must be spoken for her and Hunter to *return from* the shadows!" She reads the words aloud.

To return after you hear the toll of the bell,
Reverse the order of the words in the spell.

Magical wor♦s, for magical hearte♦,
Brings you back from whence you starte♦,
Three times three, this magic bestow,
'The sha♦ow is me; I am the sha♦ow'

The female straightens up, her eyes going from the book to the male. "This is serious. Without these words, she won't know how to return, Christopher. She is stuck in the shadows and we are not able to pass through to bring her back."

"Why not?"

"Because my love," she says gently and sadly, "You know that our kind are not able to cast spells. There is no way for us to travel to the past."

"Yes, yes, for a moment I had forgotten. Professor A.J. Reed perhaps? We know that she weaves magical spells."

The female shakes her head, her blonde hair swinging forward around her face. "A.J. is an Elfin creature, her magic is limited to the here and now."

The female looks up. "There *has* to be a way to help her, Christopher, or else our child will wander the shadows for eternity!"

As the female glances toward the windows, Lively turns from his perch there, cocks his head to the side, and looks directly at her. Their eyes lock and she whispers low—

"Lively."

THIRTY-EIGHT

The mists swirl mysteriously and the sounds of a nighttime forest echo eerily around Hunter and me. It reminds me of every spooky horror movie I've ever seen. Being scared by those movies was frighteningly fun but the mists and the sounds here are simply frightening. We're alone here.

I've tried my best to center myself with calmness and it seems to be working a little. Both Hunter and I are sitting on the path and I'm trying every combination of words from the spell in the hope that one of them might work. So far, I've struck out. According to my watch, we've only got nine minutes left out of the thirty that were allotted for our return. Each minute is precious.

"You said that everything has to be said three times three. You're doing that right, Lilith? You are, right?" Hunter asks me for the fifth time. I know he's as scared as I am, so I smile at him wearily and nod my head.

"Yup, three times three. Something's got to work and it will." He nods back at me and squeezes my hand.

"What about calling out to your parents?"

"I tried that, Hunter but I don't think they can hear me. They'd come to me if they heard me call."

"Maybe our guide here, the Shadowcat? Can you mind-call it?"

"Tried that too. Nothing."

The Shadowcat is nowhere to be seen. I was kind of wishing that if it knew we were still here, it might return to help but I guess it was only our guide for a one-time deal. I stand up and try another combination of words, repeating them slowly and precisely. Something, something has to work! I look at my watch again. I can't seem to stop checking the time. Seven minutes left! Desperately I begin saying combinations of words over and over again, mixing them up until the words jumble in my mind. I am so frustrated I could cry.

"I am so sorry Hunter. I got you into this, this—going back in time deal. It's all my fault."

Sensing my frustration, Hunter holds me tightly. "No, you didn't. I wanted to come with you, Lilith. Anyway, if we're going to be stuck here, and I'm not saying that we *are* going to be, well, at least we'll be together. Neither one of us is alone in this. That's one good thing."

We stay huddled together on the shadowy, eerie path while the last four precious minutes tick by. Then a sound of movement, a feeling of something or someone nearby alerts us and we jump to our feet. Through the mists some being casting a large shadow against the dark trees, is approaching us. Hell's Bells! It's coming directly to where we're standing. A werewolf, an otherworldy creature, something dangerous! Maybe it's coming because I can't find the words that will return us to our own time? I look at my watch. Three minutes only. Suddenly the shadow stops and I hold my breath. We're doomed!

Then, I hear a voice in my head. A mind-speak. Hell's Bells, it sounds like Lively!

"Lively, is that you? Where are you?"

"I'm in the turret room. My cat spirit cast that shadow to get your attention."

"Well, oh boy, have you got it! How is it that I can hear you mind-speak? I can't contact my parents."

"You and I, we're connected, Lilith. Remember? Witches and cats? Even though you're only half-witch, I can find and connect with you anywhere and in any time. In witch parlance, I'm your familiar, although I prefer the word partner."

Hunter grabs my wrist and looks at my watch. "Two minutes left."

"Lively, we're stuck here. I can't find the words of the spell to return!"

"That's why I contacted you. I can give them to you. Do you still have the candle?"

"Yes, but it's not lit anymore."

"Blow on it."

"Blow on it? But how—"

"It's a witch's trick. Blow on it and it will light."

I do and it does. Hell's Bells! Who knew? "Okay, it's lit." I look at Hunter who mouths the words "One and a half minutes left."

"Listen carefully," says Lively. "Say these words three times three. Ready?"

"Yes, yes. Please hurry!"

"The shadow is me; I am the shadow."

Hell's Bells! "That's it? That's all?" I am stunned.

"Just say them, Lilith."

"Of all the combos I tried, I never, ever thought to try *that* one."

Hunter nudges me. "Lilith, please, try it! We've only got less than a minute left!"

"Lively, are you sure this will work?"

"Say them!" Lively's mind-speak sounds loudly in my head.

"Amsterdam, Rotterdam, damn, damn, damn! Okay! Here goes."

Holding the candle close to my heart with one hand and grasping Hunter's hand with the other, I say the words to return. With the first few words a whooshing sound and the deep toll of a bell surround us. Shadows swirl before us, inky deep shadows. I repeat the sentence three more times. Thunder rumbles and lightening pierces the forest. As I say the sentence for the last three times, haunting howls echo throughout the shadowland. I close my eyes. And—

"They're here, they're here! Oh my dears! Sweet Lilith and young Hunter! They're back!"

The tremulous voice of Mr. Paget greets us. Opening my eyes, I see nothing but shadows and mists swirling slowly around us. I watch fearfully until they disappear and reveal that Hunter and I are back in the turret room. Hell's Bells! It worked, the reverse spell worked. I look around for Lively, afraid that his spirit may have been left in the shadowlands but I see him standing calmly next to my parents.

Hunter seems to be in a trance, looking around the room as if he can't quite believe that we're actually back in Midnight Ink and still all in one piece. I smile and begin to say something but never get the chance. The room suddenly begins to spin and the next thing I know I find myself flat on my butt on the hardwood floor. Everything is a blur as everyone, including old Mr. Paget, helps me to my feet. My dad guides me to a chair. "Here Lilith of the Angels, sit down. Get your bearings. You've been gone for almost four hours in the shadows."

Lively jumps up onto my lap and I have never been so glad to see him. I bury my face in his soft fur and hold him close. My familiar, my partner. "I love you, Lively. You saved us from being stuck in the shadowland! How did you know to come get us?"

"I sent him." The female kneels next to my chair and kisses me, then Lively. "Lively told me his spirit could reach you no matter where you were." She massages his ears. "He let me know that you two are connected through time, space, all dimensions—every place and period. I couldn't reach you myself, Lilith, so I showed him the words that would ensure your return."

"How did you know we couldn't return?"

"The Book of Lost Spells alerted us." She goes on to tell me how the book began to act erratically, opening and closing its cover, flipping pages rapidly. How it opened to the Shadowcat spell and my mom saw the shining dagger next to the last word of the spell. Then, finally the book flipped to the last page where another dagger was shining, marking the part of the spell that needed to be said in order to return from the past to the present.

"I should have recognized the meaning of that dagger when you showed me the spell." Her beautiful glittering eyes fill with blood tears. "I'm so sorry."

"Mom, no, please don't be upset. It's really my own fault. That dagger? I kind of thought it was just a sign letting the spell-caster know that the spell was very powerful. You know, a warning to be careful when casting it. I should have stopped to think about what it really meant. I was careless."

"No, darling. I should have been more alert to the spell. I've been distracted. Lately we've been more focused on—." She stops.

"Focused on what? Is there something that I should know about, Mom?"

"Focused on, oh nothing really, just—things. Anyway, you're back here and we are all so grateful to Lively. Right, Christopher? Mr. Paget?" She smoothly changes the subject. "And, many, many thanks to the Book of Lost Spells. It alerted us to your danger. Look, see? On the table? It's shimmering with light, happy that you're back."

I look at the book, its pages softly lit with a magical light. My mom is an expert at what I call 'topic diversion'. It seems to work. I'm definitely diverted.

We stay quiet for a few minutes, each one of us lost in our own thoughts about what has happened and our immense relief that Hunter and I made it back safely. The heavy silence is broken by Mr. Paget.

"Oh, goodness. Oh dear! You two must be starving, simply starving! Perhaps we can get some of those lovely scones and some clotted cream to go with them. You remember them, Lilith? We can order them again. Yes, oh, yes, you need to have some food."

The male and female agree to order the food but Hunter shakes his head. "I *am* hungry, Mr. Paget, Mr. and Mrs. Angel, and I'm sure Lilith is too. But, besides the scones and cream can we *please* also order a large peppers and onions pizza with extra cheese? And maybe some mozzarella sticks?"

We all laugh. We're on our way back to being normal. As normal as life can be for a half-witch with wings, her vampire parents, a werewolf for a boyfriend, and dear, sweet otherworldly Mr. Paget.

THIRTY-NINE

fter an hour of devouring all the food delivered to Midnight Ink—we left the scones and clotted cream for Mr. Paget while Hunter and I dug into the pizza and mozzarella sticks—I downed a can of ice tea and began to tell everyone about our amazing trip to the shadowlands.

"It was just as you described it, Mr. Paget. Exquisite howling, so beautiful."

Mr. Paget beams at me and nods his head shyly. "Yes, dear Lilith. So beautiful. Yes, it was."

I tell them everything about the werewolves running through the forest. Their beauty, their grace, and then I tell them about the Ghost Wolf. "Do you think it was Gideon, Dad? This werewolf's fur was just as you once told me Gideon's was—he actually glowed!"

"It really did, Mr. Angel. And I know this sounds crazy, but, even though we were just shadows and not really in their time and all that stuff, I swear he looked at me and knew who I was."

"He may have felt a strong presence and may have even seen your shadow," says my dad. "He is a hyper-sentient creature after all. There's so much about time and dimensions that we don't really know, even though, as otherworldly creatures, we know a lot more than our human counterparts."

"How did you know that Gideon was a Ghost Wolf? Did you ever see him as a werewolf?"

"Once," answers the female, "only once. A beautiful creature. We had seen werewolves before, in the course of our travels, but none like Gideon. It was before we had found you, darling. We had come here to find a safe and quiet place to stay, we were tired of always moving from one place to another and needed a permanent home. The name Summer Valley was so lovely and so peaceful sounding. We happened to be in the forest just before morning right after we had fed."

The male continues. "Gideon came upon us. He knew what we are, he had sensed it. He had also sensed that we meant no harm to any creatures in the area. We, too, sensed that he meant us no harm. He was magnificent, a true Ghost Wolf, so rare a creature that many, including us, believed that the Ghost Wolf was a myth or a legend.

"As the full moon was fading and giving way to the first rays of daylight, he changed into his human form. The change from wolf to human was an incredible sight to behold. The power of the wolf!" The male pauses as if he's remembering that night. "Then Gideon told us to come back when the full moon would be gone and he'd talk to us then. We did as he asked.

"He met us in the forest three days later and told us all about the area—that it was peaceful, and that it posed no threat to otherworldly creatures like us as long as we were willing to hide our true nature and harm no one.

We told him that we had long ago discovered that we could survive quite well on the 'small sip', but that there were times when we needed something more. That, of course, meant that we needed to find a blood bank. It was Gideon who introduced us to Rudy who told us that he would help us should we ever be in need of that 'something more'."

The female's beautiful green eyes glitter brightly. "Gideon is the reason we decided to settle here. We bought the house and Midnight Ink and became residents of Summer Valley. When we found you, my darling Lilith, we knew our decision had been a good one. It's a perfect place to raise a child."

"What else did you learn?" asks Mr. Paget turning to me. "Did you see anything else? Did the fog impede you seeing anything at all?"

"No, we saw everything, even with the fog. The werewolves did become confused by the fog but it didn't affect us. We saw the grey she-werewolf become totally disoriented and saw her run into Old Mr. Ringwood. She knocked him down and," I turn to Mr. Paget, "your winged messengers were right—she and Ringwood, Sr. did seem to know each other. He was completely unafraid of her and she seemed almost reassured by his presence.

"He stroked her head and tried to comfort her by saying, 'Shhh, it's all right girl. Only a fog.' It was apparent that he knew her and she knew him," says Hunter earnestly. "She would never hurt him deliberately. Those scratches on his arms and those scrapes on his neck were accidental."

"And, we saw who really killed Ringwood, Sr. and it wasn't that werewolf or any other wolf."

"*Who* killed him? You said *who* not what." My dad looks at me.

"His son, C. Thomas Ringwood, the one who owns the riding stables now—he killed his own father."

Hunter and I take turns telling my parents and Mr. Paget about what we saw. How C. Thomas shot the terrified grey werewolf twice as she ran for cover and told his hands that the wolf had attacked his father, to find and kill it while he tended to the old man. How he waited until he and his father were alone and poured something from a small bottle into his mouth then held him down until he stopped moving. My parents, vampires who have seen murder and death in their long, long lives, say nothing, their faces watchful and unreadable.

Afterward, he took a knife and cut deeply into the surface teeth marks so it would look as if his father had been killed by a wolf's bites. I tell my parents about a blur in the darkness that seemed as if it were watching C. Thomas. "It was the injured grey she-werewolf. Even though she was in pain and fearful of being shot again, she came back to try to help Ringwood, Sr. But, she was too late. She left when the Ringwood hands returned."

"The grey wolf?" Mr. Paget interrupts us gently. "You saw what happened to the grey she-werewolf—afterwards?"

"Yes, we did." I go on to tell him all we saw. The she-werewolf wounded by C. Thomas, the white alpha-male trying to help her—I recount everything including the tragedy of watching her try to change back into human form as werewolves do when badly injured or dying. "We saw both werewolves go to a small, very old building but the forces of the past wouldn't let us follow all the way. We don't really know what happened after that, Mr. Paget. I'm sorry."

"I have to believe that the Ghost-Wolf you saw was Gideon," says my dad pacing around the room. "It would make sense."

"Okay, then let's assume that we did see Gideon. That means that he was the alpha-male of the pack in Summer Valley. Who was the grey he tried to help? The large alpha-female."

"Alpha-female? Of course!" My mom turns quickly to my dad and says, "Galina! That grey had to have been Galina!"

"Galina?" Hunter sits forward, a strange look in his eyes. "Did you say

Galina?"

"Who's Galina?" I ask, curious.

The male leans toward me and says gently, "Galina was Gideon's mate. She's Hunter's mother. We met her in the forest that long-ago night when we first met Gideon."

I knew Hunter's mother had died when he was barely two years old but we never talked about her at all. I sensed that, even with all his positive energy and happy-go-lucky personality, not having a mother was a painful topic for him. I didn't even know what her name was until just now.

"My dad just told me that she had died when I was a toddler—he never gave any details, just a vague mention about her heart. Is it possible that tonight I saw *my mother* doing a moon run and then being shot by Ringwood?" Then, "She must've died in that building, Lilith. Trying, and failing, to change back to her human form probably put an enormous strain on her heart so, I guess my dad didn't really lie about what caused her death. He just didn't tell me all of it." He puts his head down on the table and the female hugs him tightly.

I'm stunned and can only imagine how Hunter feels. To see his mother in such distress and pain is horrible. I look at my beautiful, vamp mom and can't imagine seeing her in such agony and not being able to help her.

Hunter's mother was the werewolf shot by C. Thomas. The tuft of grey fur, he found in his father's fingers and kept all these years would match Hunter's grey fur exactly. No wonder C. Thomas wants to find the wolf he saw on his property. He believes that Hunter's fur, caught in his trap last month, was from the same wolf he tried to kill fifteen years ago.

After a long few minutes, Hunter raises his head and looks at me. His can-do-it attitude surfaces. "Okay. Now I know what happened. and now I want to bring C. Thomas Ringwood to justice, not only for killing his own father, but for the death of my mother, Galina."

FORTY

W e sat around the table in Midnight Ink for another hour, talking about what Hunter and I had seen and found out. At one point, Mr. Paget became very excited and seemed stressed. His whiskers bristled and he sniffed the air as if some long-ago scent might help him. He was trying to remember something one of his winged messengers had told him a long time ago about Mr. Ringwood, Sr. He apologized as he tried to remember exactly what he had been told.

"Oh, dear, oh dear, I should have remembered. I am so forgetful sometimes. It was something about Mr. Ringwood, the father not the son. Oh, no, now what was it? I can't seem to remember! It had something to do with—oh, dear! It was some years—five or six years—before that horrible night when the fog came. It was summer and very hot, I know that.

Something, something, I cannot recall it!"

"It's all right Mr. Paget. Whatever one of your messengers told you, it was so many years ago. Don't be upset," I touch his hand soothingly. "Really, you'll remember. Don't worry."

"Oh my goodness, I hope so. It seems as if it was something that might be important. Perhaps if I go home and lie down it will help me to remember." He gets up to leave and my mom walks with him toward the outer room. The chimes tinkle lightly as the door is opened and then we hear, "The water, yes, that's it. It was the water."

The water? We all look at each other as Mr. Paget shuffles hurriedly into the back room. "It's the water, that's what my beloved winged messenger told me!"

"What about the water, Mr. Paget?" I help him to a chair. "Tell us."

"The older Mr. Ringwood, he-he-he, oh dear, excuse me. Water, yes, water. Oh, dear me, now *I* am getting thirsty." Hunter gets a bottle of iced tea and pours the contents into a glass for Mr. Paget. "Thank you, thank you, young Hunter." He drinks, sighs deeply, and drinks again. "Dear Lilith, do you remember what I told you about the grey she-werewolf and Mr. Ringwood, Sr. seeming to know each other? You saw it for yourself when you were in the past."

"Yes, I remember and it was true. They recognized each."

"Indeed they should have. It was because she had no reason to fear him and he had no reason to fear her or any of the creatures that inhabit the forest. The older gentleman, Mr. Ringwood, Sr., had become a conservationist, you see. He cared for all the life in the forest and simply wanted to protect innocent animals. Yes, oh, yes. I seem to remember it all now." He gulps the tea and smiles. "When the creeks were dry in the hot summer months, he left out huge round troughs of water for the wolves and all animals of the forest. He couldn't allow them to be thirsty, I assume. That's what one of my beloved messengers told me. Oh, dear, how could I have forgotten to tell you that bit of information?"

"So he put out water for the animals and was concerned about their welfare." Hunter is walking around the room. Like Deidre Pace, old Mr. Ringwood took care of the wildlife, neither one knowing they were being kind to werewolves—and neither one knowing that werewolves, feared and hated by so many humans, never forget a kindness.

"Oh yes, young pup Hunter, yes. He must have been a good man. I never saw him myself. Oh no, no I never did, but my beloved messengers knew about him and told me."

My mind is whirling and my thoughts are centering on a reason for C. Thomas to murder his own father. Did it have to do with his having become a conservationist, someone who cared about the forest and its inhabitants? But, why would he kill him for that? I'm also curious about exactly what he put in his father's mouth. Hell's Bells! It had to be some kind of poison. And that faint sweet smell—what was that? I think of what I had learned at that lecture on plant and flower poisons. How easy it is to poison someone with something from nature.

While my parents talk to Mr. Paget, Hunter and I slip away. We need to make plans and soon. This is our case, the first one we have and I want us to work it like crazy and bring a murderer to justice. We have to find a way to prove that C. Thomas killed his father and we have to have a solid reason for it.

I oversleep on Saturday morning, drained by the emotion of all that we saw in the past. It amazes me to think that the past is still occurring, still happening so to speak. The idea of a Block Universe seems to be true. It's a long line of happenings that really never stops. In one way that's a comforting thought but in another way, it's frightening. Wars, horrors, sadness, pain, murders, all still being enacted.

Swinging my legs over the side of the bed, I see Lively in the window, head up, alert, his eyes fixed on something outside. "What's up Lively? Birds?" He doesn't move or respond in mind-talk. I walk over to the window and look out. Nothing at all is there. At least I don't see anything. Shrugging my shoulders, I walk to the bathroom for a shower, thinking that all cats, even one like Lively, are enigmas, mysterious, beautiful creatures that we may never fully understand.

After my shower I towel dry my hair, get dressed and check to see if my parents are home. They are not and it's after 10:00 AM. Oh, well, they're old enough, seriously old enough, to take care of themselves, but I still wonder what's been going on that makes them stay out well after the sun has risen.

I'm meeting Hunter at Midnight Ink and we're going to plan how best to trap C. Thomas and have him brought in for the murder of his own father and to avenge Galina's death.

In a little over three weeks there will be a full moon and I want this settled before then. Even though Hunter assures me that he will be extra careful and not venture out of the forest, I'm worried. With his promise of a ten thousand reward for the grey wolf, dead or alive, C. Thomas is attracting a lot of crazies—with guns and bows and arrows. I am betting that not one of them is even contemplating a capture, they're out to kill. Even with the local police on the alert, there might be too many nutcases for them to stop. Money makes some people do crazy and cruel things.

A hand-printed Closed sign on Midnight Ink greets me as I unlock the front door. Inside, all is quiet and peaceful which is something I love about the closed book store. My parents have given me permission to keep

Midnight Ink closed all day. They know that Hunter and I need to work in the turret room undisturbed.

"If you need our help with anything, just ask," said my dad last night. "We have faith in you, Lilith of the Angels, but—just in case, we'll be available."

A light tap on the window lets me know that Hunter has arrived. He's brought two tall macchiato coffees and doughnuts. Good, I'm hungry and the coffee will energize us.

"Hey," Hunter flashes his winning smile at me and hands me a coffee. He looks refreshed and ready to begin.

"What did Gideon say when you went home last night?"

He shakes his head and takes a sip of coffee. "Nothing really. Just asked me if we got the school project done and all. Told me to thank your parents for having me stay over."

We go upstairs and settle in front of the windows with a view of the small town of Summer Valley and the distant glimpse of the forest beyond. Coffee and a glazed doughnut make me feel good and prepared to begin our case. Hunter asks me if I have any thoughts about how we're going to proceed.

"Well, I think that we have to get proof that C. Thomas *is* the actual killer of his father. You remember that faint, sweet smell?" Hunter nods. "I've been thinking about that smell. The sweetness of it was from a flower—it had to be. I think, no, I *know* that the smell was coming from that bottle. That lecture on poisonous plants we attended at the Hall of Criminal Justice? The lecturer said that there's one flower native to California that's particularly poisonous—the beautiful, sweet-smelling, and deadly, Oleander. C. Thomas probably ground it up and put it in a bottle. It was missed because of the obvious marks on Ringwood, Sr.'s neck and, also because of C. Thomas's word that he had seen the wolf attack. But— shouldn't there have been outward signs of poisoning on the body?

Shouldn't a qualified M.E. have seen those signs?"

"So he poisoned his own father with crushed Oleander," muses Hunter. "Is there anyone we know, or know of, who might be able to tell us where we can get access to the original M.E.'s report? Someone who knows about poison and the signs of poisoning a M.E. might notice?"

I nod and finish my doughnut. "I know just the person."

FORTY-ONE

R udy down at the blood bank looks like a typical California grad student who loves surfing. Tanned body, blonde surfer streaks in his hair, coupled with a ready smile, and hazel eyes that smile all on their own, he isn't someone you'd think helps out thirsty vampires or is friends with fierce werewolves.

The thing is that Rudy is not an otherworldly creature himself—he's completely human. A human who not only knows, and wholeheartedly accepts, otherworldly creatures like my parents, Hunter's dad, and Mr. Paget, but has been completely welcomed into their lives. I'm quite sure that if Rudy ever needed help, all the creatures who know him would come to his aid.

He has his Bachelor's degree in ancient mythology, which is how he came to know that many stories of otherworldly creatures were actually not simply stories—they were true. Once he met and befriended Mr. Paget, he made it his business to protect and aid all creatures. Now he is studying for his Master's degree in botany, specifically the area of poisonous plants.

Rudy lives in a loft above the blood bank. As Hunter and I are pulling up in front of his place we see him coming back from a run. He jogs over to my car and greets us. "I just saw your parents last night," he says nodding at me. "How're things going for you two? Graduation is coming soon."

"So far, so good," I say, then ask him if we can talk somewhere private.

"Sure. Let's sit on the bench over there. I've got to hydrate after that run."

We walk across the street and wait while Rudy downs a bottle of Gatorade. "So what's on your mind?"

I start right in. "Poisonous plants. It's kind of a project we're working on."

"End-of-the-year class project, huh?" I smile but don't answer. "Interesting subject and right in my area of expertise. What do you want to know?"

"If a person was poisoned by the Oleander flower, how would a Medical Examiner know that was the cause of death? Without doing an autopsy, I mean."

"Well, an autopsy is usually done when the cause of death isn't obvious, but, as to your question—the first sign of that flower poisoning would be in the nails. Oleander leaves its mark by staining the keratin in the nails a slight bluish tinge. A good coroner would notice that." He looks at me curiously.

"Would a good M.E. notice that detail, even if there was a more obvious cause of death?"

"Sure."

"But what if the M.E. was told that someone was killed in another, more brutal way, like an attack. What if someone said they saw the attack?

Would the M.E. still do extra tests?"

"From what I know, even if the cause of death seems obvious, a M.E. is usually obliged by law to do normal testing and that includes ruling out other injuries or poisons. Notice I said *usually*. The M.E. would need the written permission of the next of kin to perform a complete autopsy. Without that permission they can't proceed."

"This would be in the Medical Examiner's report then? Even the part about the next of kin's refusal of an autopsy?"

"It would have to be." He looks at me curiously. "This is one hell of a topic for a project. You sure there isn't another reason for your questions?"

"No other reason, just one other question. How long are Medical Examiners required to keep their reports?"

"I think it's usually twenty years. But seriously? A woman I knew who worked at the county M.E.'s office told me that nobody ever really throws anything away there. According to her, they just file them and forget them."

"Thanks Rudy.

"Good luck with that class project."

"Sorry?"

"Your class project?" he laughs. "The one you just asked me about?"

"Right, yes, thanks!"

As we go back to my car, I whisper to Hunter, "We have to get into the county M.E.'s office as soon as possible. Tomorrow's a half day at school. We'll go right after our last class. Who knows what type of security we may have to go through to view the report."

Hunter and I leave the school grounds running. Once in the student parking lot we take off on his Vespa going excruciatingly slow so as not to attract the attention of the principal who monitors the lot after school. I wish I could just fly there. It would be quicker but it's day time and I can't risk having anyone see me fly. Still, just the thought of flying starts the familiar itch in my shoulder blades.

It takes us twenty long minutes to get to the county courthouse and another seventeen minutes to locate the Office of the Medical Examiner. Unfortunately, a Google search of the M.E. who worked there fifteen years ago shows that he himself is no longer with us. My hopes of actually talking to him are squashed.

Thank goodness you don't have to be a relative to view the Medical Examiner's files. Inside the squat, unassuming building, I tell the clerk, who's busy on her cell phone, that we're interested in seeing the M.E.'s report on Ringwood, Sr. and give her the date. I'm prepared to give her the excuse that we're doing a paper for our Criminal Justice class but, without even looking up, she pushes a sheet toward me and says, "Sign your names and the time you came in. When you leave, write down the sign-out time." She slides over a key attached to a plastic holder. "Files are boxes in room 561 in the basement.

"Aren't the files computerized?" asks Hunter who puts everything in his life on his laptop. A snort of laughter and a shake of her head tells him no.

"They're paper files in cardboard boxes. All in *chronological* order with sub-files inside in *alphabetical* order. They're in boxes on shelves. Each shelf has a date on it. Good luck."

"Do you need our IDs?" Hunter and I already have our driver's licenses in hand.

"Nope. Just sign the sheet." She never once looked up from her phone. So much for security.

Room 561 is at the end of a long, dingy hallway in the basement. The key sticks in the lock and gives me a problem opening the door until I jiggle it back and forth hard. The door opens with a loud squeak. Hunter feels for a light switch next to the opened door and a glaring white overhead light comes on. Looking at the rows of boxes stacked three to a shelf, I feel overwhelmed. Sighing, I begin walking down the aisle and checking the, thankfully highlighted, years on the shelves. I count back fifteen years and find the shelf I'm looking for. The boxes have letters on them written in black marker. A-E, F-J, and so on. The one on the bottom of the pile shows the letters Q-U. The file for Ringwood has to be in that box.

Hunter helps me take down the top boxes to get to the one we need. There's no desk or chairs so, after we place the box on the floor, we sit down next to it to go through the contents. There are quite a few files packets but thankfully they are all in alphabetical order as the clerk said they would be.

"Radclif, Rawlings, Reardon, Reese, Reston," I read off the names on each yellowing file. "Rice, Riggins—got it!"

I take the file that says Ringwood and open it. Hunter hangs over my shoulder as we read the M.E.'s report on cause of death.

"Complete autopsy has not been authorize◦ or permitte◦ by relative. State law confirms relative's right to autopsy refusal an◦, as cause of ◦eath ◦oes seem to be apparent, I will procee◦ with that. From outwar◦ anatomic fin◦ings I fin◦ the cause of ◦eath to be massive arterial bloo◦ loss from an attack by a wil◦ animal. Teeth marks on throat an◦ scratches on arms appear to be from a larger than normal canis lupis, a wolf. Eyewitness account of a wolf attack confirms fin◦ings." It's signed, Simon Calender, M. E.

That's it? I flip the page over and read the coroner's detailed observations of the marks on the body, but there's no mention of poison.

"This can't be all," says Hunter stands up abruptly. "We saw him being poisoned. Is there another page to this report? Check the file packet."

A look inside the packet shows nothing. Amsterdam, Rotterdam, damn, damn, damn! In frustration, I turn the packet upside down and shake it hard. Nothing falls out but I hear a rustling sound inside. Putting my hand inside the packet, my fingers touch what feels like loose paper wedged into the cardboard folds. I slide it free and remove it. It's a folded hand-written note with the heading, "Ringwood Findings-Personal Addendum to Report". I wave Hunter over next to me and together we read what's written there.

*"Personal notes of S. Calen*er*: I fin* that the fingernails of the victim of an allege* wolf attack have a slight bluish tinge which is in*icative of having ingeste* poison, possibly plant base*. From the small, but telling, amount of the nail *iscoloration, it is my conclusion that the man ha* sufficient poison in his system to have been the actual cause of his *eath. As a full autopsy was a*amantly refuse* by the relative of the *ecease*, I was unable to biologically verify poison as the cause. However, it is a strong possibility, an* my own personal consensus, that the man either ingeste* a toxic plant himself, or was given the poison which cause* his *eath."*

Pulling out my phone, I take a picture of the official report and the hand-written note. The coroner believed that Ringwood's death was caused by poison. That fact, and the fact that C. Thomas refused an official autopsy, knowing full well that it would definitely show his father was poisoned, gives us solid evidence of foul play.

"Now we just have to get the murderer to admit it." I say to Hunter who looks at me skeptically.

"How are we going to do that?"

"I have no idea."

FORTY-TWO

I seriously meant it when I told Hunter that I didn't know how we would get C. Thomas to admit he had poisoned his father. I have no clue how I am going to make that happen.

Hunter has been unusually quiet on the way back to Midnight Ink. He seems very preoccupied and I'm guessing that it has to do with the Ringwood case, but I'm wrong. When I ask him he tells me that he can't understand why Gideon never told him about being the alpha male of a pack of werewolves who ran in Summer Valley or that his mother, Galina was shot by C. Thomas Ringwood.

"Why would he not tell me all about him and my mother?"

"He was trying to protect you, Hunter. Parents do that. He wanted you to grow up happy and carefree."

"And I did. You're right, he was only trying to protect me. Maybe I would've been a different person knowing that my mom was killed. I mean it was hard enough for me just knowing that she died, that she wasn't around like other kids' mothers were. But, still, I wish he had told me." He sighs deeply, as if a heavy burden has been placed on his shoulders. We ride the rest of the way in silence, both of us caught up in our own thoughts and plans.

Two nights later there's a tiny sickle of a moon visible from the tree top in my back yard. I've flown up here to think about what I'm planning to do. The moon will be full in a few short weeks. The ten-thousand-dollar reward to trap or kill a large grey wolf, in the area of the Ringwood estate is, I'm positive, attracting too many crazies here in Summer Valley. C. Thomas has to be approached and soon.

After we left the county M.E.'s office we went straight to Midnight Ink. The male and female asked no questions, and since there were very few customers, Hunter and I settled upstairs in the turret room that's now our office. Once there, Hunter and I spent considerable time discussing how we might get C. Thomas to own up to the murder and got nowhere fast. We reviewed the personal notes of Simon Calender, M.E. again.

"He wrote this note, Hunter. That means he strongly suspected that Ringwood, Sr. wasn't killed by a wolf as his son told him had happened—he was poisoned."

"I get that, Lilith, but it means nothing unless we can prove C. Thomas poisoned his father."

When Hunter left to go home to have dinner with his dad, I stayed upstairs looking out of the floor to ceiling windows watching Hunter ride away on his Vespa and looking at the distant forest.

From downstairs I heard the occasional tinkling sound of the door chimes as a customer entered the book shop. The soft voices of the male and the female sounded muffled as they answered customers' questions about books, new and old.

It grew dark and I still stood in front of the window, staring toward the distance and thinking. And then an idea formed in my mind. The Book of Lost Spells. That's a possibility. After all, a line at the beginning of the book says that, '*It goes wherever most nee•e•*' and I definitely need its help now. The great thing was that as soon as I thought about it, the book moved from its hiding place, glided slowly across the room, and landed on my desk.

I searched and searched for a spell that would make someone be compelled to tell the truth but what I found didn't make sense. It wasn't really a spell at all. No candles, no magical words to say—it was simply a poem called, *Truth-Seeker*.

To make a liar speak what is true,
You must show them the real you.
The lie they have spoken, the truth will bar,
Once the liar sees who you really are,
Whatever they fear, your power will be,
Use that power, it is your key.

The poem has an ancient asterisk next to the word *key* that I take very seriously. No messing up this time as I did when we went into the shadows of the past. I want to read the whole thing. I flip to the back of the book, locate the page number and asterisk, and find that the best time to confront a liar is the short span of time before the full moon rises to its zenith on its first night. Hell's Bells! Just before a full moon! That's dangerous because if I want Hunter to come with me, he'll be changing into his wolf self. Can I risk that? Maybe it's a risk that I may have to take.

I read the poem over again. *You must show them the real you.* Now what does that mean? I'm Lilith Angel, high school senior, graduating soon, getting ready for college, and hopefully, opening a criminology agency. Add to that, a girl who wants to pass Advanced Calculus with at least a B-.

But, wait a second, in reality that's only *part* of who I am. The real me, the one only a few see, and know, is different. I'm Lilith Angel, the half-witch who has wings she can call up in a heartbeat and can fly up into the sky. That's it! That's what the poem means. The super-superstitious C. Thomas Ringwood has to see me as who I really am—an otherworldly creature.

So now I sit on the highest branch of this tree in my parents' garden and think about what I have to do first. Tomorrow morning right after classes are over, I'm going to talk with Hunter and together we're going to work on a precise plan to get C. Thomas to admit to the murder of his father by playing on his worst fears—his superstition. His fear is my power and Hunter's power as well.

Right now, though, I need to fly. Hunter is home with Gideon, my parents are out at least until dawn, and Lively is snuggled down in the soft pillows of the window seat. I'm alone.

Leaping from the topmost branch, I spread my wings out and catch a strong breeze that is wafting over from the ocean. Breathing in a smell of salt water, I half-circle the garden and soar out toward the forest. My wings are powerful and carry me away smoothly and easily. Tonight is mine.

I force myself to concentrate on the final exam notes I'm taking in Advanced Calculus. On the way to school I was bursting to tell Hunter what I want to do but there wasn't enough time for us to discuss anything in depth. I figured I would wait until after school when we're alone at Midnight Ink.

In class, the notes I've diligently copied down are long and complex but I am finally feeling a bit more confident about actually passing the course. Mr. Mendelsohn tells us that after we're done copying, we can relax for the last fifteen minutes of class. "I realize that for you soon-to-be graduates, senioritis has set in," he says. We all laugh. It's been a long year for him too. He's suffering from his own form of senioritis called end-of-year-teacher-burn-out.

Some kids talk quietly, some take out their phones, and others, like me who are terrified of not passing the final exam, study the notes we took.

"Not a gun, a bow and arrow."

"Aren't those illegal? It's considered hunting so it's still against the law, right?"

"I never knew there were wolves in Summer Valley. This has to be a rogue wolf, then. Maybe rabid. Don't the authorities usually kill rabid animals?"

"Well, we *tried* to go to the forest and find the wolf but the cops are keeping people from going anywhere near there and also any places near the Ringwood property."

"They can't keep everybody out. There has to be a way in to get that wolf. I mean, ten thousand dollars! That's a helluva reward."

Students near me are talking about what's been going on ever since C. Thomas posted that damned reward for the capture of a large grey wolf alive or dead. It's bad. The local police have warned those idiots who have gone searching for a wolf, that anyone in possession of any type of weapon or anyone who sets traps, will be arrested. They've issued warnings to C. Thomas, too. There is absolutely no hunting or trapping allowed in Summer Valley.

The tiny kernel of an idea that the Book of Lost Spells has planted in my brain is becoming a full-blown plan.

FORTY-THREE

It will be dangerous for Hunter to show his true self to C. Thomas, but, as much as I hate it, it's risk we may have to take. I'm in the turret room with Hunter and the Book of Lost Spells. "This is all it says, Hunter. The problem is two-fold. First we have to confront C. Thomas in the hours just before the full moon and, secondly, we have to show him our real selves. That means you have got to make the change to your wolf self and let him see you."

"I can do that. Right before the full moon rises to its zenith. I can actually make the change even earlier before nightfall if I concentrate hard enough."

"I know, you've told me that but, don't you see? It's dangerous for you. The law says no hunting is allowed in Summer Valley but we'll be on the Ringwood property. You already know he has traps and probably a gun."

"Look, we've got a couple of weeks to prepare and plan our strategy. This is something I want and need to do." He grabs my hand. "You know that, right? This is personal."

I nod my head. I completely understand what he means. "All right, then I'm going to ask my parents to help us. We may need some protection and believe me that is something they can definitely give us."

"Okay. Let's talk to them as soon as they get here. We probably do need all the help we can get." He looks at me. "But, Lilith, I don't want you worrying about me. I'll be careful."

"You better be." I say firmly.

The male and the female arrive around six o'clock. Midnight Ink is quiet and empty. We sit down at a reading table, too far from the door to be seen but close enough to be able to hear the chimes if a customer enters. I tell them our plan and how we hope to get C. Thomas to confess to a fifteen-year-old murder.

"It'll have its share of danger, especially when Hunter makes the change to werewolf," I say suddenly more concerned than ever now that I've said it out loud to my parents.

Hunter looks at me. "It has to be done. It's the only way, Lilith." He turns to my parents, "We both know that, Mr. and Mrs. Angel."

An inscrutable look passes between the male and female. Vamps are hard to read. They can block any creature from reading their thoughts but it's more than that. Vampires can create a kind of enchantment, a glamour, that hides, or completely changes what you believe they are thinking. I can tell nothing from their passed looks except that they know what's at stake and the danger of what we're planning to do.

After a few minutes of silence, my mom touches my shoulder. "Darling, we'll help you. We can protect you and Hunter so that you have no distractions while confronting C. Thomas Ringwood."

"First, we'll deal with the stable hands," says my dad, his eyes glistening. "Then we'll patrol the area nearest the Ringwood stables. We won't hesitate to stop anyone who dares comes near either of you."

As scary as it may sound to have vampires as guards who will stop anyone who dares come near, I know what they will do. They won't kill anyone the way vampire myths say they will. They'll just take a small sip of their victims' blood, which will make the victims pass out into a deep sleep for a couple of hours.

It's fourteen days until the next full moon "The full moon will be completely at its zenith at 9:44 PM," says Hunter, checking his phone. "That means that I should start to make the change around 9:00 or so. I'll do it in the forest."

"Mr. Paget's winged messengers told him that C. Thomas usually sits on his patio outside around 10:00. I'll be up in one of the highest trees on the border of the Ringwood property. Hunter will howl to get his attention and then I'll swoop down and confront him. I'll video his confession on my phone."

The male and the female tell me that they think I should practice my flying as much as possible. "Practice quick flights upward and also your landing skills. Fly near the forest so you're familiar with the area."

That surprises me but also makes me feel good. They are so aware that I'm almost eighteen and really do need to stretch my wings, pun intended!

The night wind is soft and gently ripples through my feathery wings as I take off toward the forest. It's clear with absolutely no sign of rain and I marvel at how well I am managing my flight. Landings seem to be easier as I try several of them on various surfaces. Rocky ground, grassy knolls, the rooftop of an empty summer cottage, and finally the tops of the highest trees in the forest. No problem with landing.

I'm even able to take-off by paying attention to wind uplifts and temperature changes. Warmer air makes rising easier as the hotter temps rise upward. Cooler temperatures need more of a wing push, but I am learning how to fly upward with the different temperatures. My night vision is getting better as well—my eyesight is easily adjusting to the darkness, just as Professor A. J. Reed said it would. Eyes like a hawk, she had said.

I fly with a confidence I've never had in anything I've ever done. I feel powerful as I soar and practice my landings and take-offs. My beautiful, black wings propel me with grace and ease. I feel happy and peaceful. Why did I ever not want these powers?!

As I fly back toward home a sound comes to me on the night air. The sound is from far away, muted by distance. It tugs at my heart. It sounds like a long, mournful howl.

FORTY-FOUR

In the days leading up to the full moon, I practice flying every night. During the day, I go to classes then practice for the graduation ceremony at school. It's weird living this dual life. Now I understand how Hunter feels—for most of the month he's your typical, easy-going teenage boy, but for those precious few nights of the full moon, he's a werewolf running eagerly and happily until daylight.

Our English teacher, Mrs. Holder who is in charge of graduation, asks me to please pay attention to what we're doing. "You're lost in your own thoughts again, Lilith Angel. What is the world can be more important to you than this graduation practice?"

Mrs. Holder, if you only knew! But I shake my head, mutter, "Sorry", and try hard to pay attention to the sounds of *Pomp and Circumstance* being played slightly off-key by the band as we practice marching in-line to our assigned seats in the bleachers. Hunter catches my eye as we climb the bleachers in sets of twelve students to a row. He smiles at me and gives me a thumb's up, letting me know he is thinking the same thoughts as I am.

Truthfully I should be okay with our plans, especially knowing that two vampires will be watching our backs to make sure no crazy person looking to grab a reward will get through to us. Vamps can be lightning fast when they sense danger or enemies. That's how they survived for thousands of years. My parents, as human-seeming as they appear, are still vampires with all the fine-honed skills and super-senses of their kind.

"Lilith! Your mind's wandering again. Be careful, please!" yells a frazzled Mrs. Holder.

"Okay, yes, sorry," I say, and then apologize to the girl in front of me for having stepped on her ankle. Amsterdam, Rotterdam, damn, damn, damn!

An ascending full moon plays peek-a-boo with the few clouds that move slowly across the night sky. Tonight I watch, from the top of a tree as Hunter Hollis Hopper makes the incredible change from human to werewolf and it is fascinating and thrilling to see my easy-going, makes-me-laugh boyfriend become a fearsome creature. His fur bristles with excitement as he sends a quiet howl upward toward me. He is beautiful. My own personal werewolf to love!

I send a silent plea to the universe that all goes well for us tonight. I have my phone set to video record C. Thomas telling the truth. This is our only chance. I know that the male and female, are nearby and have taken care of the stable hands a short while ago. It's quiet. It'll be just Hunter, me, C. Thomas—and my phone.

The forest edge runs along the Ringwood property line. I wait in one of the tallest trees for any sighting of C. Thomas. The muffled rustlings of the nighttime forest inhabitants are the only sounds I hear.

Sunk low to the ground in a crouch so he is less visible, Hunter walks slowly along the edge of the Ringwood property. He stays downwind and away from the stables to avoid detection by the sleeping horses there. So far so good. The night is still as the clouds part to reveal a crystal clear full moon. Close by I hear Hunter's full-moon howl, loud, impressive and strong. It's 10:00. Surely that howl must be heard by C. Thomas.

Eagerly I look toward the patio to see his startled expression, but he's not there. Where is he? I turn and watch Hunter almost belly-crawl toward the area that is directly facing the Ringwood patio. Still no sign of C. Thomas. I look back at Hunter, who for some strange reason, seems to be stuck on the grass. I watch him try lifting his paws but he can't seem to move forward. He's caught on something hidden in the lush grass. I'm about to fly down from the tree to help him when I hear the loud click of metal on metal, the sound a rifle makes when it is cocked and ready to shoot.

"Well, well, now. Look what I've found. Finally caught you, dream-haunter," says a sneering C. Thomas, pointing a rifle directly at Hunter who's struggling in what I now see is green wire mesh. "For years you've caused me fearful nightmares. You saw too much, way too much and that has haunted me for years! This time, you will not get away. Your evil luck has run out." He laughs, "Can't move, huh, Wolf from Hell? Tonight I will finally put an end to you."

As he raises the rifle to his shoulder and aims at Hunter's head, I don't hesitate. I swoop down, my legs bent at the knees. As I get closer to C. Thomas Ringwood, I shove both legs straight out, slamming my feet hard into his chest. He falls down hard on the ground, the rifle falling from his hands. Stunned he looks at me as I spiral upward. "What the hell are *you*?!"

"The truth-seeker!" I say loudly, remembering the title of the poem.

I spread my wings, allowing them to catch an updraft that has me float almost motionless just above C. Thomas who looks at me with fear and awe. I rise higher with the excitement of the moment, pivot quickly then come down lightly on the ground next to him. He scrambles backward away from me as I once again spread my wings and rise slowly upward. When I land again, I will make him tell me the truth about what happened fifteen years ago.

I'm exhilarated by my power but then I look down at Hunter—I have to help free him. This brief glance almost costs me my life because I take my eyes off of C. Thomas. In my one distracted moment, C. Thomas scrambles over to the rifle, grabs it, and aims at me. Before I can react, the bullet flies and hits my left wing tearing a hole through the glossy black feathers. An electric current runs through my body. Stunned, I plummet to earth. Hunter howls as I hit the ground.

C. Thomas stands a distance from me, the rifle in his hands. "I don't know what you are, but you must be from Hell." He raises the gun and points at my heart. "First you, then the wolf. I will finally be free of all that haunts me."

I look at Hunter. I want him to be the last creature I see. Tears streak my face as I hear Hunter whimper sadly. Then—from out of nowhere comes a howling so fierce and powerful that it stops C. Thomas from pulling the trigger. At the edge of the Ringwood property, I see a sight that has me catch my breath. Much larger than Hunter, awesome and menacing stands the magnificent Ghost Wolf, his white fur glistening with an unearthly glow that surrounds him. Gideon in all his majestic glory has changed into his wolf form and the sight is mesmerizing. He is fearsome as he lowers his head, dangerous growls rumbling from his open mouth. With his sharp white teeth bared and his mouth salivating, he looks directly at C. Thomas Ringwood.

My mind is in a whirl. Gideon! How did he know to come here?

Painfully I slowly edge over to where Hunter is trapped in the wire mesh. At least while C. Thomas is fully focused on Gideon, I can try to help Hunter get free.

"You!" shouts a terrified C. Thomas, the rifle now turned toward Gideon. "I was warned by those voodoo women that you would come! 'Fear the Ghost Wolf of Vengeance with fur that glows blindingly-hot. He comes to punish a wrong.' They were right! You're here to take revenge for what that grey wolf saw—stay away from me! Stay away!"

As he snarls viciously at C. Thomas, Gideon literally glows brighter. Talk about otherworldly! The glow of his fur is blinding—it is like looking directly into the sun on a bright, summer day. C. Thomas can't see to shoot. I work feverishly to free Hunter, my fingers cut and bleeding from the wire mesh. Hunter helps me work on the mesh, biting at it. He's almost free. "Can you take care of the rest?" I whisper. His eyes stare into mine and I know that's a yes.

I have to get the rifle away from C. Thomas. Even though the glaring light is making him unable to see well enough to get a good aim, the danger of the rifle going off and accidentally hitting Gideon is too great. Painfully I stand up and concentrate on rising upward. My left wing burns with pain but I am able to bring both wings in a downward motion that propels me up, up, high above C. Thomas. Ignoring the pain as much as I can, I know that I have only one chance to get that rifle out of his hands.

Taking a deep breath, I fly downward toward C. Thomas, aiming my legs at the rifle. I hit it square on and kick it far from his hands. It lands with a thump a distance away in the forest. My right wing bangs into C. Thomas stunning him. My landing is a bit wobbly due to my injured wing but I stand on one side of him with Gideon on his other side. When Hunter, who has successfully freed himself, runs over, the three of us surround C. Thomas making it impossible for him to get away. What a strange sight we must present! A human with wings and two snarling

274

werewolves. We stand there for a long time, no one moving.

Finally, Hunter and Gideon sit back, their heads erect, their long, sharp canines showing. They cast an unwavering gaze on C. Thomas Ringwood. There is something about a wolf's eyes that is hypnotic. Their stare is intense. Perhaps this is because they're predators who judge their potential prey or enemy with their eyes. Whatever it is, C. Thomas seems to be held tightly by their gaze, compelled to speak. I take my phone out of my pocket and aim it at C. Thomas.

"I knew this day would come. I have been warned by those who can see into the future that the Ghost Wolf would come to seek revenge on me. If I'd only been able to kill that damned grey wolf, none of this would be happening. She saw everything!"

I clear my throat and say, "Yes, she saw it all. Why did you do it?" My hope is that now that he thinks we know what he did, his answer to my question will seal the truth of what happened that night.

"My father was a wimp, a weak man. He deserved to die. Always being more concerned about that wolf than his own son. He loved that damned wolf, brought out water when we had a drought just so she wouldn't be thirsty. I've even seen him pet her. Imagine! Petting a wolf. That damned wolf loved him too."

"Why do you fear and hate wolves? Not one wolf has ever harmed your horses. Not one wolf ever harmed *any* creatures or you. Tell me why." I am angry and in a lot of pain. The pain makes me sound threatening.

C. Thomas looks at me as if I am crazy for asking that question. Then he answers me as if I should know why he hated them. "Why, because of the legend about the Ghost Wolf."

"That's just a legend."

C. Thomas shakes his head. "No, no, you don't understand. That grey wolf. She knew what was in my heart, she knew I planned to kill my father. Always, always she stared at me. I was terrified of her! After she saw me kill my father, she summoned the Ghost Wolf.

"I sought out voodoo women. They told me that the story of the Ghost Wolf was true and they said that the Ghost Wolf was patient. It would wait for the right time to get me, to bring me to the pit of Hell for my father's murder. I must always be on guard. I begged for their protection but they were afraid that if they helped me they would anger their own powerful spirits." He begins to sob. "I knew that one day he'd come for me." Staring directly at me he yells, "And you, what are you but an Avenging Angel from Hell in league with the Ghost Wolf." He begins to sob.

Well, my last name is Angel but I'm hardly from Hell. "But why did you kill your father?" I ask. My wing is throbbing and I wince with pain. Who knew that these wings, which only materialize when I want them, could be so much a part of my physical body?

"I needed money for my gambling debts—I had so many of them. He'd bailed me out before but he wouldn't give me any more money. I asked him to sell some land to help me out and he refused. Said the land was for the wolves to run free. Told me that I was a disappointment to him. He was going to change his will and leave all the land surrounding the ranch to a conservation group, another bunch of animal lovers like him. He would never sell this land to help me. I was desperate for money."

"So you killed him to get it?"

"It was the only way I could get this damned land! That night, when I saw that wolf with my father, I had an idea. After I shot her and she ran, I forced crushed Oleander down my father's throat to immobilize him. The idea of a wolf attack seemed to be a perfect way out. I saw those slight scratches she made and I used my knife to make them look like deep, deadly wounds from a wolf attack.

"But that wolf came back—two bullets shot into her and still she came back and saw what I did. I was afraid of her. But she disappeared again and when my hands and I couldn't find her, I thought she had died from her wounds.

"Everyone believed the old man had been killed by a rogue wolf. No questions asked. There were no wolves around here after that until—last month. I saw the same wolf, the same wolf!" He points to Hunter. "Fifteen years later, it came back to get me." He looks dazed. "What do you want from me?"

"Only the truth about what happened fifteen years ago," I say feeling dizzy. "And you have given us that."

"The truth. I gave you the truth."

A deep, powerful howl shatters the night followed by another howl, less deep but just as powerful. Gideon and Hunter, heads thrown back and howling at the moon. Distant howls carried on the night wind seem to respond to their howling. Is it the Lost Pack from far away in Shasta County? The echoing howls of werewolves from the past that still faintly linger in the forest? Hunter and his father continue saluting the full moon. The sounds are deafening.

C. Thomas puts his hands over his ears and screams "No no! Don't bring me to the pit of Hell! Please! I'll go and confess to the murder. I will, I promise! If I confess to all that I've done, you have to leave me alone, don't you?! You have to do that!" The howling continues and C. Thomas, looking at me in panic, faints dead away.

My wing is throbbing painfully and I call out to my vamp parents. In a heartbeat they are there beside me calmly taking in the scene before them. Gideon and Hunter acknowledge the male and female standing beside us. They know I will not be alone and with a final howl, father and son turn toward the forest. I watch them begin to run side by side, two magnificent werewolves racing under the power of the full moon. I still wonder how Gideon suddenly appeared here. How did he know what we were going to do tonight? But—I'm too tired to think further about that.

"They're running together for the first time," says the female as she gently examines my wing. "They will run together for many years to come."

My parents bite their tongues and dribble blood on my injured wing. In minutes the pain is gone and I am healed. They do the same for my cut hands. The powerful enzyme in a vampire's blood is incredibly healing.

I fly upward to test my wing, making lazy circles around the tallest trees, then land gently back down near my parents. C. Thomas is conscious, sitting up with his back resting on an old tree, still too stunned to move freely. His video confession is in my pocket and I show it to my parents.

"Nice work, Lilith of the Angels. That's enough to have him charged with murder." My dad smiles at me.

"That and the M.E.'s note. Now we just have to give all this to the police and have C. Thomas arrested."

"I think that's about to happen very soon," says my mom pointing toward the Ringwood driveway. I see flashing lights and hear the sound of police car sirens coming down the road. "We alerted Rudy. He already made the call. Make your wings disappear for now, darling. You're about to tell the police about your very first case."

FORTY-FIVE

e told them everything. Shakily standing on his front lawn, where the cops took him after finding him at the edge of his property near the forest, C. Thomas told the truth to the police officers about the night his father was murdered. After his detailed confession, he said some strange things about a wolf who saw the murder and how he *knew* that the Ghost Wolf was coming to 'get' him and bring him to the pit of Hell. The cops put that monologue down to a guilty conscience that almost drove C. Thomas mad.

His years of the guilt weighing on his mind, said one officer, forced him to finally confess to murdering his father. "We see it all the time. Guilt is a great factor in getting someone to tell the truth." I wanted to add that seeing werewolves and an alleged flying Avenging Angel from Hell will pretty much have the same effect, but I kept silent. I stood next to the police, my wings neatly disappeared, while C. Thomas babbled his way through his confession. Afterward, I gave them my cell phone with the same confession on it.

A detective took me aside, faced me squarely, and asked how, and more importantly *why*, I was involved in the case. I told a good lie and said it all started as an idea for an end -of-the-year school project for my Criminal Justice class. "There were rumors about this murder and facts that didn't add up to a wolf attack," I said referencing the picture in the old online newspaper article and my trip to the M.E.'s office. "I came here to interview him and ask him what he knew about it. He just became very agitated and started babbling."

"In the middle of the night? You came here alone in the middle of the night?" he asks skeptically. "Not the best idea now, is it? All alone with someone you believe committed a murder!"

"Actually, um, I—" Hell's Bells!

"We came here together, detective." I turn to see a very serious-looking Hunter, now changed back into his human form, walk over to us and hold out his hand to the detective. He overheard us. I notice that there's dried blood on his lip from when he bit the wire mesh netting in an effort to free himself. "We're working on the project idea together, sir. Hoping to impress our teacher with the effort. We came out here earlier, didn't expect to be here this long. I guess Mr. C. Thomas Ringwood just kept talking and the hour got late and well, that's why we're still here."

"Boy, you two must *really* be interested in Criminal Justice. That's a lot of work to do just for a school project," says the detective sarcastically. I smile and say that's what we want to study in college next year.

"Uh-huh. You call this in, son?"

"No, a friend of ours did."

"You should have his name and number from the dispatcher," I say quickly.

The detective looks at his notes and shakes his head. "Yeah, okay. Guess you were on the phone with this guy and he got concerned. Damn good thing too. This C. Thomas Ringwood doesn't seem too sane and sensible right now. Okay, you kids better get home. I'm assuming you have school tomorrow but when you get out, come on down to the police station and we'll take your official statements.

"There's no school tomorrow. Teachers' workshops," I say.

"Lucky you. So you'll come down in the morning. It won't take more than a half hour. Uh, you two need a ride?"

"No, sir. We have transportation. Our parents are coming to get us."

We watch as they handcuff C. Thomas and put him in a police car, then we say good-night and walk toward the road where my parents and Hunter's father are waiting. Though the police seem baffled by all that's occurred here tonight in regards to a fifteen-year-old murder all had assumed was a random wolf attack, they are satisfied that C. Thomas Ringwood's story is true. Hunter and I wave as the police cars and the unmarked detective's car drive past. What an unbelievable night!

Walking through the forest at night under a full moon is a magical treat and the adrenaline rush from everything that's happened makes me more alert to all the beauty of the night. I can understand why my parents are creatures of the night.

We're going to Hunter's house to let my parents refresh themselves. Too many small sips from the ranch hands and any would-be wolf hunters, have made the male and female sluggish. It's the same physical sensation humans get after eating a huge holiday dinner. Once they rest a bit they'll be fine.

I guess Hunter and I will find out soon enough how Gideon knew what we were doing and how he came at just the right moment. How he knew where we were, and what we were going to do doesn't matter. His appearance just might have saved us both.

Inside the house, my parents follow Gideon into the living room where they lie back in comfortable chairs. Hunter brings me a bottle of iced tea and one for himself. Gideon pours himself some wine. There's no talking for a while—we're all lost in our own thoughts. Then, because I'm immensely curious about it, I just have to ask Gideon, "How did you know what we were going to do tonight?"

"A human parent usually has an inkling their child is up to something that might put him or her in danger. They sense something but they don't really know what it is. But, werewolves have a heightened sense of impending danger for themselves and especially for their children. It's our highly developed wolf sense. I just *knew*." He sits back and sighs. "And, I've been stalking C. Thomas for years after what happened fifteen years ago."

"You mean after he—killed my mother." Hunter sits forward.

Gideon looks at his son and shakes his head. "Your mother, Galina, is not dead. She's very much alive."

"She's alive?! But, Dad, you told me that she was—" He can't finish the sentence.

Gideon pats his son's arm. "Tomorrow. Tomorrow, late afternoon, I will take you," he looks at each of us in turn, "*all* of you, to see her. But not tonight. It is much better to go in the late afternoon. Her mind is clearer then and she likes to see me at dusk." Hunter begins to say something more but Gideon stops him. "No more tonight, Hunter. I'm tired, so tired. This has been a strain for all of us. Tomorrow you will see for yourself and understand why I *had* to make you believe that your mother was not alive. Why I had to lie and say I didn't know the poor she-werewolf who was shot. You'll understand it all."

My parents, refreshed by a short rest discreetly tell me that we should go home now. They feel energized enough to leave and, anyway, they want me to exercise my wing by flying home.

"We'll be around you, darling, no worries. There's a lovely breeze tonight. It will carry us easily toward home. You and Hunter go outside and get some air. We'll be right there."

While the male and the female talk with Gideon, Hunter walks me outside. Once there he holds me close, burying his head in the space between my shoulder and neck. He's just been given a total shock hearing the news that his mother is still alive. Now he has to wait until tomorrow afternoon to see her. It's hard for him and my heart aches for his pain.

"I'm so sorry, Hunter, I don't know what to say."

Finally, he pulls back from me and says, "I'm okay, Lilith, I mean, I'll *be* okay. This is a lot to think about. I love my dad but, why would he keep the fact that my mother is alive from me all these years? What could be so bad about her that he's kept this a secret?"

"He said you'd see for yourself why he kept this a secret. We just have to wait until tomorrow. So, listen, we'll go to the police station first thing in the morning, hang around Midnight Ink until the afternoon, and then we'll go see your mom. Okay? I'll pick you up around 9:00?"

He nods. "Yeah, sure, okay. 9:00 is fine."

"Are you running again tonight?"

He shakes his head no. "I feel wiped out by everything. Tomorrow I'll run, but not tonight. Besides, I think this is the perfect time to tell my dad about our journey to the past. I think he'll understand. It's the right thing to do. And, hey, Lilith, listen. I just," he holds my shoulders and looks in my eyes, "I want you to know that, no matter what happens, I'm just so glad that I have you to go through all this with me. You really are a special person. Thank you for being here for me."

I want to cry at what he says. As it is, the emotion makes me rise three feet in the air and Hunter wraps his arms around my waist to keep me grounded. As he pulls me back to earth, the front door opens and I hear the male say, "Lilith of the Angels, you will never be earthbound." That makes all of us—my parents, Gideon, Hunter, and me, laugh —and that's a good thing.

I call upon my wings which appear immediately. The female carefully inspects my healed wing, running a gentle hand through the feathers and tells me that all is good. No damage. Sensing an updraft, I spread my wings and turn into the breeze rising smoothly upward. The male and female zoom straight up and hover near me. With a good-bye wave to Hunter and Gideon, we turn toward home, my parents riding the air currents and me floating gently on the breeze.

FORTY-SIX

My dad, slathered with sunscreen and wearing very dark sunglasses came with us to the police station. C. Thomas Ringwood is being arraigned today, charged with the murder of his father fifteen years ago. He willingly confessed everything that he did, including lying to authorities that his father was killed in a wolf attack. He did not mention anything about wolves or the pit of Hell this time, only said that now he was free. The detective who arrested him took that to mean that he was free from a guilty conscience which probably had tormented him all these years.

After having given our statements and a copy of the M.E.'s personal note to the police, I drive us all back to Midnight Ink where my mom is waiting. Gideon has asked us to come to his house around 4:00 PM. It's been agreed that we'll all go together. Until then, my parents have the usual mysterious 'important things' that they have to take care of, and I ask Hunter to come upstairs to our turret office, and help create a file for our first case, The Ringwood Murder.

It's not even noon yet so we have plenty of time. I know Hunter is bursting with anticipation at finally being able to see his mom and I want to make sure that I can keep his mind occupied for at least a short time. If I can get him to concentrate on putting the file together with all the evidence including the police report, it may work.

My idea works for a while, although every so often, I see Hunter stare out the window at nothing in particular, with a sad look on his face. Lively, now a pure black cat with white paws, sits on Hunter's lap and rubs his head against his shoulder. He knows how to comfort a fellow creature. Hunter gently pets Lively's soft fur and I can see him begin to relax.

A glance at the clock shows we've been working on this file for almost two and a half hours. Good. Only a short time to go. I take out my phone and order sandwiches from the local pizza place. Time to feed the wolf and the angel.

"After Galina was shot, she tried to change back to her human form but— she was too wounded to make the change. Doing that, as you well know, Hunter, requires mental and physical strength. Because of the injuries to her body and the disorientation caused by the fog, she became stuck in her wolf self."

We're standing outside Gideon's car, far from Hunter's house. All of us are looking at a large clearing sheltered within thick areas of trees. No one would know this clearing is here. It would be visible only from the air. I should know—I saw it on my first secret solo flight weeks ago. Weeks ago, when I heard the mournful howl borne on the air. It had come from here.

Inside the clearing is the same large house and beautiful open areas surrounded by tall fences that I remember seeing. At the very edge of the property, hidden by trees, is the small wooden building Hunter and I saw Gideon hide an injured Galina, when both were in their wolf forms that fateful night fifteen years ago.

We walk toward the gated property, Hunter holding my hand as if his very life depends on it. Pointing to the small building, Gideon says, "I took her here, fifteen years ago. There was only that small wooden house here then. She stayed in that small house and I fenced this entire area in for her. I wanted her to have the freedom to run here but still feel protected. This newer house was built later on. I visit her every day while Hunter is at school and in the evenings when Hunter has gone out. I bring my work here so she can sit with me and feel comforted by my presence. My Galina, my beautiful Galina.

"There are times that she's confused, sometimes snarling and at other times, emitting sad whimpers," he says. "I couldn't let you see your mother in this state, Hunter. She would not want you to see her like this either. As much as it pained me to be untruthful when you asked me, I had to say that I didn't know the werewolf who was wounded." His eyes turn dark and sad. "And I was fearful that if you knew who had shot her, you'd confront him and I feared that you might be shot as well. All Galina and I ever wanted for you was that you grow up happy and healthy. It pains me that you saw your mother so terribly wounded when you went into the past."

There's a deep silence then. Hunter is trying to understand all this and make some type of sense of it all. The silence is broken when I say, "Mr. Hollis-Hopper? When Hunter and I were shadows in the past, we felt that Ringwood, Sr. and Galina knew and trusted each other."

"Galina loved that gentle old man," says Gideon leading the way to the high gates. "He was kind to her and she never forgot that. She didn't care if he was a human, to her he was another creature of the forest. I always thought that Mr. Ringwood, Sr. knew or deeply suspected that Galina was a werewolf. But, he didn't care. He loved all the creatures. Yes, they trusted each other and cared deeply for each other." He sighs. "As injured as she was that night, she went back to try to protect him. I think she suspected that his son might harm him."

So that inky blur we saw the night of the murder *was* an injured Galina coming back to protect a man who was kind to her. A human friend she loved. How it must have hurt her to know that she was too late.

Gideon opens the gates and goes inside, then beckons us to come in and wait.

"Galina!" Gideon calls.

From the side of the house we see her come running. She is a beautiful, large grey she-werewolf. Hunter's resemblance to her is remarkable. She stops when she sees us and her gaze is one of caution. Her eyes are a strange mix of human and wolf, almost as if she is still trying to change back to human form. She sniffs the air, her head turning first to Gideon and then to us. Then emitting a low, warning growl, Galina walks in a slow crouch toward my parents and me. I step back but the male and the female seem unafraid.

"Mom?" I say as I see her approach Galina, her delicate pale hand extended, fingers downward so that the she-werewolf gets her scent. "Maybe you should step back. I mean," I cast an apologetic look at Hunter and Gideon, "she *might* hurt you."

"You won't hurt me, will you Galina?" My mother advances slowly and calmly, letting Galina sniff the air around her fingertips. "You know what I am, Galina, you can sense it. You and I, we're alike in so many ways. You know that I'm an otherworldly being, the same as you. Our kind has lived peacefully side by side for centuries with honor and respect for each other."

My heart is pounding in my ears so loudly that I'm sure everyone can hear it. My dad stands near her as my mother kneels down. Galina comes closer to her. I know my parents are vampires but Galina is bigger, more powerful—a true werewolf of immense strength. In any physical fight between vampire and werewolf, though the vamps have their own super-strength, I truly believe that the werewolf could tear the vamps apart very easily.

But I underestimate the fearlessness of my mother. She allows Galina to get close to her face, and stares deeply into her eyes. My dad tenses, but my mom doesn't flinch. Then, in an unbelievably gentle manner, Galina rubs her head against my mother's blond hair. My mom cups Galina's head in her hands and kisses her fur. It is an incredibly beautiful sight to see.

My dad approaches Galina and speaks softly to her. "We've met you and Gideon many years ago and were honored to be accepted by you, Galina."

She cocks her head to the side, a hesitant acknowledgement of having met them in the distant past. Then she looks at Gideon who is standing next to Hunter. Hunter's eyes are wide with awe. "Galina, my beautiful one." Gideon's voice is husky with emotion. "Come see our son. It is time that you knew each other again." Galina turns and walks slowly over to Gideon and Hunter. My eyes mist over with tears. The healing of mother and son is about to begin.

We left Galina just as the sun was setting and the second night of the full moon had begun, leaving Gideon and Hunter behind to stay with her for the night. Hunter promised me he'd text me later. I have a feeling that Hunter and Gideon will be doing some type of a full-moon run in the large enclosure surrounding the house. Perhaps it will give some joy to Galina to see her son run with Gideon. I hope she joins them, I really do.

Gideon was very open and forthright about everything. "No more secrets or lies," he told Hunter. "Going forward I will honestly answer any questions you have. I expect the same from you."

He told us how, after he had safely settled Galina here, he had helped the Lost Pack find a new home in Shasta County. It wasn't safe anymore to have a group of werewolves stay in this area. How he would run with them when Hunter thought he was away on a business trip. He admitted that those runs were bitter-sweet. The thrill of running under a full moon with his pack was tinged with sadness that Galina wasn't with him.

"I let Hunter run in the forest, but there were very strict rules about where he could run. I needed him to be safe. And Hunter, I followed you, I tracked you without your knowledge. I couldn't risk anything happening to you. The night C. Thomas almost caught you, I was crazy with worry."

"I'm so sorry, Dad. That was a stupid move on my part."

"A young werewolf's foolish mistake. We all do foolish things when we're young, Gideon," says my dad. Gideon nods.

I can sense the power of the moon's effect starting on Hunter and Gideon. My dad senses it too. We need to leave. I look around for my mother. "Mom? We're going to leave now."

I walk around the house and see her by an area of soft grass, a distance away. She is sitting on the ground with her arms around Galina's neck, holding her close. There's a soft whimper from Galina and I hear my mom say, "I will be back, Galina and I promise we will find a way to help you." She rests her face next to Galina's head for a few moments then gets up and comes to where I'm standing. "I'm ready, darling."

We say our good-byes and test the air for updrafts and breezes. The male and female rise swiftly into the night sky while I spread my wings and drift upward with a warm breeze. Then the three of us begin the flight home, the night air kissing our faces with a soft warmth. I float lazily and even do a few somersaults in the air, but mostly I just drift with outspread wings.

A short distance away we hear a beautiful sound—the strong and powerful howl of a werewolf, followed by the howl of another, and then, hesitantly, a third howl. There is no sadness in any of the howls.

FORTY-SEVEN

A week has gone by since I met Galina. The days of the full moon are over for this month. I haven't seen a lot of Hunter. He has been leaving right from school every day this week to see his mother. He's happy and I'm happy for him. Next week is graduation. Hunter and I agree that it's exciting and scary at the same time, but we're both looking forward to this new period in our lives.

Today he surprises me by showing up at Midnight Ink, coming upstairs to the turret room where Lively, whose math skills amaze me, was looking over my Advanced Calculus exam. I passed it with an eighty-eight bringing my average for the year to a solid ninety! To celebrate, Hunter has brought Italian subs for him and me, as well as sliced chicken for Lively. He spreads everything out on the desk so that we can eat together and talk. We have a lot to talk about.

I tell him that my parents told Mr. Paget that Galina is indeed alive. "He was so happy that she had survived the gunshot wounds. Mr. Paget is hopeful that there is something in the magical books here at Midnight Ink, and especially in my Book of Lost Spells, that can help Galina. He promised that he will look through his vast collection of books on otherworldly healing to see if he can find a way to help her, too."

"How are your mom and dad, Lilith? I miss seeing them every day."

"They miss you too. My mom said that she's going to ask Gideon when she and my dad can visit Galina again."

"That's great. Your mom and mine seem to have a special connection. Tell your parents that I'll stop by real soon. So—everything's okay here, then?"

He gives me that boyish look I love. He's been through enough with his own parents and all. I don't want him to worry about me. So I don't tell him that my parents are really distracted about something, coming home way past sunrise every day, and that I'm more than a little concerned about them.

I don't tell him that yesterday my mom told me that if I smelled anything strange in the air, I was to call her and my dad immediately. I know she means the smell of rotting roses. I'm very aware of that smell. I know that it means danger is present. I never told Hunter about the smell of rotting roses or the unexpected feeling of deathly fear that comes with it. He doesn't need to know about that either right now. He's adjusting to a new life that includes his mom and that's all he needs to have on his mind at the moment. I smile and say that my parents and I are all fine. You know, the good kind of lie you tell to people so they don't worry.

Hunter then tells me that he and Gideon are moving from their small house on the edge of the forest to the large house where Galina lives. "She can't come to our old home. The open area will only frighten her. She needs an enclosed space for running. It's better if we go live there. We'll keep the old house for when she, you know, for when she—"

"Can make the change." I finish for him and he shakes his head yes.

"You know those memories I told you about? They had to do with my mother. That muted memory I had of a grey werewolf running free. And the memory of some kind of terror. I didn't know what it was, but now I know my mind was actually accessing Galina's memories. Her freedom and then her fear when she was shot and couldn't make the change to human form. All along, it was from her."

I ask Hunter how he's coping with all this and he says he's doing okay. It's enough, he tells me, for him to be with his mother, even in wolf form, and when he's with her she stays close to his side. I understand that. He has just come back into her life and she is afraid of losing him again.

He also tells me that Gideon promised to run freely with him during the first full moon of summer, right here in the forest of Summer Valley. "I would be proud to run with you, my wonderful son," he said to Hunter.

Gideon made another promise. He intends to take Hunter to Shasta County during one full moon and formally introduce him to the Lost Pack. He told Hunter that it was well past time for his son to do a full-moon run with the original werewolves from Summer Valley. "Perhaps," Gideon said, "in time, some of the pack will think about returning here." That Hunter tells me, will be a dream come true.

"You know something, Lilith? I can't believe all that's happened over the last few months. It's strange and wonderful at the same time. But I even love the strangeness! You have powers you never realized you had. You always thought that levitating was an annoyance and yet here you are embracing the fact that you can fly. And me? I finally know what happened to my mother and that she's alive in her wolf form. That doesn't matter, not really, because now she knows me and we're finally together. Maybe someday soon, Mr. Paget, my dad, your parents, and you will discover a way for my mom to become a true werewolf again, able to change back and forth like she once did. I mean there has to be some type of magic or something for that."

I tell him that after graduation, I'm going to go over every spell in the Book of Lost Spells carefully to see if I can't find one that just might help Galina. From the corner of my eye I see the book glow with a pinpoint of light when I say that. I take that as a good sign.

"Your dad is happy, that's for sure. And he also seems relieved that he doesn't have to keep secrets from you anymore. I'm so glad you weren't angry with him for the secrets and the lies. My mom said he was only trying to shield you from the sadness of the situation."

"I *was* mad, for a while anyway. He let me think my mother had died when I was only two years-old. I grew up without a mother and that hurt for so many years." Hunter, always so happy and carefree—it seems almost impossible that he was hurting all this time. "Remember when you had that dream and you said that storms destroy?" I nod. "And do you remember what I told you?"

"I do remember every word you said. 'What happens after a storm is important. That's when the clean-up and rebuilding start. Sometimes a storm has to wash away what's not good in order to create a clean slate so we can begin something new and better.'"

He smiles at me. "Well, the storm has passed and the rebuilding has begun. I *do* have a mom and things will get better. I'm counting on only good things happening for *all* of us from now on." He hugs me tightly. "And one of the best things is that we're together, you and me. We'll make good things happen."

Finally, we talk about our upcoming new venture as criminologists, knowing that our majors in college will be in that field. We are actually going to open our agency this summer. Before he leaves, I show Hunter a graphic I created on the PC. It's a wolf with wings. He laughs and says that's great. "Any reason you created this, Lilith?"

"Actually—there is. I've been thinking about it." A deep meow from Lively who is sitting in the window gets my attention. I laugh. "Okay, Lively has been thinking about it and he kind of helped me with this idea. Anyway, I think, um Lively *suggests*, that we should name our brand-new agency, Angel-Wolf Criminal Investigators. The angel," I point to myself, then point to Hunter, "and the wolf. It fits us so well!"

"Angel-Wolf! It's perfect! I really like it, Lilith!" He brings me into a hug and we kiss for a long time until levitation takes me up, up to the ceiling. Then I slowly return to his arms and we burst out laughing as we kiss again.

Later, I walk Hunter out to his Vespa and we make a date to do something this coming weekend. As he drives off, I think about all that's ahead of us and how we're actually starting a criminology agency together. I marvel at what we've accomplished. Solving a fifteen-year-old murder, having the real murderer confess and be arrested, and reuniting Hunter with his mother.

Then I think of all that I've personally done. Embracing my powers whole-heartedly, facing my fears and learning to cast spells, and coming to a complete understanding of what it means to be otherworldly. Not to mention passing Advanced Calc. It's all good. As I go back inside Midnight Ink, I smile at the name Angel-Wolf which will become the official name for our agency. As Hunter says, it's perfect.

Back inside I think once again about my vamp parents. Something's up and I know it has to do with me. They seem more concerned as my birthday nears. I'll be eighteen in two weeks. Just yesterday, the male and female had Professor A. J. Reed cast a here-and-now protective spell around Midnight Ink and our house. When I asked why, the female said, "Everyone needs protection, darling, that's all." Strange that we never needed it before. What's going on?

I shake my head to clear any negative thoughts from my mind and head toward the stairs. Up in the turret room I pick up Lively and allow myself to rise a few feet from the floor. Lively purrs and snuggles me and the Book of Lost Spells winks a hello. My otherworldly little world. This is where I feel the safest.

As I settle back down onto the floor I look out the window and breathe in the summer day. Thankfully there's no smell of rotting roses. Right now, I would say that my 'imperfectly normal' life seems, well, pretty perfectly normal.

And I want to keep it that way, no matter what.

Read the further adventures of Lilith Angel in Book 2 of the series in

Magic & Mystery At Angel-Wolf

A Lilith Angel Book

Graduation is over, school is out, and summer is here. The warm breeze coming through the open windows in the turret room feels good. I'm here early because I want to work on a sign Hunter and I are going to put in the window of Midnight Ink, the book shop owned by my parents. The sign will be for our new agency, *Angel-Wolf Criminal Investigators*. I want it to look as professional as possible.

The opening of our agency next week coincides with my birthday and we're planning a double celebration here in our office. It's only 6:30 AM, but I was too excited to sleep, and so decided to come here. The printer opens his doors at 10:00 sharp and I want to have plenty of time to make any necessary changes to the sign before I drop it off for a professional printing.

Standing in front of the windows, I'm trying to decide where I want the sign to go when I notice that there's a woman outside the door of Midnight Ink. She's someone I've never seen before. I can't see her face because she's wearing oversized dark glasses and a scarf which covers the sides of her face. I'm guessing this woman at the door is someone new who has ordered a special book or manuscript from my parents and is impatient for Midnight Ink to open. Whoever it is, I'm not opening the door. She can just leave a message in the mailbox or come back later. I've got work to do.

I watch her look at the shop from bottom to top, her eyes lingering on the windows of the turret room where I'm standing. I quickly step out of view and peek at her from the side of the window. She stares a bit longer, then turns and walks hurriedly away. Good, now I can finish getting our sign ready.

I walk back to where I've left the sign but, halfway there, I stop in the middle of the room, my heart hammering in my chest. A heavy smell of decaying flowers, dead and moldy, rotting roses, seems to be coming from the open windows. That smell that I know, that is vaguely familiar to me. That smell that brings a chill of fear to my mind. Hell's Bells! What is it and why am I so suddenly terrified?

As Lilith plans her 18th birthday celebration with her boyfriend Hunter, she is unaware that a terrible danger awaits her. The woman who had tied her to the church railing so many years ago has come to claim Lilith's new, unexplored powers, the powers that will arrive full force when Lilith turns eighteen. This mystery woman is particularly interested in Lilith's new-found power to cast spells—spells that can be used for good or evil. And this woman has absolutely no interest in the casting of good spells—she wants to use the power for evil.

Armed with a deadly potion that can put Lilith into a deathlike trance, the woman stalks the daughter she once abandoned with the smell of rotting roses, a smell that is a muted reminder of a terrifying incident that happened when Lilith was a baby.

Can the powerful vampires who rescued Lilith from that church railing and love her as their own child, stop this evil woman before it's too late? Asking for help from the mighty werewolf, Gideon and his mate, the tragic Galina, they begin the search for this elusive woman whose very existence threatens the life of the daughter they call Lilith of the Angels.